A FAMILY SECRET

BOOK TWO IN THE FAMILY FEUD SAGA

ROSIE CLARKE

Boldwood

First published in 2009 as *A Promise Made*. This edition first published in Great Britain in 2025 by Boldwood Books Ltd.

Cover Design by Colin Thomas

Cover Photography: Colin Thomas

A CIP catalogue record for this book is available from the British Library.

Paperback ISBN 978-1-83518-150-8

Large Print ISBN 978-1-83518-151-5

Hardback ISBN 978-1-83518-149-2

Ebook ISBN 978-1-83518-152-2

Kindle ISBN 978-1-83518-153-9

Audio CD ISBN 978-1-83518-144-7

MP3 CD ISBN 978-1-83518-145-4

Digital audio download ISBN 978-1-83518-147-8

This book is printed on certified sustainable paper. Boldwood Books is dedicated to putting sustainability at the heart of our business. For more information please visit https://www.boldwoodbooks.com/about-us/sustainability/

Boldwood Books Ltd, 23 Bowerdean Street, London, SW6 3TN

www.boldwoodbooks.com

1

She was standing looking out at the park, her face half turned from him, slightly wistful, perhaps a little sad. For a moment he stood watching her, drinking in the lovely line of her face, her slim body that curved where it should. Just seeing her made him feel good to be alive, gave him a reason for pushing his tired old body to live one more week, one more day – one more hour. He had kept her here when she would have left after Simon died. His son's widow – the woman he loved in a way that a man of his age, already married to another woman, should not. He wanted her, loved her, cherished her and lived in dread that she would leave him.

Emily Vane turned, her face lighting up as she saw him. If she had been lovely before she was breathtaking now – the kind of intriguing, sensuous woman that men would always want. He knew that he could not let her go. Even if she were like a little butterfly beating her wings against a sunlit window trying to get out, he would never open that window and let her fly.

'Vane,' Emily said. 'How are you, my dear? Amelia said that

you weren't feeling too well this morning. Should you have come down?'

'The day I take to my bed, they may put me in my box and bury me,' Vane growled. 'You looked pensive just now. What were you thinking about? One of the patients worrying you?'

'No, I don't think so,' Emily said. 'I love my job at the convalescent home. You know that, Vane.'

He knew. It was a part of the honeyed trap he had set to keep her here when she'd wanted to leave after her husband died. He frowned as he recalled the way his son had treated this wonderful girl. Simon had been a fool! If only he had met Emily when he was younger. But that was the irony of life. She had married Simon and he was far too old for her.

'Something is wrong – tell me.' He walked towards her, unable to resist the temptation just to touch her cheek, the need inside a burning fire that only the wisdom of age kept from becoming a conflagration. If he had tried to make love to her she would have run away. So he took what comfort he could from having her near, loving her in the only way she would allow. 'You know that I want you to be happy?'

'Yes, of course.' Her soft laughter pleased him. 'I am happy, Vane. Who could fail to be living in a place like this? The house and the park... it never fails to lift my spirits.'

'Then they *were* low,' he persisted. 'Why?'

'I was just thinking of my sister. Her husband should be coming home soon. You knew he was a pilot, didn't you? Simon flew with his crew at one time.'

'Were you thinking you would like to visit your family? It is a while since you went.' Sometimes he had to give her the illusion of freedom, but he knew the bonds he had woven about her would hold.

'I was thinking what to buy for Frances's birthday,' Emily said.

'It has to be something I can post – unless I go down for a visit soon. I daresay my brother could do with a little help. He wrote telling me that his accounts were in a muddle again.'

'Visit your family,' Vane said. 'We can manage for a few days – just as long as you come back to us soon.' She had to come back because without her, his wealth, this ancient house he treasured, his life, would mean nothing.

'You know I shall come back, don't you, Vane. For as long as you need me.' Her soft brown eyes were on him, slightly accusing and yet forgiving. She could forgive him, but never herself – that was why her promise would hold, because she had lied to him.

'I shall always need you,' he said. 'And now I suppose I must find some work to do. This place is beautiful but it doesn't run itself.'

'And I must go down to the home,' Emily said. 'But I think I shall just pop up and see Robert first.'

'My grandson,' Vane said. 'I was thinking about buying him a pony, Emily – but perhaps it is too soon?'

'A little,' she said with a teasing smile. 'He isn't even three yet, Vane. Get him a puppy, if you like. He loves your old Sandy, but a puppy would be something for him to play with.'

'Yes, I shall,' Vane said. 'He needs a companion and I am too old to play – though we enjoy visiting the lake together. But a puppy it shall be.'

'I think I shall go into Winchester this afternoon,' Emily said. 'I'm going to buy Frances some expensive perfume. I think she will love that, don't you?'

'Yes, I am sure she will,' Vane said. 'I shall see you at dinner, Emily.'

He watched her walk from the room, the unconscious sway of her hips making him long for his lost youth, and then shook his head and sighed. She was young, he was old – he could never be more than her friend. But he could bear that as long as he could see her every day. He could bear anything as long as she didn't leave him.

* * *

Frances Danby glanced at the French gilt clock on the mantelpiece, catching her breath as she watched the long hand reach a quarter past three. It was Wednesday afternoon and that meant her father-in-law would arrive at any moment. A sick feeling clawed at her stomach, because she hated Wednesday afternoons, dreaded Sam Danby's weekly visit to take tea with her and his grandson.

She walked to the sitting-room window and looked out at the garden, watching her son playing with the boisterous puppy his grandfather had recently given him. Frances hadn't wanted the child to have a dog. In her opinion he was too young, not quite four years, but Sam had overruled her. She believed he had bought the animal out of spite.

Frances shied away from the thought. She was wrong. Surely she was wrong! Those sultry looks Sam had been giving her recently couldn't mean what she suspected. She had done every-thing she dared to show him that she wasn't interested other than to tell him to get the hell out of her life. It was impossible to speak more plainly, because it would cause a huge row in the family. Besides, Sam hadn't actually done anything she could accuse him of to his face. He lost no chance to touch her, patting her on the bottom whenever the opportunity came his way – but it was the way he looked at her that made Frances feel sick inside.

'Oh, Marcus,' Frances said aloud as she patted the soft hair she had recently had marcel-waved in front of the mirror. Her eyes were a greenish blue, her mouth naturally red and a little petulant at this moment. 'I do wish you were here.'

She was so lonely at times, despite having her younger brother living with her for the time being. In truth, Connor was more of a worry than a comfort, especially these last few months. It was all the fault of the wretched war, which had dragged on for so much longer than anyone had expected. She and Marcus had married in the summer of 1940, soon after her father's death, and it was now the spring of 1946. They had been married for more than five years but hardly any of that time had been spent together. Even though the war was finally over, her husband still hadn't been officially released from his duties as an RAF pilot.

If Marcus were here his father wouldn't keep looking at her that way! Frances's eyes flicked to the clock again, an expensive present to her and Marcus from his parents the previous Christmas. Sam would be here in five minutes. Her stomach clenched and she took a deep breath to steady her nerves. Her face looked pale, almost desperate, but that was silly! Sam hadn't made any demands but she knew what he was thinking.

She heard the crunch of tyres at the side of the house as a car slid over the gravel drive and she went to the French windows to fetch her son in from the garden. Sam wouldn't attempt anything when his grandson was in the room. She couldn't stop him looking but she was safe enough with the child there.

'Come along, Charlie,' she called. 'Your grandfather is here.'

The child came readily, his face eager, eyes bright. He was a happy child, full of life and good-natured. His grandfather's visits meant sweets, because Sam saved his ration to buy them for the boy whenever they were available.

Sam Danby walked into the sitting room at the same moment as his grandson came bounding in and Frances slammed the door, shutting the puppy in the garden. The child threw himself at his grandfather, clamouring to be picked up. For a moment, as they played their usual games, Frances was free to observe her visitor.

Sam was a man of average height, heavily built with short wiry hair flecked with grey, and a bull neck. He wasn't at all like his son. Marcus was of finer stock and took after his mother, who came from a good county family. Sam, as he was fond of telling anyone who happened to be around, was of farming stock, down-to-earth, hearty men who were used to hard work. It was hard work that had made him one of the richest men in the district, though Frances knew that he'd had his start through his wife's inheritance from an aunt.

'That's enough for the moment, Charlie.'

Frances's heart jerked as Sam looked up at her. He took a twist of sweets from his pocket and gave them to the boy.

'Don't eat all the sweets at once,' Frances said, her voice coming out sharper than she'd intended. 'We are going to have our tea in a minute or two. I baked a sponge this morning and some rock buns.'

'Save the sweets for later, eh, lad?' Sam winked at Frances. His eyes moved over her appreciatively. She was an attractive woman. She had a good figure and there was something about her that made men turn their heads to look twice. She was a bit sharp sometimes, but he liked her that way. 'Your mother makes the best rock buns ever, Charlie.' He grinned at her. 'You look like a film star with your hair that way – had it cut, I see.'

'Thank you,' she said stiffly. She was a bit nervous about her hair, because Marcus had always liked it long. She hoped he would like it the way it was now. The gleam in Sam's eyes made her stomach tighten but she managed to retain her composure. 'I'll ask Muriel to bring the trolley in, shall I?'

'You do that, lass, then we can be comfortable together – no interruptions. I look forward to our little chats. Just you, me and Charlie here.'

Frances gave him a cool nod. She left the room, her heart beating a little too fast, and went into the large kitchen, which still smelled of baking and herbs. Muriel looked at her and smiled and Frances felt better. She always tried to make sure that her help was here on a Wednesday afternoon. Comfortably plump and placid, Muriel made Frances feel that much safer.

'You can bring the trolley in now, Muriel.'

'Right you are, Mrs Danby,' Muriel said. 'I'll get off straight afterwards, if you don't mind. My lad is coming home tomorrow and I want to get things nice for him.'

'You must be so pleased to have Bob home,' Frances said, forgetting her own problems for the moment. 'We're the lucky ones, Muriel, and I do understand. Yes, you get off. I can manage – and I shall see you next week.'

She returned to the sitting room, Muriel following with the two-tier wooden trolley.

'Ah, Muriel,' Sam Danby said, smiling pleasantly. 'I hear your lad is coming home. If he wants a job on the lorries you tell him to see me. Bob was always a steady lad. I'll be pleased to take him on.'

'Thank you, Mr Danby. I'll tell him.' She looked pleased because he was an important man in the village and she was flattered that he wanted her son to work for him. 'Excuse me, I'm off home now. I've got a lot to do.'

'Going to kill the fatted calf? The lad deserves it from what I hear. Got himself promotion and a medal. Our lads are heroes, Muriel.'

Muriel beamed at him and left the room. Frances poured tea and placed a cup beside him on the small, occasional table.

'What will you have to eat, Sam? Muriel has made egg sandwiches and there's your favourite buns.'

'I'll have some of those sandwiches and two of your buns, lass. I missed lunch today. Had something to do.'

'Have you been busy?' Frances made an effort. 'You have the land and the lorries – besides the London property. It will make things easier for you when Marcus comes home, I expect.'

'I daresay.' He patted her bottom as she came closer to hand him his plate. Frances moved away quickly, holding back her feelings of disgust. 'You've got a rare figure on you, Frances. Marcus is a lucky dog!'

Frances suspected that he had deliberately changed the subject. She had tried talking to him about his various businesses before and he invariably ignored her. She thought there was something hidden, something he didn't want her to know. Sometimes she sensed a darker, sinister side to Sam – but perhaps that was just because of the way he looked at her. Everyone else seemed to respect him even if they didn't exactly like him.

'You haven't heard anything from Marcus, have you?' she asked, because she couldn't trust herself not to say what she really wanted to tell him.

Sam frowned. 'I should be the last to hear. He will ring you or his mother first. I'll see him when he gets home. It shouldn't be long now.'

'No, thank goodness,' Frances said. She saw his eyes narrow and looked at her son. 'Charlie, you're dropping bits of egg on the carpet. Stop it, please.'

'You go into the garden, lad,' Sam said. 'I'll see you again before I go. I might have something else in my pocket for you.'

Frances wanted to protest but couldn't. Her stomach was tying itself into knots and she avoided looking at Sam as her son went outside. She watched him give most of his sandwich to the puppy.

'That dog is a nuisance. It is licking Charlie's fingers and he's eating his bun. He could pick up all kinds of things from an animal like that, you know.'

'The lad likes it,' Sam said. 'You're too strict with him, Frances. A bit of dirt won't hurt him. I worked on the land when I was a boy and I didn't have anywhere to wash my hands when it was docky time.'

'You spoil him,' Frances said, a flicker of annoyance in her eyes.

'Mebbe I do,' Sam agreed. His gaze narrowed as he looked at her. 'You could be a bit warmer to me, Frannie. I like you, lass. We could be friends – mebbe a bit more if you wanted.'

'You are Marcus's father!' Frances stood up, feeling shocked. What was he implying? She wanted to scream at him to leave but as usual she was hampered by the need to prevent a damaging breach. 'Please, Mr Danby, don't...'

'I speak my mind,' he said and got to his feet. She felt her stomach clench as he came closer, fearing that he meant to grab her. 'You needn't worry. I shan't force anything on you, but I've fancied you for a while now. If you get tired of waiting...' He broke off as the telephone shrilled and Frances rushed to answer it.

Her hand was trembling as she picked it up, her voice breathy. 'Hello. Frances Danby.'

'Are you all right, darling?'

'Marcus!' Relief flooded through her as she heard her husband's voice. 'I've been thinking of you all day, wondering what you were doing.'

'That's what I like to hear,' Marcus said, deep-throated with emotion. 'It's good news, Fran. I've finally got my papers. I'll be home sometime next week and this time it's for good.'

'That's wonderful!' Her voice broke on a sob of relief. He was coming home at last and the nightmare of the past few years would be over. 'I've missed you so much, darling. It seems so long since you were home.'

'It's nearly two months,' he agreed. 'I know everyone thinks the war is over and we can all go home, but things have to be cleared up, Fran. We've got to get our men home as well as a lot more stuff that doesn't get into the papers – but I've done my stint and it won't be long now.'

'I can't wait.' She turned her head as she sensed Sam behind her. He nodded his head and walked past, letting himself out of the front door. She almost sagged with relief. 'No, it won't be long.' She cradled the phone to her ear. 'I'm so glad, Marcus. So glad.'

She could hear a car engine starting and wheels spinning on gravel, and she knew her father-in-law was leaving. Perhaps he would curtail his visits once Marcus was home. He must know she wasn't interested in him in that way. Surely he would leave her alone now!

'Emily,' Amelia said as she saw her come in, her arms laden with parcels. 'Did you enjoy your shopping trip? You seem to have bought a lot.'

'It is so nice to see things in the shops again,' Emily said. 'There were so many things we simply couldn't get during the war, even if we had the coupons, but it is getting better at last. I found some lovely French perfume for my sister's birthday – and

I bought some Yardley Lavender water for you, Amelia. I know you like it.'

Emily smiled at Vane's wife. She was dressed in jodhpurs and an old jacket, the elbows patched with leather. She never wore make-up and used the lavender water only on her handkerchiefs, but it was her favourite and helped her when she had one of her headaches, which came more often these days.

'Thank you,' Amelia said. 'That was very thoughtful of you. A letter came for you this afternoon. It is on the hall table.'

'Oh, thank you,' Emily said. 'It is probably from my brother Henry. I have been expecting him to write. I'll read it after dinner.' She smiled at Amelia. 'How is Vane? I thought he looked a little tired this morning.'

'He ought to rest more,' Amelia said and frowned, 'but he won't listen to me. He might listen to you, Emily. You know he values your opinion.'

'Oh, I doubt anyone could keep Vane in bed if he didn't want to be there,' Emily said. 'Excuse me. I must just pop up and see Robert. Has he been a good boy?'

'You know he is never any trouble,' Amelia said. 'Vane brought him a puppy home from the farm. He is insisting on having it in the nursery, though Nanny isn't too happy – and I can't blame her. He is too young for a dog, Emily.'

'Oh no, surely not,' Emily said and laughed. 'It does children good to learn about looking after animals. Nanny must be firm. The puppy stays in the kitchen area until it is house-trained.'

She ignored Amelia's look of annoyance and ran up the stairs, depositing her small pile of parcels on her bed before going along to the nursery. Robert was her darling, the light of her life, and she couldn't wait to see him with his new puppy.

* * *

Connor was out late again that evening. Frances glanced at the clock and saw that it was almost nine o'clock. She hadn't delayed supper for him, because he often didn't come home until bedtime. He preferred to stop with his friend Peter at Alice's house. He had declared his intention of living with Daniel and Alice when his brother came home. If she were honest, Frances would be relieved to see him go. She stood up, thinking that she would leave something on the kitchen table for Connor and go upstairs. She wouldn't sleep yet, but her brother could let himself in.

As she went out into the hall, the telephone rang. She picked it up, hoping it might be Marcus again, though she knew that wasn't likely. He wouldn't ring twice on the same day.

'Good evening, Frances Danby speaking.'

'Frances.' Emily's voice came over the phone like a breath of fresh air. 'Are you all right, love? You sound a little tired – or upset?'

'Yes, I am a little. I was just thinking of going to bed,' Frances said. 'Connor hasn't been home all evening. I don't know where he gets to at night.'

'You worry too much,' her sister said. 'Connor is nearly sixteen, Frances. He isn't a child. Some of the soldiers who died out there weren't much older than he is now.'

'I suppose so,' Frances admitted. 'I forget that most of the time. He still seems a little kid to me.' She sighed. 'What have you been doing? Are you at the house?'

'No, I've been trying to make sense of the accounts for the home. I was about to leave and then I thought I would give you a ring.'

'I'm glad you did. We don't talk to each other enough, Emily. With you living so far away and me stuck here. If I could drive I would come and see you, but it is such a drag on the train.'

'You sound miserable – are you?'

'No, not really. Marcus rang me earlier. He will be home sometime next week, and this time it is for good. He was finally given his release papers today. It's over, Emily. It's really over at last!'

'That's wonderful.' Emily's pleasure lit up her voice. 'I mean, I know that the war was officially over some months ago, but it is taking ages for some of the men to be demobbed. Vane has been doing his best to help get things moving for some of the families around here. He has been stuck in meetings for weeks – but none of that matters. You must be so thrilled, Frances.'

'Yes, I am,' Frances said. 'We've been married for nearly six years but it seems as though we've spent only a few weeks together.'

'Yes, I know. I often wonder to myself where the past few years have gone. Before the war we were all at home and Father was alive. So much has happened to us all. I know it has been hard for you with your husband away in the RAF, Frances, but you have your son. How is little Charles, by the way?'

'Very well. Naughty but beautiful,' Frances said, laughter in her voice. 'How is the Vane heir?'

'Robert is fine,' Emily said. 'Amelia and Vane are always fussing over him, which is good in one way because I have my work at the convalescent home. If he so much as whimpers Amelia has him out of his nursery and on her knee. I tell her she is spoiling him, and so does Nanny, but she won't listen. She says he needs a little fuss. I believe she thinks I am a bad mother.'

'No, of course you're not,' Frances said at once. Emily had had a rough time one way and the other, losing both her husband and the man she loved to the war. 'I expect you are busy a lot of the time...' She hesitated, then: 'Will you be closing the convalescent home now that the war is over?'

'I shouldn't think so. Not for the foreseeable future anyway. We are still having men referred to us. Some of them are so badly injured that they may never go home. In fact, quite a few don't have homes to go to any more. Either they lost them and their families during the Blitz, or some people don't want them back. Some don't even get visitors. Their wives never come near them because they can't bear to look at their injuries.'

'Oh, that's awful.' Frances felt close to tears at the thought of all those ruined lives. 'You are so good with them, Emily, and you enjoy it – don't you? Does it make up for... other things?' Frances couldn't bring herself to say the words. Emily had discovered that her husband had a male lover and that her marriage had been nothing but a sham. Simon had married to give his father the heir he wanted for the Vane estate, but after being badly burned in a plane crash, he had been on the verge of going to America with his lover for treatment when he had a sudden relapse and died.

'Sometimes,' Emily told her. 'When I'm feeling a bit low I come down and talk to some of the men. I soon realise how lucky I am.'

'Yes...' Frances was quiet for a moment. 'I think I must be one of the luckiest women alive. I feel so guilty when I think of all the wives who have lost their sweethearts and husbands, brothers and cousins. Marcus is coming home and I've got everything I ever wanted.'

'You were always lucky,' Emily said, 'but you shouldn't feel guilty about it, love. Lots of other men are coming back too. Has Alice heard when Daniel might be home?'

'I saw her yesterday,' Frances said, thinking that they were lucky as a family. Daniel was her only brother to go to war, and he would be home soon. 'You knew that Daniel was with a batch of prisoners the Red Cross evacuated immediately after the war was finished, of course. I think he is in some sort of halfway camp now, being rehabilitated. Alice is hoping that he might be home in a couple of weeks.' Frances smiled as she thought of her sister-in-law's happiness. Alice had clung to her belief that her husband was alive when all the signs were that Daniel had been killed, and in the end she'd been proved right. He had been captured while working with a resistance group in Greece and out of his mind after a severe blow to the back of his head for some while. But at last he had recovered and Alice had begun to receive his letters. Ever since then, she had walked around lit up like a beacon.

'Well, at least that is something to look forward to,' Emily said. 'Alice was so certain he wasn't dead when she got that official telegram – and she was proved right in the end.'

'Yes, it was a relief to us all when that happened. Emily, I wanted to talk to you about...' Frances broke off with a little sigh of annoyance. 'There's someone at the door. I had better answer it. I'll talk to you again soon. Come down and see us when you can. It's ages since you did.'

'Yes, I'll try. I had a letter from Henry today. He needs my help with the farm accounts – and he doesn't sound at all well, Frances. You should go and see him if you get a chance.'

'Yes, I will,' Frances promised. 'I must go now.' She replaced the receiver and went to open the door, frowning at the thought of her eldest brother being ill. She hadn't seen Henry for ages. They got on all right, but didn't have much in common. 'Oh, it's you.' Frances stared at her youngest brother in annoyance. 'I was on the telephone. Why didn't you let yourself in? I hope you haven't lost the key I gave you?'

'No, I forgot it this morning,' Connor said. 'Sorry I made you answer the door. I should have found a ladder and climbed in through the bedroom window.'

'Don't be ridiculous,' Frances said. 'Of course you shouldn't. We would have the police round here thinking there were burglars.' She raised her eyebrows. 'I suppose you want some supper?'

'No, thanks,' Connor said. 'I went over to Henry's after school and Mary got me some supper. I've been helping to feed their pigs.'

'Is that what I can smell?' Frances wrinkled her nose. 'You had better put those clothes out to be washed tomorrow – and wash yourself before you get into bed.'

'Yeah, all right.'

Connor went past her and up the stairs. Frances suspected that he would ignore her. She had no control over him whatsoever and it worried her that he was getting into trouble. She was annoyed that he had interrupted her conversation with Emily. They didn't talk often enough as it was. She thought about ringing back, but Emily would probably have gone up to the house by now and she might get Amelia Vane if she rang there. Frances didn't like Lady Vane very much. She suspected her of trying to keep Emily from visiting her family, though Emily always denied it.

Yawning, Frances tried the various doors and windows, making sure they were locked before she went upstairs. Marcus would be home soon and then she wouldn't have to do these things; he would do them for her. It would be so nice to be looked after, to have someone to lean on. She had a feeling that her problems with Sam Danby were nearly over. Marcus would protect her once he was home.

The thought of Marcus's homecoming warmed Frances as she went upstairs. Suddenly, she was excited, feeling like a bride again. She had loved Marcus all her life and being married to him was all she had ever wanted of life – but the war had spoiled things. She smiled and hugged her pleasure to herself because the war was over, and so were the loneliness and the fear that had hung over her for months.

* * *

Emily walked up to the house, because it was a lovely still night. She hadn't bothered to bring her car earlier and she didn't mind walking alone at night; at least, she didn't mind being alone on Vane's land. She felt safe here, protected from the dangers of the outside world.

During the early years of the war she had worked for the fire service in Liverpool. She had been caught out in raids several times, witnessing the utter destruction that the bombing had caused, and the grief. Terry had been a fireman too, and it was his devotion to duty that had caused his death. She smiled a little as she thought of her lover, the father of her child. If he hadn't been killed doing his duty, she would probably have left this place long ago.

'Emily, is that you?'

Vane's voice broke into her thoughts, startling her, making her feel slightly guilty. There was always an element of guilt in her thoughts concerning Vane, because she had lied to him about Robert – at least, she had allowed him to believe what he wanted to believe: that her son was also Simon's and therefore his grandson.

'Yes,' she answered, thrusting the guilt to a far corner of her mind. 'It was such a lovely night that I thought I would walk.'

'Yes, the stars are wonderful tonight,' Vane agreed. 'I came out to smoke a cigar. You know Amelia hates them, and I wanted to be alone.'

'It is good to be alone sometimes,' Emily said. 'Shall I go and leave you to your thoughts?'

'No, let me walk back with you,' Vane said. 'I don't want to be alone when I can have your company.'

Emily nodded. She knew that he preferred her company to Amelia's, but she took no advantage of it. They all lived in harmony together most of the time – and that was best.

'I think I shall visit my brother soon,' she said. 'Just for a few days.'

'We shall miss you,' Vane said. 'But you must do as you want, Emily.'

'Oh, I shan't be away long,' Emily said. 'I told you I would stay while you needed me, and I shall.'

'Good,' he said, smiling as they walked the rest of the way in silence.

2

'Where are you off to, Connor?' Frances asked a week later as she saw him standing in the bus queue for Ely, a small, nearby market town. His friend Peter Robinson was with him, and he gave her a nervous look as she stopped. 'Shouldn't you be at school?'

'We've got a day off,' Connor told his eldest sister. 'We're going to have fish and chips at the shop on the market place, and then go to the Thursday matinee at the pictures. It's a western.'

'Have you got enough money?' Frances asked. She frowned as the bus arrived and he hopped on without answering her. She often worried about him these days. He had become very moody during the time that Daniel was believed dead, and she knew he hated living with her. He spent as much time as he could with Henry or at Alice's house. 'Don't get into any trouble,' she called after him, though she knew he wouldn't hear, and he wouldn't listen if he did.

Frances wheeled her bike through the High Street to the shop she favoured with her weekly order. There were two grocery shops in the village and both thriving, because despite the regular bus service into Ely it was easier to have the goods delivered from a local shop, especially if you had children. It would have been different if she had learned to drive, as Emily had at the start of the war, but somehow she had never bothered. Marcus or her late father had always been there before the war, and then, after she'd married, she'd been busy with other things.

She had left Charlie with Muriel that morning. He was a noisy, happy child, and he would be fine playing in the garden with the puppy he loved so much. Perhaps Sam Danby had been right about that, she thought and then frowned, because she didn't want to think about her father-in-law. She gave a little shudder and then dismissed him from her mind.

Entering the small shop, which smelled strongly of carbolic soap, vegetables and tar, from the wood kindling piled in the corner, Frances found that Alice was already there ordering her goods. She turned as she heard Frances speak her name, a smile on her lips.

'Frances, how lovely to see you. I was going to come and visit you after I'd done my shopping. I've had a letter from Daniel. He will be home sometime next week.'

'That's good news,' Frances said. 'I told you that Marcus would be back this week, didn't I?' Alice nodded, smiling happily. She was a pretty girl with soft hair and a gentle smile, though a little plumper than she had been before the birth of her son. 'We must have a little party, a get together for all the family. I telephoned Emily yesterday and she has sort of promised to come down for a visit, but I am sure she will if you tell her that Daniel is coming home. He was always her favourite.'

'Yes, I know. Dan is very fond of her too,' Alice said. She looked down at her son, who was by her side and pulling at her skirt for attention. 'Yes, darling. You shall have a sweetie if Mummy can get some.' She laughed as she saw Frances frown. 'I expect you think I spoil him, but he looks so much like Dan sometimes that I can't help it.'

'I don't let Charlie have sweets often,' Frances said. 'I don't think they are good for him.'

'Oh, Frances,' Alice said. 'That's a bit strict, isn't it? Surely you relent sometimes?'

'Well, for a special occasion,' Frances said, a slight flush in her cheeks. 'He has them once a week when his grandfather calls.'

'Well, I suppose it is good for them to learn discipline,' Alice said, though she looked doubtful. 'Not that we can get sweets all the time anyway with the rationing.'

Alice turned away then as the shopkeeper spoke to her. Frances felt a little warm, because she didn't like to be criticised over her management of the child. It wasn't fair, because she only wanted what was best for her son.

'Why don't you come back with me?' she suggested to Alice. 'We can have lunch together, if you like.'

'I can't stop for lunch,' Alice said as she paid for her goods over the counter. 'Mum wants to go into Ely later – but I can stay for a cup of tea and a chat.'

'I've made some buns this morning,' Frances said. 'Marcus's father comes for tea on Wednesdays. He likes rock buns so I usually make a few for him, but there's enough for us too.'

Alice agreed, waiting while Frances paid for her order. They walked back through the village street together.

'I didn't know it was a school holiday today,' Frances said. 'What is it for this time?'

'I don't think it is,' Alice said, wrinkling her forehead. 'I'm sure Peter went to school this morning as usual.'

'He was with Connor in the queue for the bus to Ely when I

came by,' Frances said. 'He told me it was a holiday and that they were going to have fish and chips and go to the pictures.'

'Peter hasn't got enough money for that,' Alice said. 'If he is going to the pictures, Connor must be paying for him.'

'I wouldn't have thought he had enough money either,' Frances said. 'I know he does a paper round at the weekends, but he doesn't get much for that – a couple of bob perhaps.'

Alice looked concerned. 'Perhaps they've been saving their pocket money, or they might have done a little job for someone...'

'Yes, perhaps,' Frances agreed. She couldn't think where else Connor would get spending money. Henry certainly hadn't got any to spare for his younger brother. She knew from his wife that he was at his wits' end finding the cash to pay the farm workers, because they had met in the street the previous day and Mary had come back for a cup of tea and a chat. 'Of course Clay might have given him a few shillings.' Clay was her second eldest brother – but he didn't see the rest of the family often since the brothers had fallen out over the land after their father's death.

'Does Connor see much of him?' Alice asked. 'I didn't think they got on very well since Clay fell out with Daniel and Henry?'

'I really don't know whether he sees Clay or not,' Frances replied, feeling a little guilty. She had never known what had caused the row between Daniel and Clay, but it had been some-thing to do with their father's second wife, Margaret. She had picked that much up from something Emily had let slip, but she hadn't really wanted to discover the truth. Clay was the least favourite of her brothers and it was months – nearly a year – since she'd seen him. Henry wouldn't speak to him at all these days.

'If Peter is getting into trouble, Mum will half kill him,' Alice said. 'I know Mr Brown wanted a word with her a few weeks back. Peter is going to be apprenticed to him as a carpenter when he leaves school this term. She wouldn't tell me what was wrong, but I think it might be to do with taking time off from his Saturday job without asking.'

'No wonder Connor hopped on that bus quick,' Frances said, feeling cross. 'If he has been missing school I shall have something sharp to say to that young man! He leaves in the summer and I've had my work cut out to keep him there until then, because he wants to leave, but his teachers say he could do something really worthwhile with his life if he tried. I think he should go to college.'

Alice made no comment. She knew that Connor hated living with his sister, though she wasn't sure why. It might be to do with the fact that Frances had gone ahead with her engagement and wedding too soon after her father's death, and that Connor had decided that she hadn't cared about his father dying – or him!

'Don't be too angry with him,' Alice pleaded, half-wishing she hadn't told her sister-in-law anything. She liked her husband's youngest brother and wouldn't want him to get into trouble because of something she had said. 'He's had a rough time these past few years.'

'No more than a good many other lads.'

'Connor was terribly upset when he thought Daniel had been killed,' Alice reminded her.

'Yes, I daresay, but he has known that his brother is all right for a while now. Besides, being worried doesn't excuse his behaviour – especially if he has been getting into some mischief.'

'No, I suppose not,' Alice said, but she couldn't help thinking that the lad was still missing his father and that Frances might have been a little kinder to her young brother. 'Well, Dan will be home soon. I daresay he will sort him out.'

'Yes,' Frances agreed. 'If Connor will listen to anyone it's Daniel. He certainly takes no notice of anything I say to him.'

* * *

Frances heard the peel of the doorbell with a sinking heart. Each week she hoped that her father-in-law would forget to come or be too busy, but he was as regular as clockwork in his visits. She went to open the door, putting on a smile that did not reach her eyes.

'Frances,' Sam said, leaning forward to kiss her. She turned her head sharply so that his wet lips found her cheek and not her mouth. 'You look lovely as always. How is my boy today?'

'He is in trouble for pulling the puppy's tail,' Frances said coldly. 'I told you he was too young, Sam. The poor creature yelped with pain and I had to smack Charlie to teach him a lesson.'

'You're too hard on the child,' Sam said and frowned. 'I don't suppose he meant to hurt the dog – and I doubt any lasting harm was done. Dogs are resilient creatures.'

'That's as may be,' Frances said, feeling resentful because she had known he would take the boy's side. He always made her feel as if she were the wicked witch instead of Charlie's loving mother. 'But if you had waited a couple of years, he would have been old enough to understand.'

'I'll talk to him,' Sam replied. 'You make too much of things, Frances. Get that from your mother, I shouldn't wonder. She was always the nervous type.'

Frances bit back the angry retort that sprung to her lips. She would have liked to say a lot more, but she was living in her father-in-law's house. He had supposedly bought it for her and Marcus as a wedding gift, but as yet it remained in his own name. They could always move, of course, but this house had been in her family until her brothers had been forced to sell to pay their stepmother out. There wasn't another house in the village as nice, apart from Sam Danby's own house of course.

She turned and led the way into the drawing room. She always entertained Sam in the large formal room, because the sitting room she favoured was too intimate and she did not want the smell of him to linger there. He was a large man who sweated when it was warm, and his clothes had a tang of tobacco smoke and perspiration.

'Please sit down,' she said in a cool tone. 'I shall fetch Charlie downstairs and then we'll have tea.'

'Why not sit with me on your own for a few minutes?' Sam Danby asked. There was a suggestive leer about his thick lips that made her shudder inwardly. 'You could be a little warmer towards me, Frannie. I'm a generous man when I'm pleased. You know I like you.'

'Excuse me, I must fetch my son.' Frances walked hurriedly from the room, wishing that she hadn't sent her son upstairs earlier. He had deserved the punishment, but her father-in-law would never make that kind of suggestion to her with his beloved grandson in the room. The thought of his touching her in the way his manner seemed to suggest he wanted to touch her made her feel sick inside. She paused outside her son's bedroom for a moment, the revulsion swirling inside her.

Oh God, how long must she put up with this? She had hoped Marcus would be home by now but he had been delayed and it would be the weekend before he was here. Taking a deep breath, Frances went into the bedroom and picked Charlie up. He was lying on the bed looking at his books, his face stained with tears.

'Mummy is sorry for smacking you,' she told him. 'But you hurt the dog and you mustn't do that, darling. Come along now, your grandfather is waiting.' He patted her face with his rather grubby hands and smiled at her, making her heart turn over. She loved him so much and it wasn't his fault. He wasn't old enough to understand. 'That's a good boy,' she said and set him down. 'Go to Grandad now, love.'

She followed as he bolted down the stairs, taking a deep breath before she entered the sitting room. Perhaps this was the last time she'd need to endure this ordeal. She could talk to Marcus, tell him how she felt without making a big thing of it.

* * *

It was nearly nine thirty when Connor came in that evening. Frances was still up, sitting in the room she liked best, working at her knitting. She heard her brother trying to creep up the stairs and went out into the hall after him.

'Where have you been until this time of night? And why weren't you in school today?' Her voice was angry, raised because she was emotional and she had been worried about him.

'We had a day off for good behaviour,' Connor said, but he couldn't look at her and she knew he was making it up.

'Don't lie to me,' she said, glaring at him. 'You are such a troublesome boy, Connor. Surely you know that it is in your best interests to stay on at school and learn all you can? Do you want to be like Henry? He left to work on the farm when he was fourteen and he can hardly manage the accounts.'

'Henry's all right,' her brother said, a sullen slant to his mouth. He looked at her resentfully. They had never been close and he missed Emily and Daniel. 'At least he doesn't nag the way you do, Frances.'

'He doesn't have to look after you,' she snapped, because she was tired and upset. 'And where did you get the money for the pictures? Don't say that Peter Robinson paid because he doesn't have any money, Alice told me so.'

'Alice doesn't know everything,' Connor said. 'We helped out for a few hours on Mr Robinson's farm and he gave us five bob each.'

'That sounds extraordinarily generous of him,' Frances said, not believing a word. 'I can always ask him, you know.'

Connor stared at her, mutiny in his eyes. 'I don't care what you do. It's none of your business anyway. I shan't live here with you once Dan gets back.'

'Dan hasn't got anywhere to live yet,' Frances said. 'And Henry doesn't need the worry of you getting into trouble. The last thing I want is the police coming round here again. I told you the last time that I wouldn't put up with it.'

'We were only scrumping in Granny Hern's orchard,' Connor said and grinned. 'She's an old witch. She runs out after the kids with her stick and waves it at them. We only done it for a dare.'

'You "did it", not "done it",' Frances corrected. 'Don't they teach you anything at that school of yours?'

'Not a lot,' Connor said and grinned at her. In that moment he looked very much like Daniel, and she softened towards him. 'Nothing I want to learn leastwise. Can I go to bed now?'

'Yes, go on,' Frances said and gave him a reluctant smile. 'Don't wake Charlie. I had a terrible time getting him to sleep tonight. His grandfather gets him too excited. He has now promised to buy him a pony of all things!'

'Dad bought us boys ponies,' Connor said. 'What's wrong with Charlie having one? You rode when you were younger. Henry told me about it. He taught you.'

Frances bit her lip. 'Yes, well, that was different. I was eleven when I started to ride. Charlie is much too young.'

'He won't come to harm if someone looks after him,' Connor said. 'You can't keep him in cotton wool forever, Frannie.'

'Don't call me that!' She was reminded of Sam Danby's words

earlier that afternoon. He often called her by that name and she
hated it. Her bruised feelings made her sharper than she
intended. 'Go to bed – and behave yourself. Marcus will be home
this weekend and I'll get him to take a strap to you if I find out
that you've been up to something dishonest.'

'Marcus isn't my father – and he isn't my brother either,'
Connor said defiantly. 'If he takes a strap to me he'll be sorry –
and so will you!' He ducked his head down and ran up the stairs,
leaving Frances to stare after him in frustration. The trouble with
Connor was that for the past four years there had been no one he
respected around to discipline him. Henry was busy, tired and ill,
he couldn't be expected to administer physical punishment, and
she hadn't tried. In fact, she had closed her eyes to what her
young brother was doing, because she didn't want to know.

She would be glad when Marcus was home – and Daniel too.
Perhaps then Connor would realise he couldn't continue to run
wild.

Everything would be better once Marcus was home!

Frances looked at the clock for perhaps the fiftieth time in an
hour. When he'd phoned her the previous evening, Marcus had
said he hoped to be home by lunchtime and it was now half-past
four in the afternoon. Where could he have got to? She jumped
to her feet as she heard the sound of a car engine outside,
running to the door eagerly.

'Marcus!' she cried as he got out of the car. 'I was starting to
worry.'

'Sorry, old girl,' Marcus said. He took two strides towards her,
sweeping her up in a bear hug and swinging her off her feet. 'I
was late getting away – bit of a get together with the lads – and

then I called to see Mother. Father wasn't there but it was her I wanted to see.'

'Oh.' Frances felt a bit resentful. He ought to have come straight home and visited his parents another time. 'I thought you would be here for lunch.'

'Mother wrote to me, asked me to call,' he said. 'She was worried about something and wanted to talk when Father wasn't around, that's all. Anyway, I'm here now – where is Charlie?'

'Connor took him for a walk,' Frances said. 'He was a bit fretful. I expect they will be back soon – but we have a few minutes alone.'

'Missed me that much?' Marcus lifted his fine brows. Frances felt her heart turn over. He wasn't in the least like his father. His aristocratic looks were a part of what had made her fall for him in the first place, and they must have come from his mother. 'It's all right, darling. I'm home to stay now. You won't have to cope with everything alone. Mother told me you find Charlie a bit of a handful, but now I'm here and it won't be so hard for you.'

'Oh...' Frances wasn't sure how she felt about Marcus talking of her with his mother that way. 'He is strong headed sometimes – and your father spoils him. He bought him that puppy and now he is talking about buying him a pony for Christmas. Charlie isn't old enough to start riding, Marcus. I don't want him to have a pony yet, but your father won't listen to me. He says I'm too strict with the boy.'

'Well, I'm here now,' Marcus said. 'We'll see how things go, darling. Father is a bit domineering sometimes, I know – but I see no harm in Charlie having a pony as long as he doesn't ride it alone.' He smiled at her. 'Come here and kiss me. I haven't seen you for months.'

Frances felt her knees weaken as she walked into his arms. His smile had always affected her this way. She had fallen in love with him when she was still at school, and the time they had spent apart during the war had only made her long for his return.

'I do love you,' she said, lifting her face for his kiss. For a moment she melted into his body, feeling the familiar rush of desire. 'Marcus... it's so good to have you home. I've been so lonely for you.'

'Me too,' he said, kissing the bridge of her nose once before releasing her. 'Have you any whisky in the house, darling? I could really do with a drink.'

'Yes, I think there is some left from the last time you were home,' Frances said, feeling oddly disappointed. His kiss had aroused her as always but she'd felt an odd reserve in him, as if he were holding back. 'We could go upstairs for a while...'

'Later,' Marcus said easily, searching for and finding the whisky bottle in the sideboard. 'I shall have to go into Ely tomorrow and see what I can find to fill this up. I like a few drinks, Frances. It's a way of life you get into, having a drink with the lads after a tough operation.'

'But it is over now, isn't it?' Frances looked at him anxiously. 'You won't have to go back?'

'No. I am officially a civilian again,' Marcus said, but something flickered in his eyes that bothered her. 'I shall have to find myself some kind of a job, I suppose.'

'But won't you work for your father?' Frances had somehow taken it for granted. Sam Danby owned a substantial amount of agricultural land in the area, but he also ran a small fleet of lorries, and she suspected that there were other businesses.

'I'm not sure,' Marcus told her with a frown. 'We never got round to discussing it. I went straight from college to the RAF and...' He shrugged. 'I can't see myself managing the farm. Perhaps the lorries, or one of his other businesses.'

'Does he have others?' She looked at him curiously. She knew there was some property in London, but Sam was close-mouthed on the subject.

'Yes, I think so. I can't imagine all the money comes through the lorries or the land. As you know, he has some sort of property in London. Mother says he goes up two or three times a month. He doesn't tell her anything, of course, but I might prefer property management to anything else.' He finished his drink and poured himself the rest of what was left in the bottle. 'Damn! You haven't got any more anywhere?'

'No, I'm sorry,' Frances said. 'I didn't think about it. Besides, you never used to drink that much.'

'Didn't I?' Marcus looked moody. 'It's the damned war. It was hell some of the time, and then when it's over... something happens. You keep going somehow while you have to, but...' He shook his head. 'Don't worry about it, darling. I expect I shall—' What he meant to say was lost as the kitchen door banged and then his son came running into the room followed more slowly by Connor. 'Hello there, my boy!' He picked the child up, swinging him round and up on to his shoulder. 'Why don't we go and see what I've got for you in my case?'

Frances listened to their excited chatter and her son's screams of excitement as they left the room. She glanced at Connor, too wrapped up in her own thoughts to notice the look in his eyes. If she'd realised he was feeling excluded from the family reunion she might have said something, but she had a horrid sinking feeling inside. She had built up this homecoming in her mind so much and now she felt flat. It was almost as if Marcus had become someone different, as if she hardly knew him.

* * *

'You don't need to take Robert with you,' Amelia said, stroking the small boy's head as he clung to her skirts. 'He will be fine with us, Emily. Why don't you have a little time for yourself? Make it a longer holiday this time. You don't get to see your family that often these days.'

'But they will all want to see him,' Emily said and held out her hand to the child. Sometimes Amelia's attitude towards her son irritated her a little, but she tried not to let it show. 'Come to Mummy, darling. We are going in the car now.'

Robert looked up at Amelia for a moment and then let go of her skirt a little reluctantly. He toddled unsteadily towards his mother on his chubby legs, giving a squeal of delight as she caught him up and hugged him. He patted her face and chuckled, chattering in his own way. As yet he had a limited vocabulary, but Emily smiled as she heard the word 'Mumma' repeated several times. At least he knew who she was, even though Amelia spent far more time with him than Emily did as a rule. He called her 'Melia'. As Emily bore him away, taking him out to the car, he waved to her over his mother's shoulder.

'Melia isn't coming today,' she told him as she gave him to Nanny, who was waiting to receive him onto her lap in the back seat of the car. 'Be a good boy, darling. We have a long drive down to see Uncle Henry.'

Emily had decided to stay with her elder brother at the farmhouse rather than with Frances, because she knew that Marcus had just come back after months away. They would naturally want some time alone together, even though Frances had invited her to stay for a few days.

'You know you are welcome here, Emily,' she had said when she'd telephoned. 'After all, it was your home until you married.'

'Thanks, but Henry wants me to stay with him,' Emily had told her, because she couldn't say that Frances's house didn't feel like home any more. It was too neat and tidy, too cold in a way. Vanbrough was a huge house, but it had a lived-in feeling, the furniture in the family rooms well-used and loved. Vane left his things just where he liked, and his ancient golden Labrador dog followed him everywhere. 'I'm going to do the accounts for Henry, and he has plenty of room in that rambling old house of his.'

Emily wasn't sure why she had been reluctant to stay at her old home, but it was Marcus's house now – and Frances's. It wouldn't have been the same and she might have felt awkward. Henry was looking forward to seeing her and so was Mary. Daniel was staying at Alice's parents' home for the time being, though Emily knew that Alice had been searching for a house for them for some weeks. She would be able to see them too, and their son Danny.

'Everyone ready then?' Emily glanced over her shoulder and smiled before starting the car. Nanny had come prepared with books and games for the journey. 'Off we go then. You will like Uncle Henry's farm, Robert. There are lots of animals.'

Emily glanced back and saw that Amelia was at the door of the great house, staring at them in an odd intense way that made her feel slightly uncomfortable. What did that look on her face mean? Was it just that she hated to part from Robert – or was she becoming too possessive? Sometimes now Amelia acted as though she thought the child was hers.

No, she was making too much of it! Emily waved at Amelia, and then released the handbrake. As she drove along the road that ran through the park, she was aware of ancient trees and a feeling of peace. She never failed to be moved by the beauty of the old house and its grounds, and she knew that she was very lucky to live in such a place – even if she did sometimes feel guilty because of her secrets.

Vane believed that Robert was Simon's child. He had taken it for granted when she'd told him that she was pregnant, and somehow she hadn't been able to confess the truth. Amelia had guessed that she had conceived during a brief love affair with another man, but Vane had no idea. For the past couple of years since her son's birth he had delighted in his heir, telling everyone who would listen what a wonderful, clever boy Robert was and spoiling him whenever he got the chance.

He would be terribly disappointed and hurt if he ever learned that Robert was the son of Emily's lover, a fireman who had died when he went back to rescue a colleague from a burning house in the Blitz. Emily frowned as she turned onto the main road, which ran past the estate walls. Vane would be entitled to be angry with her for lying.

Of course, she hadn't exactly lied. She had simply allowed him to believe what he wanted to believe – and Amelia had begged her to do it. Unable to give Vane an heir herself, now that Simon was dead, Amelia had wanted Emily to stay on with them. She adored Robert. It was natural that she should miss him when his mother took him away.

Emily made an effort to shrug off her slight feeling of unease. She was looking forward to her visit with her family. It would be good to see them all again, especially her brother Daniel.

Emily's face wore a frown of concentration as she drove through the traffic. Daniel had had a terrible time. Captured by the Germans in Greece, he had spent the last years of the war in a prison camp. She knew his letters to Alice had been cheerful, because Alice had let her read bits of them, but he'd written to Emily personally once and she had guessed at the things he didn't say.

Would his war experiences have changed her brother? Emily wondered. Daniel had been closer to her than any of the rest of her family before the war, and she worried about him. He was lucky to be coming home when so many men never would. Emily's contact with the soldiers who had suffered terrible injuries had made her see the horror of war for herself. Sometimes she sat by a dying patient and talked to him for ages, holding his hand until the end. Each death left a little scar on her heart. War was so futile. It made her angry to think of all the men who had died, and all the women who had lost their loved ones.

Alone in her bedroom after a patient had been lost, she would weep for the pity of it and for the lover she herself had lost. Terry had been so brave, dying to help others. She had loved him so much and they had had so little time together. Feeling the sting of emotion in her throat, she forced her thoughts back to the present. Terry was dead but she had her son – his son.

Forget the past! She must think about the future. She was committed to Vane and the convalescent home. She owed it to the men and also her father-in-law. By letting him believe that Robert was his grandson, she had sealed her own fate. And she was happy with that – most of the time.

It would be good to see Daniel and Frances – and all the others, of course. Except Clay. She hadn't spoken to the second eldest of her brothers for ages, because she knew what he had done. Connor had heard Clay and Daniel fighting, and he'd told her that the reason for the fight was because Clay had raped their stepmother.

Emily's stomach curled with disgust. How could he have done that to their father's widow? Emily hadn't liked Margaret much, but she was still angry with Clay. Because of what he had done, Margaret had demanded more money from Daniel. He would need that money now that he was home. She knew only too well that Henry was in deep trouble with the farm. If he managed to stave off bankruptcy it would be a miracle.

Emily had some money of her own. It wasn't a fortune, just a few thousand pounds that had come to her from Simon's estate. At first she hadn't wanted to touch a penny of her late husband's money. Her marriage had been a sham and she wasn't interested in the legacy, but Vane had insisted it was hers.

'It is your independence,' he'd told her. 'If you get sick of us, Emily, you can go and live your own life. Not that I want you to go, my dear. You know I would love you to stay with us – but I don't want you to feel trapped.'

Vane was such a dear! Emily smiled at the thought of him. She had been in awe of her father-in-law once but now she had become fond of him. He treated her with kindness and respect and she admired him, because he was everything his son hadn't been.

The money from Simon's estate was just sitting in the bank doing nothing. She didn't think it was enough to pay Henry's debts, but she might be able to help Daniel get started again. She would talk to him when she got the chance, because she doubted that Clay would pay his brother the money he owed him.

* * *

'Damn you, Clay!' Daniel Searles said, glaring at his elder brother. 'You owe me that two thousand for paying Margaret off. She was going to report you to the police. You would have spent the past five years in prison if I hadn't saved your neck.'

'More fool you,' Clay retorted. 'Don't threaten me, Dan. It won't do you any good. I don't have the money to pay you. Things have been hard for me as well as everyone else. Ask Henry what it has been like trying to keep things ticking over.'

'Henry was saddled with a huge bank loan, as you know very well.'

'That was his problem.' Clay shrugged and spat on the ground. He had thickened over the years, his features coarsening as he'd lost much of the good looks that had been his in youth. He was younger than Henry but still well into his thirties, a man who had indulged in the pleasures of the table as well as of the flesh. 'If you give me time I might be able to raise five hundred.'

'I want all of it,' Daniel said. He clenched his fists, knowing that he didn't have the strength to thrash his brother as he would have once. The prisoner of war camp had taken its toll on him as it had on all the men, but he wasn't broken in spirit like some of the poor devils he'd known. His physical strength would come back in time; he'd had Alice and his son to come home to and now he was back with them he would get on in leaps and bounds. 'I'll take the five hundred for now, Clay – but I want the rest of it.'

'You'll have to wait.' Clay glared at him. 'I'll do what I can and that's all I'm going to say.' He glanced back towards his house. His wife had come to the door to look at them. 'Dorothy has dinner ready. You can stay if you want?'

'No thanks. I've promised Alice I'll go to look at a house with her this afternoon.' He gave his brother a hard look. 'I want that money and I'll do whatever I have to in order to get it.' His gaze shifted towards the house and Dorothy. 'Give my love to your wife.' His words carried an underlying meaning and Clay threw him a look of hatred.

'Don't try that or you will be sorry!'

'Don't push me too far or you're the one who will regret it,' Daniel warned.

He turned his back on his brother and got into the old truck he was driving. It had stood idle in one of the barns since he'd been shipped out to Greece, but he had got it going again and the engine sounded sweet as he started it up. He had always had a talent for repairing engines – that was how he'd got left behind when the British evacuated Greece. If he'd abandoned that ammunition truck when the engine died on him, he might not have ended up as a prisoner of the Germans.

There was no point in looking back, no point in dwelling on what had happened to him. Daniel had ridden out the war as best he could, using his time to study mechanics. He'd formed an odd sort of friendship with one of the guards. As a prisoner of war, Daniel had received parcels from the Red Cross and occasionally from home. He'd seen Hans looking at his chocolate bar with naked envy and he'd given him half, because towards the end of the war the Germans had been short of luxuries too. After that, Hans had brought him books and manuals about engines and tools. Daniel didn't know until after the war how he'd managed to find English copies. He'd discovered then that Hans had had an English grandfather, who had worked on the earliest cars in the Daimler factory.

They had parted on amicable terms. Hans had wanted to keep in touch, but it wouldn't happen. Daniel wasn't interested in the past. The war and everything that had happened to him in the camp was over. He was home now. All he wanted was to forget and get on with the future. His dream was to open his own garage, but for that he needed the money Clay owed him.

He frowned as he drove through the village. Somehow he was going to get that two thousand. It would make all the difference to their lives. The farm would have to be sold, because the bank was making threatening noises. They would be lucky if they salvaged enough to pay off their debts. Daniel had already transferred the two fields he owned independently into Alice's name. At least that would ensure they had something left if it all went down – which was looking increasingly likely despite the efforts he'd made since his return.

It wasn't going to be easy for a few years. Daniel hated the idea that he might not be able to provide a decent living for Alice and their son. He'd made such plans for the future. Sitting in that wretched camp, it was all that had kept him sane.

Damn Clay for what he'd done to Margaret! She might have been a calculating bitch who had taken them for every penny she could get, but she hadn't deserved to be treated like that! Daniel had given Clay a thrashing and he'd extracted a promise that his brother would repay the money after the war, but he still wished he could turn Clay in for the criminal he was without destroying the innocents in the family. Clay was trying to wriggle out of the payment, but Daniel wouldn't let him.

As he drew up outside his father-in-law's house, he saw that another car was already parked outside. He didn't recognise it, but as he went into the house he heard laughter. That was Alice and Emily! He grinned as he walked into the small back parlour. The room was overflowing with people, and he thought that the sooner he and Alice got their own place the better.

Emily turned and saw him. She gave a screech of delight and rushed into his arms, responding warmly to his hug of affection.

'Dan! It's so lovely to see you again.' She drew back, looking at him anxiously. 'You're a bit thinner but Alice will soon feed you up. You haven't changed much otherwise. I was afraid you might have.'

'I was lucky,' Daniel said with a lazy grin, consigning all the fear, hunger and pain to oblivion. 'It could have been a lot worse. Some of the chaps were shot trying to escape. I was part of a tunnel group, but it collapsed before my turn came and we couldn't get enough wood to shore it up. After that I decided to sit it out. Hans told me it couldn't be long so I waited for the surrender.'

'Hans – was he a German?' Emily's brows rose. She was used

to everyone hating the enemy, and Daniel's voice seemed to indicate tolerance.

'I gave him chocolate from my parcels and he brought me manuals to study. I could probably pass any exam on mechanics I choose to sit now.'

'Oh, Dan.' Emily breathed a sigh of relief. Daniel was all right! There were bound to be bad memories and hidden scars, but he could cope with them. He wasn't broken in spirit like some of the men at the home. 'Thank goodness! You're just the same.'

'Not quite,' he admitted with a wry look. If anything, he had come out of it harder, tougher. 'But I've been lucky. I was sorry about Simon.' He looked at her oddly, uncertain of how she felt about her husband's death.

Emily nodded. 'It was a shame. We all thought he was getting better. He was going to America with a friend for treatment. They told us it was quite sudden. Vane had a heart attack afterwards, but he is much better now – thank goodness.'

'Are you happy staying there?'

'Yes, of course,' Emily said, though it wasn't completely true. Sometimes she wanted a lot more, but she didn't know what. Terry was dead and she was sure that she would never love another man in the same way. 'I wouldn't know what else to do, Daniel.'

'No, I suppose not,' he said and looked at the small boy playing with Danny on the floor. 'But you've a beautiful boy. And, hell, at least you've got a decent car, Emily. My old truck is all I can manage for the moment.'

'Vane bought it for my birthday. It isn't new, of course. No one can get new cars yet, but it is in lovely condition.' She smiled at her brother. 'Would you like to drive it? You can take Alice to see that house she has been telling me about.'

'Are you sure?' Daniel was pleased. 'It's generous of you, Emily. I'll take good care of it. But what about you? You don't want to drive my truck?'

'I'm going to see Frances when you and Alice leave. When you come back you can leave the car there for me if you will. I promised to have dinner with her and Marcus so you have plenty of time.'

'Great.' Daniel glanced at Alice. 'Get your coat on, love. I'll just have a look at the car with Emily.'

He went out and Emily followed, leaving Robert inside for the moment. She handed Daniel her keys and watched as he got into the driving seat, looking at the controls.

'It's a nice car, Emily.'

'I like it,' she said. 'I should like a private talk one day before I leave, Daniel.'

'Anything wrong?' He lifted his brows.

'No, I just want to talk.'

'Tomorrow morning? I'll come to the farm at ten.'

'Lovely,' Emily agreed. 'Have a nice afternoon with Alice. She is so excited about the house.' She turned as Alice came down the path wearing her best blue coat. 'Enjoy yourselves. I'm going to fetch Robert and walk to Frances's house. She says she wants to chat.'

'Don't do anything I wouldn't,' Alice said and giggled. Her face was lit up with excitement. Everything she had ever dreamed of was coming her way.

Emily smiled and waved them off. Her sister-in-law was such a pretty girl and so happy to have Daniel home. Tears stung Emily's eyes. It was lovely to see Alice so excited, and she sensed that Daniel was all right. He had changed in small ways but he wasn't crippled either in mind or body. No one could ask for more than that after what he'd been through.

3

'I love your hair,' Emily cried as she kissed her sister's cheek. 'It really suits you.'

'Do you think so?' Frances pulled a wry face. 'Marcus isn't too keen. He liked it long but I suppose it will grow again.' She looked at Emily's hair, which was still long, though caught up in a shining swirl at the nape of her neck.

'It would be a pity not to keep it short now,' Emily said. 'You really do look wonderful, Frances – more sophisticated. I have been thinking that I might have mine cut when I get time.'

'Well, perhaps I shall keep it shorter than I used to have it.' Frances put a hand to her hair. 'Marcus hasn't said that he doesn't like it. I just sense he doesn't.' She shook her head. 'I'm being silly! How are you, Emily? Still busy, I expect?'

'Yes, as a rule,' Emily replied. 'The home takes up a lot of my time, but I take Robert for walks in the park most days. I don't neglect him.'

'Of course you don't,' Frances said. 'If Amelia says that, she is wrong.'

'She doesn't exactly say it but I know she thinks it.' Emily pulled a wry face.

'That's like me,' Frances cried with a laugh. 'She probably doesn't at all – and Marcus probably likes my hair.'

'I am sure he does.' Emily watched as Frances fiddled with her rings. 'Is anything wrong – really wrong?'

'No...' Frances stood up and went to the window, looking out at the two small boys playing with the puppy. Robert was toddling after his older cousin, gamely trying to keep up. 'At least... Marcus is a little odd since he came home. He seems on edge and...' She turned to face Emily. 'I think he drinks too much whisky.'

'Oh, I see.' Emily sat in silence for a moment. 'Give him time to settle, love. He has been living on his nerves for years. Those flyboys went through hell, you know. Sometimes it catches up with the men afterwards.' She hesitated, then, 'He doesn't have nightmares, does he?'

'No, nothing like that. It's just the drinking – and he is restless. Sometimes, I don't think he wants to be home with us. He goes out in the evenings, and I think it is to drink with other men.'

'Is everything all right between you – you know what I mean?'

'Oh yes!' Frances blushed. 'I thought at first he might have met someone, but that side of it is fine.'

Emily laughed. 'Then I shouldn't worry too much if I were you. It's just that he is getting used to civilian life again.'

'Yes, I suppose so.' Frances smiled. 'You've seen Daniel and Alice? At least they are happy.'

'Alice is glowing,' Emily agreed. Her gaze narrowed as she studied her sister's face. 'There's something else, isn't there?'

'Yes,' Frances admitted on a sigh. 'It's Sam Danby.'

'Your father-in-law?'

'Yes.' Frances caught her breath. She hesitated for a moment and then, suddenly, it all poured out. The way Sam looked at her, the way he lost no excuse to touch her and how it made her feel.

'I can't stand being near him,' Frances said. 'I've tried being cool and distant but it doesn't work. He has started hinting now. I want it to stop but I don't know what to do.'

'Why don't you tell Marcus?'

'It's difficult. They aren't the best of friends anyway and it would make things worse. They might have an awful row. I should feel terrible if it caused a split in the family.'

'But it may be the only way – unless you could talk to his wife?'

'Tell Rosalind?' Frances was horrified. 'I couldn't do that, Emily. She doesn't like me much as it is.'

'Of course she does,' Emily said, but Frances shook her head. 'How do you know that?'

'I just know it,' Frances said. 'I suppose all this sounds silly to you, but I find it upsetting.'

'No, I don't think it is silly,' Emily said, 'but I do think you should talk to Marcus – or Mrs Danby. Or simply tell Mr Danby that if he doesn't behave you will refuse to let him see his grandson.'

'Yes...' Frances looked struck. 'I suppose I could do that if I have to. It's not something I'd do unless it got too bad – but it might be the way out of this mess. He adores Charlie. I hadn't thought of that, Emily. Thank you.'

Emily wished she hadn't said anything. Sam Danby was a hard man. If Frances tried to stop him seeing his grandson she might be treading on dangerous ground.

'Would you like me to tell Marcus for you?'

'Oh, no,' Frances said. 'I can hear a car outside. That must be

Marcus. Let's forget about it now. I'll think it over and decide what is best another time.'

* * *

Frances went to the door with Emily. It was gone nine and her sister wanted to get back to the farm, because she was afraid of keeping Henry up late. He had to be up early in the mornings and, as she had told Frances earlier, Emily was worried about him.

Frances watched as her sister got into the smart saloon car that Lord Vane had given her, feeling a pang of envy. Emily seemed so independent, so calm and self-assured. If she still felt grief over her lover's death, she didn't let it show. Frances wished that she could be more like Emily, or that her life was less complicated.

She was still feeling vaguely envious of her sister as she returned to the sitting room. Marcus was at the sideboard, helping himself to yet another drink. She wondered how many he'd had that evening, noticing that his hand trembled a little as he raised the glass to his lips.

'Do you think you should drink that, Marcus?' she asked. 'I should have thought you'd had more than enough already.'

'Should you indeed?' His eyes slanted round to look at her. 'What the hell do you know about it?'

'You drink far too much,' Frances said. She knew he was angry, but somehow she couldn't stop the words. 'You're not the same when you drink too much.'

'Damn you!' Marcus glared at her. 'Who asked for your opin- ion? I shall drink when I like and as much as I like – and if you disapprove you can go to hell!'

'Marcus!' Frances stared at him with hurt eyes. What had

happened to the man she loved? He would never have spoken to her like that when they were first married. He seemed like a stranger – a man she did not know and did not like much. 'Please don't speak to me like that. I am your wife.'

Marcus lifted his glass to salute her, a sardonic expression in his eyes. 'Wives are for f—' He sneered. 'Not for giving one a lecture. So shut up and go to bed if you don't like what I'm doing.'

'You're drunk,' Frances said. 'I refuse to be spoken to in that way, Marcus. I am going to bed now, alone. You can apologise in the morning.' She turned and left him, walking from the room with as much dignity as she could muster.

Upstairs, Frances turned the key in her bedroom door. She was upset and angry. It was the first time Marcus had ever been rude or abusive towards her and she didn't like it. He reminded her vividly of his father when he was drunk.

She shuddered as she undressed and crawled into bed. She hoped Marcus wouldn't try to get into her room, because nothing would make her unlock that door tonight.

Emily sighed as she closed the farm accounts. It had taken her ages to struggle through them, but at least now they were done Henry would have something to fight those ridiculous tax demands with, because the farm had lost money for years. She stretched her shoulders, feeling sad that after all his hard work, her elder brother was practically bankrupt. It was surely only a matter of time before the bank called in their loans. They would lose the land, and Henry would be lucky if he could manage to hold on to his home. She would have to try and help him if it came to that, Emily thought.

She went to the window of the back parlour and looked out into the long garden. Mary was feeding the hens that roamed free, scattering the scraps under an apple tree at the far end of the garden. Robert was helping her by chasing them whenever he got near enough, and he was having a wonderful time. It was a peaceful scene, but she knew well enough that her sister-in-law was worrying herself over Henry's health more than the state of his finances. His cough seemed much worse now and she had noticed him rubbing at his chest, but he was still refusing to visit the doctor.

'Have you finished?' a voice said from behind her, and she turned to see Daniel standing in the doorway. 'What's the verdict – is it as bad as Henry feared?'

'It couldn't be much worse,' Emily said. 'I doubt he will be able to hold on to this house once the bank calls in its loan – but I shall help Henry and Mary if they will let me. I have a few thousand that Simon left me. I don't need it, because Vane makes me an allowance for my work at the convalescent home.'

'Do you enjoy working there?' Daniel said. 'Alice said you had been through a tough time, but she wouldn't tell me the details – other than that Simon was dead. She said you would tell me if you wanted me to know.' He raised his brows at her.

'I was a fool to marry him,' Emily told him with a wry smile. 'You were right, Dan. You said that I should wait, get to know him properly – and I ought to have listened to you. The marriage was a sham from the beginning. Besides, there was someone else. I fell in love with him when it was too late, but we had a little time together before he was killed. He was a fireman and he went back into a burning building for someone – and it collapsed on top of him.'

'That's rotten luck,' Daniel said, looking at her affectionately. 'I'm sorry, Emily. I can't tell you it will be all right one day, because it wouldn't help even if I did. I suppose it helps having a child.'

'Yes, it does.' Emily took a deep breath. 'I haven't told anyone else the truth, Dan, not even Frances or Alice – but Robert is Terry's son. Vane thinks he is Simon's but that isn't possible.'

'Emily...' Her brother stared at her in dismay. 'That's a bit dangerous, isn't it? What if he finds out?'

'You won't tell him and I shan't,' Emily said, but there was a niggling doubt at the back of her mind. Amelia had guessed the truth and she just might use it if she was angry enough.

'But that means living a lie,' Daniel said, gazing at her uncertainly. 'It's a bit of a mess, Emily. You shouldn't have lied to Vane about a thing like that. It isn't right or fair.'

'I didn't lie to him. He assumed that the child was Simon's and I didn't tell him otherwise.'

'It's the same thing,' Daniel said. 'And it's not like you, Emily. I wouldn't have expected you to do something like that.'

'Oh, don't look at me like that,' Emily said, stung by his words. She already felt guilty enough without his censure. 'I know I ought to have told him, but he was just recovering from a heart attack – and Amelia begged me not to disappoint him. He had just lost his only son and I hadn't the heart to hurt him like that.'

'I see.' Daniel nodded but she could tell that he wasn't convinced. 'Well, it doesn't seem like a good idea to me – but you know your own business best.'

'I can't tell him now. He adores Robert,' Emily said. 'Besides, what harm can it do?'

'I don't know,' Daniel said. 'As long as you can live with it, I suppose it's your affair.'

Emily was uncomfortably aware that he was right, but she was upset that he seemed to think it was all her fault. He hadn't been there – he hadn't seen the pleading look in Amelia's eyes or the delight in Vane's. And she'd been particularly vulnerable at the time, unable to face telling Vane that she was carrying her lover's child.

'Anyway, let's forget it,' Daniel said, as she was silent. 'I'm worried about Henry. He's ill but he won't admit it.'

'Yes, I know,' Emily agreed. 'Mary begged him to go to the doctor this morning, but he said he was too busy.'

'I think it will finish him when the farm goes,' Daniel said. 'You and Frances will lose out, Connor too.'

'It doesn't matter about me, and Frances is all right,' Emily said. 'Connor is still at school but when he leaves I'll do what I can for him.'

'You can't help us all, Emily,' Daniel said with a wry grin. 'Besides, all that lad wants is to work on the land. He could do better for himself if he stayed on at school, went to college and earned a degree, as Frances wants him to – but he hates school and I doubt if he will stay past the end of the summer term. He would have left at fourteen if Frances had allowed it.'

'We'll see what happens when it comes to it,' Emily said. 'Actually, I do have quite a bit of money going spare, Daniel. Not enough to save the farm – but I could help you out with the garage you want.'

'No, thanks,' Daniel said swiftly. 'I can manage for the time being. Clay owes me two thousand and I intend on getting my money.'

'Clay isn't like you or Henry,' Emily said with a frown. 'I don't trust him these days – and he will wriggle out of paying you if he can.'

Daniel coughed and swore beneath his breath. 'I would have thrashed it out of him once – but I don't think I could do it now.'

'You will get better,' Emily said, looking at him anxiously.

'Alice said the hospital told her there were no lasting effects of the rotten experiences you've had, Dan – or was that just for her sake?'

'No, I shall be fine once I get over this,' Daniel said. 'It's the remnants of a fever I had when I was in hospital, but nothing to worry about. In a few months I shall be back to normal – but I don't have that long to wait. I've told Clay I want my money now.'

Emily nodded, looking doubtful. 'Well, I wish you good luck,' she said. 'But my offer still stands. If you need money, come to me. I will make it a loan if you would prefer, until you are as rich as Sam Danby.' She smiled to show that she was merely teasing. 'Seriously, Dan. I'd like to help if I can.'

'Thanks, love,' Daniel said. 'I shall remember if I'm desperate, but I had some back pay owing when I was demobbed, and that will tide us through for the moment. Alice's father has given us some money towards the house – he promised that when we married. We're putting down a hundred pounds and I'll manage to pay the rest off a bit at a time. Jack Martin has offered me a gentleman's agreement. He's a friend of Dad's from way back, but you might not know him?' Emily shook her head. 'Well, he offered and I accepted. We don't need to go to the bank for a mortgage, because he's the sort you can trust.'

Emily was about to say that she would lend him whatever he needed to settle his debt now, but the door opened and Mary, Henry's wife, came in, leading Robert by the hand. She was a plump woman with dark hair, never pretty but with a smile that made you feel warm right through.

'This young man wanted his mummy,' she said and smiled at Emily. 'I hope you've finished those books now, Emily. I've put the kettle on and we can all have a nice cup of tea.'

'Yes, I've finished,' Emily said and bent down to scoop Robert up in her arms. 'And after we've had our tea, I think I shall take

Robbie to see the calves. You would like that, wouldn't you, my darling?'

'Can we go now?' Robert asked and patted his mother's face with slightly grubby hands. 'Want to see the bull too.'

'Well, I'm not sure about that,' Emily said, laughing. 'But we'll see what Uncle Henry says later.'

* * *

'I'm sorry, Fran darling,' Marcus said when he came in that morning. 'I know what I said to you last night was inexcusable – but I hope you will forgive me? I was upset about something, but I shouldn't have taken it out on you.'

He moved towards her with the intention of kissing her. Frances turned her cheek, still angry with him.

'That was a disgusting thing you said to me last night. I am not sure I can forgive you, Marcus.'

'I can't remember exactly what I said.' Marcus ran his fingers through his thick dark hair. 'I know it must have been pretty bad for you to lock me out like that – and I do apologise. I had things on my mind, Fran.'

'Well, let's forget it,' Frances said, because she didn't want to carry on the quarrel. 'But please don't drink so much, Marcus. It upsets me – and it frightens me too. You're not the same when you've had a lot to drink. You're more like your father.'

'God forbid!' Marcus cried, and there was an expression in his eyes that shocked her. 'I'd rather be dead than turn out like him, Fran.' He saw her startled look of surprise and laughed harshly. 'I never did like him much – but to tell the truth I can't stand to be near him these days. When I think of what he's done...'

'What has he done, Marcus?'

Marcus shook his head, his expression one of distaste. 'You

don't want to know, Fran. Just be careful of him if he comes round when I'm not home.'

'You don't need to warn me about that,' Frances said. 'He is always giving me looks, touching me. I haven't wanted to tell you, because I didn't want to cause trouble between you.'

Marcus laughed again, but there was no humour in his eyes. 'We've had an almighty row. I doubt if he will come round for a while – but if he upsets you again, tell me. I would rather he didn't come, but I suppose I can't cut him off altogether, because of Mother.'

'Yes, all right,' she said. 'Are we friends again?'

'Yes, of course. Come here, darling.' Marcus drew her into his arms, and this time she offered her lips for his kiss. She sighed and nestled her head against his shoulder, feeling the relief flow over her. 'I really am sorry about last night. I won't let it happen around you again, Fran – but I can't promise not to drink. I need it. It isn't just what I've learned about Father, it's the war... All your friends dying... The fear of waiting for the next call.'

Frances looked up at him, seeing the haunted look in his eyes. 'It must have been awful for you.'

'It was bloody,' Marcus said. 'I know it is over and that I'm home again, but it isn't easy to forget. The drinking is a habit I picked up. We all did it whenever we got the chance, because it helped to deaden the fear – and the hell of going up, knowing that each day might be your last.'

'But you *are* home,' Frances told him. 'You're here with me and Charlie – and you don't have to worry about being shot down. We can be happy together if you let go, Marcus. You have to let go of all that.'

'I'll try for your sake,' Marcus said. 'Anyway, I shall have to pull myself together, because I need to look for a job.'

'Look for a job?' Frances was shocked. 'But I thought you were going to work for Sam?'

'Yes, so did I,' Marcus said. 'But I've changed my mind. I would rather go into a factory after...' He shook his head. 'He thought he could buy me with his dirty money, but I told him to go to hell. Mother told me she thought something wasn't right about that property in London, but I thought she was imagining things. She will be sickened when I tell her what I've discovered.'

'What have you discovered?'

Marcus shook his head. 'No, I can't tell you, Fran. It is too disgusting. I'm not sure what to do about it at the moment, but I've told him what he can do with it. I don't want to be involved in any of that.'

Frances was puzzled. She had always sensed that there was a darker side to her father-in-law. He was so secretive about his business in London. She wished that Marcus would tell her, but he was obviously too angry and too distressed to discuss it for the moment.

'Emily wants to take us all out to the Lamb Hotel in Ely for dinner while she is here,' Frances said, deciding to change the subject. 'She said tomorrow evening – will that be all right for you?'

'Yes, why not?' Marcus said and laughed, a genuine laugh this time. 'Don't look so worried, my darling. I promise to be a good boy and behave.'

'Oh, Marcus.' Frances shook her head at him. 'I'm so glad you're home. It was awful when you were away. I don't want to quarrel any more. Please, don't let us quarrel. I love you so much.'

'We shan't quarrel,' Marcus said and put his arms around her. 'I wouldn't mind something to eat now. I have an appointment this afternoon. It's a job managing a small farm machinery depot.

Doesn't pay what I had expected to earn, but we shall be lucky if I get it.'

'I hope you do,' Frances said fiercely. 'I don't want you to work for Sam if it makes you unhappy.'

'I've got a bit of money in the bank,' Marcus told her. 'We're not on the bread line yet, old girl. Although, if he wanted, he could throw us out of the house.'

'He wouldn't?' Frances felt a little tingle of alarm. 'It was supposed to be a wedding present.'

'Yes,' Marcus agreed. 'If he'd put the deeds over to us at the start it would be settled – but I shan't beg him, Fran, and I'm not going to work for him. If he cuts up nasty, I shall find us somewhere else to live.'

Frances turned away to make some sandwiches for their lunch. She didn't mind that Marcus had quarrelled with his father, or that he wouldn't be earning as much as he had expected – but she would hate to lose the house. It was a question of pride. Frances couldn't bear to be pitied, and she knew how people would talk if they had to move out into a smaller place. But perhaps Marcus would make up with his father or find a job he really liked. It wasn't fair, because the house was supposed to be theirs.

* * *

'Lose the farm?' Connor stared at his brother in dismay. 'But Henry can't lose the farm. He was going to give me a job when I leave school.'

'I'm afraid Henry doesn't have much choice,' Daniel said. 'The bank is calling its money in and that means everything will have to be sold. He hasn't told Mary yet, but he only just heard this morning. He will be lucky if he can cover the debt and hang on to his house.'

'I shall have to work for someone else then,' Connor said. 'I might ask Alice if her father will take me on.' He looked gloomy, because he had been so sure that he would be working for Henry. 'You'll be short of money too then?'

'Yes, it will be tight for a while,' Daniel said. 'I've scraped up enough to put a deposit on the house Alice wants, but I'm not sure how we shall manage. I've still got those fields along the Ely Road, which I've signed over to Alice to make sure they don't get seized by the bank as well as the family land.'

'Couldn't I work for you then?' Connor asked, looking hopefully at him. 'I wouldn't want more than a few bob and my keep.'

Daniel hesitated. He had intended giving his fields to Connor when he got sorted out, but with the bankruptcy hanging over them and Clay refusing to pay what he owed, he couldn't afford to do it yet.

'I was thinking of renting them out on a short lease,' he said. 'Henry put them down to grass and someone asked if he could have them for grazing this year. I've said yes, on the provision that I get them back next year. I might put them down to arable then, Connor, but for the moment I can't afford it.'

'Oh...' Connor turned away, his disappointment obvious to his brother. 'All right. I'll talk to Mr Robinson, ask him if he has any work – or if he knows of someone who will give me a job.'

'Have you considered staying on at school for another year?' Daniel said to his retreating back. He felt guilty because he was aware that Connor had been expecting to live with him and Alice. Daniel knew that Alice wouldn't have minded having him with them, but he didn't feel it was fair. She had a new house to cope with as well as their son and him. Besides, Daniel wanted some time alone with her. They had never had a real honeymoon, except for one night at the Lamb Hotel in Ely, because he'd had to go back to his unit. Yes, they needed a little time to get used to each other. Perhaps in a couple of months or so. 'Think about it, Connor. It might be the best thing.'

Connor didn't answer him. Daniel felt as if he'd let his brother down. It might have been different if he'd had the money Clay owed him. He could have started the little business he wanted and let Connor farm the fields he still owned. As it was, he wasn't sure how long he would be able to hang on to them. He might have to sell, though they wouldn't bring in even enough to finish paying off what he owed on the house.

* * *

'I wish Henry had come with us this evening,' Mary confided to Emily as they drove back to the farm. 'That was a lovely meal, and it was nice having the family all together. Except for Clay, of course, and we don't count him as family any more. I sometimes feel so sorry for Dorothy. Clay never takes her anywhere.'

'She is a fool to let him get away with it,' Emily said. 'But I don't have time for Clay. He isn't like any of the others.' She sighed as her thoughts drifted back to the time before her father married for the second time. 'What Clay did to Margaret was disgusting. And he has never treated Dorothy as he ought. I have no idea why she married him.'

'No...' Mary was thoughtful, then: 'Henry has always been good to me, Emily. I know he isn't as clever as Daniel, and perhaps it is his fault that the farm is in trouble – but he's a good man.'

'Yes, of course he is,' Emily said warmly. She was very fond of her eldest brother, Mary too. 'It wasn't all Henry's fault. The war made things difficult for him – and Clay didn't exactly play fair. If he hadn't insisted on taking his share of the estate out when Margaret did, forcing us to borrow so heavily, it might not have gone so badly.'

'You've helped him all you could,' Mary said. 'But he needed Daniel to put him right on things. If Dan had been here...' She sighed as they drew up outside the house. 'That's odd, there are no lights. I know the boys are staying with friends, and your Robert is with Alice's parents, but Henry said he would be working at home.'

'Perhaps he was tired and went to bed. You said he had admitted to feeling not quite right earlier.'

'He half promised to go to the doctor tomorrow,' Mary said. Her voice was breathy and Emily sensed that she was anxious. She locked the car and followed her sister-in-law up to the back door. It was odd that the kitchen was in darkness, and she had an uneasy feeling that something was wrong. She was almost expecting it when Mary switched on the light and gave a cry of alarm. 'Henry!'

Henry was sitting at the kitchen table, slumped forward, his head on his arms. There was something odd about the way he was positioned, somehow stiff and unnatural. Emily's heart jerked with fear as she went to him. She felt for a pulse, but his skin was cold and she knew even before Mary lifted his head and looked at his face.

'Oh, Henry,' Mary said on a sob, cradling his head against her ample breasts for a moment. 'Not tonight, love. Not when I'd left you alone. I've never left you alone before.' She looked at Emily, her face working with grief. 'He made me come with you, said I should go and enjoy myself – and now look what he's done. I just wish I'd been with him.'

'You probably couldn't have done anything. Henry has been ill for a long time, Mary. He ought to have seen a doctor ages ago.'

'He always said he was too busy, told me not to fuss so much,' Mary said, tears sliding down her cheeks. 'Oh, Emily. He was such a good man. He didn't deserve this.' She caught back a sob of despair. 'He felt he had let you all down.'

'Of course he didn't,' Emily said, her throat tight with emotion, because she had been so very fond of her brother. He was slow and inclined to get things in a muddle at times, but kind and dear. She put her arms about Henry's wife, letting Mary cry, stroking her shoulder. She had done something similar many times in the past with relatives of dying patients, but this struck home because Henry was her brother and she loved him very much. 'Henry was a dear, and he did his best. It wasn't his fault that it all went so wrong. You mustn't ever think that we blame him, Mary.'

'No, it wasn't his fault.' Mary raised her head. Her cheeks were wet with tears but she was making an effort to control them. 'It wasn't his fault that the war came and he got in such a muddle with all the regulations, but he blamed himself.' She fished for a handkerchief in the pocket of her serviceable coat and blew her nose hard. 'What do I do now? I suppose we need the doctor and...' Words failed her. She looked at her sister-in-law, clearly at a loss. 'What am I going to tell the boys?'

'Leave that until the morning,' Emily suggested. 'Would you like me to telephone for the doctor? I'll ring Frances too and ask her to contact Daniel. Alice's father isn't on the telephone but Marcus will go along the street and tell him. Unless you want to do it yourself?'

'I would rather you did it,' Mary said. 'I'm going to put clean sheets on the bed, because they will lay him there for the moment, won't they?'

'Yes, I expect so. Until we can make the arrangements for the undertaker to come. Do you want Henry to stay here or be taken to a chapel of rest?'

'He stays here until the last,' Mary said. 'He would come back and haunt me if I sent him away. Excuse me, I must make sure we're tidy before anyone comes.'

Emily watched as her sister-in-law hurried away. She knew that Mary was merely making an excuse to tidy up, but she needed to be busy, because she wasn't ready to face what had happened.

Emily bent down to kiss Henry's cold cheek. 'Poor old love,' she whispered. 'I am so sorry, Henry. So sorry, my dear.'

She touched his head once more and then walked out into the hall to make the necessary phone calls. She must telephone the doctor first, but the police would also have to be informed because Henry had died suddenly. It was all so sad and she wasn't sure that Mary would get her wish and keep Henry at home until the last. There might have to be an inquest into his death, because it had happened so quickly.

She decided to phone Frances first, because she needed Daniel to be here. Emily had coped with this situation so often at the convalescent home, but this time it was different. This time it was her brother, and she wanted to sit down and weep, but she had to be strong for Mary's sake.

* * *

'I wish you weren't leaving immediately,' Frances said as they walked out of church together some days later. 'It is all so horrible. Mary is wandering about as if she doesn't know what time of day it is, and I keep thinking of Henry dying alone.'

'Don't, love, there's nothing you can do to change things.' Emily gave her a hug. Frances was tearful, fishing for her handkerchief. 'Yes, I know. It is awful, but it was his choice, Frances. He didn't want to come to the hotel with us that evening, and he insisted that Mary went alone. I'm just glad that Robert was with Alice's parents, and that Henry's boys were staying with friends.'

'That is what I mean. He was completely alone. It must be terrible to die all alone.' Frances shuddered and dabbed at her eyes. 'Poor old Henry – except that he wasn't so very old. He wasn't even forty, Emily. He just seemed to be old, perhaps because he was ill, or the worry of the farm was too much for him. I loved him. He didn't deserve to go that way.'

'Yes, I loved Henry too,' Emily agreed, feeling her throat tighten. 'Apparently, it was his heart, and he knew that he might not have much time left. He had been to see Dr Merton, but he'd kept it from all of us, just carried on as he always did. I suppose the fact that he had visited the doctor made it easier with the certificate.'

'Emily! How could you?' Frances looked shocked. 'You seem so cold, so calm, as though it was just one of your patients and didn't matter.'

'Everyone matters,' Emily said, holding her pain inside. 'I care, of course I do. It is just that it meant they didn't need to take him away, and Mary wanted him at home.' She could see that her sister thought she was uncaring, but she'd shed her tears for Henry in private.

Emily left Frances and went to her sister-in-law. Mary was looking rather lost, her eyes wearing a faraway expression as if she wasn't here in spirit. She was just standing there aimlessly, but she smiled as Emily came up to her.

'The church was full. Henry would have liked that, wouldn't he? I am sure he never expected so many people to be here today.'

'He would have been pleased.' Emily put a comforting arm

about her waist, feeling her tremble. Mary was bearing up, but only just. 'Henry had a lot of friends. People liked him – and they respected him for what he was, Mary. You could always trust Henry.'

Mary blinked hard. 'Dorothy is here, you know,' Mary said. 'Clay didn't come, but Dorothy said she wanted to be with us. Wasn't that kind of her?'

'Yes, but she is like that. Clay might have come, though.' Emily felt a flicker of anger against her brother.

'It doesn't matter. Henry wouldn't have wanted him here. He never forgave him for what he did to Margaret – or for taking his share out of the land when he knew Henry couldn't afford to pay him.'

'No, I suppose not.' Emily looked at her, sensing her unease. 'You'll be all right, Mary. I have to go back because I am needed. Daniel will look after you – and the house is yours. You don't have to move if you don't want to, and then you could sell.'

Mary looked bewildered. 'Are you sure? I thought everything had to go in the sale, but I don't understand these things.'

'You mustn't worry about anything. Daniel will take care of everything.' Emily kissed her cheek. 'I'm going to say goodbye to him. I'll write to you soon, Mary, and I'll ring you now and then, as I did Henry. You can always telephone me if you want me.'

She left her sister-in-law as other friends came up to them, making her way to where Daniel stood with Alice and Connor.

'Can I talk to you for a moment, Dan?'

'Yes, of course.' He glanced at his wife. 'Go and have a word with Dorothy, love. She looks a bit lost over there. You go to Mary, Connor. Ask her if she needs any jobs doing at the house. Even if it's only chopping a bit of wood. She'll be glad of some help, I daresay.'

'It was good of Dorothy to come,' Emily said as the others went off. 'Clay ought to have come with her though.'

'Just as well he didn't. Mary blames him for all the worry Henry had over the farm – and I agree with her in part. Some of this is down to Clay.' Daniel's handsome face was tight with anger. 'Clay has a lot to answer for.'

'Yes, I agree,' Emily said. 'I have to leave now, Dan. You know what we've arranged about Mary's house – and if anything is salvaged when they sell the farm it goes to Mary and the boys.'

'Yes, of course. She will be all right. Her brother has already offered to take her in if she wants. She won't starve, Emily.'

'I know that, but she may prefer her independence.'

'I'm not sure what she wants, but we'll give her time to decide.'

'I feel awful about leaving you with all this, Dan, but I'm needed at the home. Amelia has been on the phone almost every day.'

'You told me. Besides, this is my responsibility. You've done your bit with the house.'

'Mary isn't to know that I bought it from the bank,' Emily said. 'Besides, it's only money. She needs more than that – but it is you, Alice and Frances who will have to supply the things I can't.'

'We'll manage,' her brother said with a wry smile. 'Stop worrying, Emily, and go. Robert looks anxious.'

'Nanny is looking after him,' Emily said, though she could see that her son was pulling at Nanny's hand in an effort to break free. 'I keep thinking – if I hadn't given Nanny the night off she might have been there with Henry.' She caught back a sob. 'No, it wouldn't have changed anything. Dr Merton said his heart just gave up because it was worn out.'

'He was a victim of the war like so many others,' Daniel said with a grim look. 'If I had been here I could have taken some of the strain, but I was stuck in that damned camp sitting on my backside and twiddling my thumbs. Don't blame yourself, Emily. Blame the war or fate or the government, but not yourself.'

'No, I shan't,' she promised. 'I'll go then – but don't forget what I said the other day. If you need money...' Daniel shook his head, making her smile because he was the same old stubborn Dan. 'I know it isn't what you want, my dear, but it's there if you need it. Take care of yourself and Alice – and little Danny.'

Emily walked away from the church to her car. Nanny was waiting patiently, but Robert was pulling at her hand. He broke away from her as she came up to them, stumbling towards her on his chubby legs. Emily bent down to sweep him up in her arms. She held him close, loving the clean fresh smell of his soft body. Her love flowed towards him, wrapping about him. He was so precious and she loved him so much. She hugged and kissed him, setting him down again next to Nanny, who captured his hand.

'Shall we go home?' she asked. 'Is everything packed, Nanny?'

'Yes, madam,' Nanny replied. 'I daresay you will be glad to be on your way. These occasions are very sad.'

'Yes,' she agreed. 'Very sad. My brother wasn't old, Nanny. He just seemed that way.'

Emily was thoughtful as she started the car and moved off. She wasn't sure how long it would be before she came down again. Since her marriage, she had always stayed with Henry at the farm when she visited. It was as if something had gone, cutting off her links to the past.

She realised that she would no longer think of this village as home. Daniel, Frances and Connor were still here, but they didn't need her and her home was at Vanbrough House now. Her future belonged with Vane and Robert. And Amelia, of course.

4

_____

Emily was standing staring out at the night sky when Vane entered the small sitting room. She sensed he was there, though he didn't speak, and turned to smile at him.

'Come in, Vane. You're not disturbing me.'

'You seemed lost in thought. I wasn't sure if I was intruding.'

'No, of course not. I was about to order some hot cocoa before I go to bed, but I don't suppose I can tempt you?'

'I would prefer a brandy,' Vane said and chuckled as he saw her fine brows lift. 'I know the doctor says that I ought not to indulge, but what is the point? I shall live as long as the powers that be intend and no longer.'

'Do you really believe that?' Emily asked. 'Is the future all mapped out for us? Do we have any choice?'

'Are you thinking of yourself?' Emily shook her head. 'Your brother? It was sad to die at that age. If he was in trouble you should have asked me, Emily. I might have been able to arrange something with my bank – an extended loan or something.'

'Henry would never have agreed. He had no head for book work, but he was a good farmer and a proud man. If he could have hung on for a while, Daniel might have sorted things out, but it was too late.'

'A pity, my dear,' Vane said. 'I am very sorry.'

'Yes, so am I,' Emily said. 'I think I shall go and ask for my cocoa now. Goodnight, Vane.'

'Goodnight, my dear. I missed you and I am glad you're back.'

Emily smiled but didn't answer as she left the room. He stared after her. The smell of her perfume lingered, filling his senses. He was disturbed by some news of his own, news which might mean that the convalescent home would close. He must think of something to keep Emily busy and fulfilled or he might lose her.

* * *

'I was sorry about your brother,' Sam Danby said when he met Frances in the high street a few days later. 'I would have come to the funeral but I was in London.'

'Henry was ill,' Frances replied coldly. She lifted her head, giving him a proud stare because she did not need his sympathy. 'It's Mary I feel sorry for. She is alone in that big house and she doesn't know what to do with herself.'

'No, I suppose it is very difficult for her. Her boys are both at school, aren't they?'

'Yes. Why do you ask?'

'We need help in the house. Rosalind likes your sister-in-law. She wondered whether she should offer her a little job.' He held up his hand as Frances glared at him. 'No, please don't look at me like that, Frannie. I'm not saying she's only fit for house-work and I'm not taking advantage. She must be finding it hard with the bankruptcy sale coming up soon. I only wanted to help.'

'I think we can look after her ourselves,' Frances said. 'Daniel has given her a little money and Marcus is giving the same.'

'That son of mine is a damned fool!' Sam muttered angrily. 'What does he mean by working for that tuppenny-ha'penny firm when he might be his own boss?'

'Marcus makes his own decisions,' Frances said. 'If you will excuse me, I must get on. I have a lot to do today.'

'I miss having my tea with you,' Sam said. 'Why don't you bring the boy to tea with Rosalind? She was saying that she hasn't seen you in ages – except at the funeral, of course.'

'I shall ring her,' Frances said. She wasn't particularly fond of her mother-in-law, but Rosalind had done nothing wrong. It was only right that she should see her grandson now and then. And Sam couldn't touch her or give her those looks in front of his wife. 'Yes, I should like to visit soon.'

'Good!' Sam looked pleased with himself. 'I'll tell her later. She will have something to look forward to. Get off then. I shan't keep you from your work.'

Frances walked away. Marcus would be pleased she was going to have tea with his mother. He might hate his father, but he still saw his mother as often as he could, usually when his father was out.

He had been very good about his drinking since the night Henry died. Frances hadn't noticed him drinking anything more than a glass of wine with his dinner. Things were better between them again. He was loving and charming, as he had always been. She believed that it was all going to be perfect again, just the way she had planned it when she married.

* * *

'I was sorry to hear about your brother,' Amelia said as they were drinking tea together in the front parlour some days after Emily's return. 'It was a sad business, because he was quite young, wasn't he?'

'Yes, he was and it was awful,' Emily agreed. 'I knew he was ill but I didn't expect him to die like that, so suddenly. The worst thing was that we had all gone out to dinner and he was alone.'

'Yes, that was unfortunate,' Amelia agreed, her fine brows lifting as she looked at Emily. 'I worry about Vane. He's had one severe attack. Another might kill him.'

'He seems to be much better. He is always working or going to meetings.'

'Yes, I know – but if he were to be really upset over something...'

'What are you saying, Amelia?'

'Vane would be most upset if you left us.'

'I have no intention of leaving.'

Amelia smiled her satisfaction. 'Vane thought you might decide to go and live near your family. I told him he was worrying for nothing. We are both so fond of you, Emily. Vane missed Robert terribly when you were away. He is all we have, you see. It would upset him if you took the boy away from us.'

'Yes, I know that,' Emily said. She felt a tingle at the nape of her neck. Amelia was smiling. Nothing she had actually said could be taken as a threat, and yet it felt that way. 'But I have not thought of leaving. This house is home to me now, Amelia. Robert loves it too.'

'Yes, he does,' Amelia said. 'That is good, because it will be his one day – the title too. You wouldn't want to jeopardise that, would you, Emily?'

'No...' Emily hesitated. The threat was veiled but it was there beneath the surface. 'You don't need to worry, Amelia. I'm not going to take Robert away again – not for quite a while. Now that Henry is dead and the farm is to be sold it doesn't seem the same.'

'Such a pity that it had to happen,' Amelia said. 'Was there no way your other brothers could save the farm?'

'Unfortunately not,' Emily said. She stood up, feeling that she had had enough of Amelia's questions for the moment. 'I'm going upstairs to see Robert for a few minutes, and then I shall go down to the home to see how things are.'

'Yes, of course you must,' Amelia agreed. 'Robert is quite tired, I think. He had a lovely time in the gardens this morning. Vane gave him a model boat and we sailed it in the lily pond. Don't look so alarmed, Emily. Nanny was there too. He was perfectly safe. You must know that I always take care of him. I would never let any harm come to Robert. He is such a little darling and we all love him. Besides, he is Vane's heir, isn't he?'

'Yes, we do love him,' Emily agreed, ignoring what she felt was a taunt. 'But in future I would rather you asked before letting him play near water, Amelia.'

She left the room before Amelia could answer. It irritated her because Amelia took so much for granted. She behaved for much of the time as if she thought Robert belonged to her. Emily tried to be understanding. Amelia had wanted to give Vane an heir but it had not happened. That was a shame, but it didn't give her the right to act as if Emily's son were her own.

Sometimes, Emily wondered if she ought to devote more of her time to Robert, and yet the home was important to her – and to Vane. He relied on her to run it and she enjoyed having the responsibility. No, she couldn't give it up, she decided. Besides, it would be unkind to deny Amelia her part in Robert's life. She loved him and he loved her. Emily was foolish to be jealous. She must share him with Vane and his wife.

It was the price she had to pay for letting Vane believe that the boy was his grandson.

* * *

'Are you sure you want to do this?' Daniel asked of his sister-in-law. It was just two weeks since the funeral and she was talking of taking a job with the Danbys. 'You don't have to work, Mary. The rest of us will make sure that you don't go without. Connor is willing to look after the pigs and that will bring in a few pounds every now and then.'

'Connor has been a good boy,' Mary said and smiled. 'Henry always kept a few pigs in the orchard, apart from the rest of the livestock. We never sold them, just killed one when we needed it.'

'And you still can if you wish.'

'I think I shall sell them.' Mary shook her head and sighed as Daniel protested. 'You've all been so kind, but I can't expect Connor to keep giving up his free time. I've still got my home and a little bit in the bank, which I didn't expect – but I don't mind giving Rosalind Danby a hand a couple of days a week. I like her and she made it sound like a favour to her. She sat here in my kitchen and told me she was lonely, asked me if I would come and do a bit for her if I had the time. I shall be cooking and doing light housework. She already has a cleaner. I thought it was kind of her to offer and it gives me some independence.'

'Well, if it's what you want,' Daniel said. He had already given her as much as he could afford, but he knew Emily would have sent a regular payment if he had asked. He frowned as he thought of something. 'You won't come to the sale tomorrow? It's machinery and bits and pieces – the horses too.'

'No, I shan't come,' Mary said. 'Shall you go?'

'Yes, I believe I shall,' Daniel replied. 'I might buy a few things myself. Danby thinks a lot of it will go for a song. Money is tight at the moment – and it happens at bankruptcy sales.'

Mary frowned. 'That sounds so awful. Bankruptcy sale. I can't imagine what your father would have thought, Daniel.'

'He would have been angry,' Daniel said. He wasn't happy about it himself, but he was brushing through as easily as he could for her sake. 'It might not have happened if Father hadn't married again. Margaret wanted her money when she went off, which left us with a huge debt. It was worse because Clay demanded his share too. The way things were during the war with all the restrictions, Henry didn't stand a chance of paying it off.'

'You would have managed it better,' Mary said. 'Henry often said it. He knew all there was to know about the land, but he wasn't a businessman. The interest kept mounting up and he just ignored it because he couldn't find a way to pay it off.'

'It wasn't his fault. If Clay hadn't wanted out, Henry would have had the help he needed. Two heads are always better than one.'

Daniel left his sister-in-law busy in her kitchen. She was baking cakes for a church bazaar and seemed to have settled down well enough. He had been worried about how she would cope, but now that the funeral was over, she seemed to have accepted her situation – at least she wasn't wearing her grief on her sleeve. He didn't particularly like the idea of her working for Rosalind Danby, but he couldn't forbid it. On top of the bankruptcy it felt too much like humiliation, but Mary didn't see it that way.

He was frowning as he got into his truck. Clay hadn't come up with any money as yet. It was about time he paid his brother another visit.

* * *

Frances looked at the pretty gilt clock on the mantelpiece. The sale of farm goods would be starting in half an hour. She knew that Daniel was going, but she couldn't face it. She didn't even want to go to the village shop, because she knew that people would be talking about the sale. Some of them would laugh behind their hands. They would take pleasure in seeing the downfall of the Searles family – and it *was* humiliating, whatever Daniel might say to the contrary. Henry had allowed things to slide and Frances felt he had let them all down. She knew that he had been ill in the past few months, but she didn't understand where all the money had gone. There had been plenty when her father was alive.

She decided that she would catch the bus into Ely and get her hair done. She preferred the hairdresser there to the village salon. Besides, she would avoid all the sly looks and sniggers if she went into town.

* * *

Daniel watched as the auctioneer knocked down the farm machinery for a fraction of what it was worth. He ground his teeth, swallowing his bile. All this was so damned unfair! And there was nothing he could do about it. The bank had taken over and they didn't care that the carts and tractors could have been sold for more money, and the horses! They were good stock. Sold privately, they might have made at least fifty pounds more than they had today. All the bank wanted was to recover the debt. Daniel had hoped that something might have been saved from the mess, but now he realised that they would be lucky to clear the debt.

'Rotten shame,' Sam Danby said, coming up to him as the last of the horses went for next to nothing. 'I thought this might happen. Your brother should have sold to me a year ago. I would have bought him out and given him a fair price.'

Daniel nodded, a grim expression on his face. He wanted to tell Danby why Henry would never have sold to him, but he bit back the bitter words. Henry hadn't trusted the man, but it may have been better to swallow his pride and taken a decent offer rather than let things get to this fiasco. He would probably have persuaded Henry to let him handle it if he'd been home.

'Henry thought he could get through,' Daniel said in defence of his brother. 'It is a pity but he was too ill to manage the business. If I had been home it might have been different.'

'Great shame. Don't like to see it, Dan. If you're interested in selling those fields of yours, I'll give you a good price.'

'Thanks,' Daniel said. 'I haven't made up my mind yet, but I'll speak to you first if I sell.'

'Good man,' Danby said. 'I think I'll get off now. I have an appointment in Ely. It's a sorry day, Daniel. Your father wouldn't have liked this.'

'No, he wouldn't.'

Daniel cursed inwardly. As if he needed reminding! Robert Searles would have fought tooth and nail to keep his land! He felt as if he had failed his father. The shame of seeing the family brought to this sat like a sour lump in his chest. Yet he had been powerless to help while stuck in that damned prisoner of war camp. He felt icy shivers down his spine as he recalled the hell of those wasted months and years. The nightmares still haunted him and they didn't always come in the hours of darkness.

He'd had enough of this shameful business! Daniel turned and walked off. Clay had promised to give him the five hundred pounds this afternoon. He had wanted the whole two thousand, but Clay wouldn't budge. Daniel knew that he might have to settle for what he could get. At least for the time being.

With five hundred pounds he could at least get started. There was a barn behind the house he'd bought for Alice. He could work on renovating second-hand cars there for a while – until he could find enough money to set up the garage he wanted with a forecourt, showroom and petrol pumps. It was a long way from what he had planned, he reflected grimly, but it looked as if he was stuck with a bad deal.

He had arranged to take the pigsties and a few pigs from Mary, which would give her a little money. He had room in the orchard that backed on to the house in the fens, and he would keep hens and chickens there. Perhaps a few geese as well, and of course he would grow all the vegetables they needed.

He frowned as he recalled what had got him into this fix. He had given into Margaret's blackmail the night Clay had raped her. He ought to have refused, let her call the police. Clay deserved a prison sentence for what he'd done to her.

Daniel shook his head, smiling grimly as he admitted to himself that he could never have done it. Poor Dorothy would have been wretched over it, and Frances would have felt humiliated. Emily would have hated it too, though she would have got on with things – and she was away from it now. He was glad she hadn't been here today to see the way things had gone.

Daniel felt some of the bitterness ease as he thought of his favourite sister. Emily had wanted to help him get started, but a man had his pride. He wouldn't ask Emily for money unless he was desperate.

* * *

Frances frowned as she approached the bus stop in Ely and saw the bus drawing away. The hairdresser had kept her waiting while she finished putting the dye on someone else's hair, and that meant Frances was stuck here for at least another hour. Muriel was looking after Charlie, but she would be wanting to get off home soon.

'Want a lift?'

Frances looked to her left and saw that Sam Danby had drawn up to the kerb in his car. It was a large, shiny Daimler and very expensive. She hesitated, because the last thing she wanted was to be alone with him, and yet she couldn't let Muriel down or she might lose her.

'Yes, all right, thanks,' she said. 'I've just missed the bus.'

'I saw it leaving,' Sam said and smiled at her. 'Hop in then, Frannie, and I'll soon have you home.'

Frances did as he suggested. She pulled her coat over her knees, sitting primly, her hands on her lap. Sam glanced sideways at her and smiled but made no comment.

'Your hair looks very nice,' he said as the car nosed out into the road. There wasn't a great deal of traffic in Market Street, just a lorry and one other car. The only time the street was really busy was on a Thursday when everyone came in from the villages for the market.

'I like the way they do it here,' Frances said, putting a hand to her bouncy style. 'I'm not sure that Marcus does. He liked when it was longer, but it is easier to manage like this.'

'Marcus doesn't know what he wants,' Sam said with a sneer. 'Your hair is modern and pretty. It suits you – and you should do what you want, not what he says.' He took his eyes off the road for a moment. 'Does he give you enough money, Frannie? For yourself, I mean. You should have good clothes and nice jewellery. A woman like you deserves the best money can buy.'

'Marcus hasn't got that much to spare for the moment,' Frances said. 'He helped Mary, as I told you – but don't think we're short, because we're not.' They didn't have a lot to spare but they were managing for the moment.

'Marcus is a fool,' his father said again, sounding annoyed. 'If he came to see me we might be able to sort this out, but he is as stubborn as his mother.'

'I think you can be pretty stubborn too, Sam – when you want.'

'You're right about that, Frannie.' Sam took his left hand from the steering wheel, laying it on her knee for a moment. 'When I want something I just keep after it until it comes my way.'

Frances removed his hand from her knee. 'I am grateful for the lift, Sam, but let's get something clear. I am Marcus's wife and I don't play fast and loose.'

'No, you don't,' Sam said and obligingly returned his hand to the wheel. 'That's a pity because I like you. As a matter of fact, I fancy you something rotten. I know you don't fancy me, Frannie, but just remember that I could do a lot for you. I wouldn't ask much, just to visit once a week. You could be nice to me and I would be nice to you – a mutual arrangement. Marcus doesn't need to know.'

'What would Rosalind think if she knew what you had just said to me?'

'It wouldn't surprise her in the least,' Sam said. 'She gave up caring what I do a long time ago. We live our own lives. I don't interfere with her and she leaves me to do as I please.'

'Oh...' So much for Emily's idea that she could speak to his wife. 'I don't think I could agree to anything like that, Sam. I love Marcus and I wouldn't want to let him down.'

'Well, I have to respect that for the moment,' Sam said. 'I'm not going to force anything on you, Frannie – I like you too much.

It is a pity you weren't more amenable to my suggestion, but there's always another day. You might change your mind in the future. My offer will still stand when you realise that Marcus is never going to amount to much.'

'That's a horrid thing to say about your own son!'

'But it is true,' Sam replied, glancing at her face. 'Don't poker up, Frannie. You know it in your heart even if you aren't ready to admit it yet. Marcus is weak. I don't know where he gets it from, certainly not me. Rosalind's father was a bit of a drip, thought himself above trade and all that stuff, so maybe that's who he takes after. You're an ambitious girl, Frannie. You want more than the life Marcus is offering you. When you decide you've had enough of being a housewife, come to me. I could show you a different sort of life, believe me.'

'You are saying things you shouldn't,' Frances warned him. 'I'm going to let it go because I don't want more trouble in the family – but I shall never be what you want, Sam.'

'No?' His brows rose and there was a hateful smile on his lips. 'If Marcus keeps drinking the way he does, you will change your mind soon enough. I'm a patient man, Frannie. I can wait a bit longer.'

Frances bit her lip. How did Sam Danby know that Marcus drank too much? She had imagined that he was cutting back, that he was almost normal again, his nightmares behind him. How had Sam got hold of the idea that his son was drinking too much?

* * *

Frances looked at the clock on the mantle. It was almost eight o'clock and she had been expecting Marcus home for dinner more than an hour ago. She had had to put his meal in the oven to keep warm and she knew it would have spoiled by now. She had tried to eat her own, but most of it had gone out in the bin because she couldn't get the food down. She was worried sick because Sam Danby's words kept echoing in her mind and she was afraid that Marcus had been drinking more than she'd imagined.

Hearing something in the hall, she looked expectantly towards the parlour door. Surely Marcus would come in and tell her that his car had broken down on the way home or that he had been kept late at work? She heard something fall and then the sound of footsteps going upstairs. She went out into the hallway, seeing that an umbrella stand had been knocked over, the walking sticks and other paraphernalia lying on the floor. Frances bent to pick them up, her heart beating faster than normal. Was Marcus drunk? Surely not? He had promised he wouldn't do it again! She hesitated and then went upstairs. A light was on in the bathroom, and as she paused outside the door she heard a retching noise – he was being sick. Perhaps he was ill!

She opened the door and looked in, seeing Marcus on his knees in front of the toilet, his head bent over it as he vomited.

'Are you ill?' she asked, hesitating to approach him.

'Get out of here,' he muttered. 'Leave me alone or you'll be sorry.'

Frances backed out of the room. Her throat was tight and she wanted to weep. Marcus had been drinking, his sickness self-imposed. He had broken his word to her!

Sam must have known that Marcus was drinking too much. He had hidden it from Frances when he was in the house, but other people had known. She felt angry and humiliated, imagining what people must be saying and thinking. As if it wasn't

enough losing the farm! Did Marcus really have to get himself
into this state?

She went back downstairs and picked up a copy of *Vogue*
magazine that she had purchased in Ely. The illustrations of
beautiful girls in expensive clothes made her feel even more
resentful than she already was. It was ages since she'd bought
herself anything good. Marcus wasn't mean, she knew that, but
he simply didn't have the money for clothes like this – and as for
jewellery...

Frances shook her head. She wasn't going to let herself think
about things like that, because that would mean that Sam had
won. He had tried to taunt her, to make her realise what was
lacking from her life – from the life she had imagined would be
hers when she married Marcus. He came from a wealthy family
and she'd had every right to expect that she would have all the
luxuries she could desire.

Frances stared at herself in the mirror. It wasn't that she was
greedy or dissatisfied with what she had now. She would be
perfectly content if only Marcus didn't drink so much. But he
was changing, becoming a man she didn't know or like very
much.

* * *

'Oh, Sam,' Rosalind Danby said as her husband came in that
evening, 'I wondered if you could advise me. There are rats at the
bottom of the garden again. They are after the rabbit food, I
suppose.'

'We should get rid of them,' Sam said. 'The war is over,
Rosalind. We don't need them for food – and I've never been
fond of rabbit anyway.'

'I keep them for Charlie's sake,' Rosalind said. 'He likes to pet them – not that he comes here very often, but he likes to stroke them when he does.'

'Keep them then,' Sam said, because if he cared about anyone's wishes it was his grandson's. 'You can leave the rat poison to me, Rosalind. You wouldn't understand what you were buying. A lot of the stuff they sell you at the ironmonger's doesn't work. I know where to get something stronger.'

'Oh, well, if you think so, Sam,' Rosalind said. 'I am sure you know best. Can I get you some cocoa – or would you prefer a drink?'

'I'll get my own,' Sam said. 'Don't fuss, woman. You know I can't stand it. Just get your own and let me be.'

Rosalind turned her head. She had put up with his rudeness, his coarse manners and his careless dismissal of her as a person for years. Sometimes she felt as if she couldn't bear it any more, but she didn't know what else she could do. She was trapped here with Sam, and as far as she could see there was no way out.

* * *

'I'm sorry, Fran,' Marcus said when he came down the next morning. It was half past nine and he was dressed in a pair of grey slacks and an informal shirt. 'I was a bit the worse for wear last night.'

'You had been drinking,' she said, giving him a reproachful look. 'You promised you wouldn't, Marcus.'

'I have tried to cut back,' he said, looking at her sheepishly. 'But something happened – I was sacked yesterday. Not doing the job properly, so they said, but that's a lie – there was another reason. Jackson couldn't look me in the eye when he told me. I swear he had no reason to complain of my work. He sacked for some other reason.'

Frances looked at him doubtfully. She hated his drinking and what it did to him, but he was still her husband – and she was still on his side.

'Sam gave me a lift home from Ely yesterday after I missed the bus. You don't think...'

'That is exactly what I think,' Marcus said wrathfully. 'He probably gave Jackson a huge order for farm machinery on the condition that he sacked me. He wants me to go crawling back to him, Fran – but I would rather starve.'

'Oh, Marcus,' Frances said. She went to him, putting her head against his shoulder. She wasn't sure that getting Marcus to work for him was the whole of Sam Danby's plan. He might want to humiliate him, to make her see that he wasn't the successful man his father was – because he wanted her. 'I'm so sorry, love. So very sorry.'

Marcus moved away from her, a look of belated pride in his eyes. 'No need for you to be sorry, Fran. It's not your fault. I know I shouldn't have let it get to me that way – but I couldn't help it. I thought I was doing a good job and then...' He shook his head. 'I needed a drink and one led to another, but it won't happen again. I give you my word.'

'What will you do now?' Frances said. 'That was a good job and there aren't so many about these days.' She didn't like the idea of Marcus having to take a menial job in a factory.

'Mother said she would give me some money,' Marcus said. 'I could start a small business myself – perhaps in haulage. It won't be like Father's firm because I'll only have one lorry for a start, and I'll do long-haul journeys. I think there is more money in that over time. You'll see, I shall soon make a decent living for us, and then I can employ others – and I don't need *his* dirty money to start me off. Mother's money came from her family. It doesn't have the taint of his filthy hands on it.'

Marcus sounded so bitter that Frances wondered what was behind his hatred of Sam Danby. Before the war they hadn't always got on, but they had rubbed along most of the time. Just what was it that Marcus had discovered about that property in London that had made him despise his father so much?

* * *

Vane saw Emily coming across the lawn towards the house. Her hair was swinging loose about her shoulders, soft and slightly waving. He was glad that she had not cut it in the modern fashion, because he liked it this way. She had such an air about her these days, something she was totally unaware of, he was sure. It made people turn their heads to watch her, and it brought her respect.

He knew he was right to choose her. She was the chatelaine that Vanbrough needed, the one who would bring life to this house he loved so dearly. He had chaffed against the bonds when he was younger, but as he grew older and discovered the disappointments of life, it was the house that had sustained him – and it would sustain her when he was gone.

Vane rubbed at his chest, feeling the pain that sometimes spread as far as his arm. It lived with him almost constantly these days and he knew that it couldn't be much longer. He would have to leave her soon – his Emily. It was a terrible burden he meant to lay on her shoulders, but there was no one else.

Would she accept it? He knew that he could not force her, but he believed that she felt it too – this love that had tortured him and delighted him for so many years. Vanbrough would live on through Emily and her son. He could go to his grave happy in the knowledge that she would not betray his trust.

Smiling, he went out to meet her. There was not much time left and he could not bear to waste a second.

5

'I wish you had come down for harvest,' Frances said when she telephoned her sister one cold and wet day in September. 'Alice had a party at hers and it was really nice. The house is big and old – and I wouldn't fancy living out in the fen the way they do – but it was hot that day. She had a table out in the back yard and it was lovely. The children had a treasure hunt and lots of little presents. Alice cooked a huge amount of food and made fruit squash, and we all had a wonderful time – but I missed you. We don't see enough of you, Emily.'

'I couldn't get away,' Emily said, feeling a little regretful that she had missed such a nice family get together. 'Alice asked me to come and stay, of course, but I was needed here. We always have a summer party for the patients and their relatives, and we had a good time here too. Nurse Rose organised a treasure hunt, which was great fun.'

'You devote all your time to that place,' Frances said, and Emily detected a note of resentment in her voice. 'I wanted to talk to you. I know we can talk on the telephone, but it isn't the same.'

'No, I don't suppose it is,' Emily said. She heard something behind her and glanced over her shoulder. 'Look, I have to go, Frances. Someone needs me. I will ring you this evening – and I'll try to get down again soon.'

'You're always saying that,' Frances said. 'You haven't been near since Henry died. Anyone would think he was the only brother you had!' She put the receiver down with a little bang.

Emily looked at the telephone for a moment. Frances was right in a way; she had neglected her family since Henry's death. It wasn't that she didn't care, but they'd had one crisis after another here. Oh, she wasn't sure why she was reluctant to leave Vanbrough at the moment. Amelia hadn't made any threats recently, but she was becoming more and more possessive of Robert.

Emily sighed and got up. She knew why she had been summoned. One of their patients had taken a turn for the worse in the night. He was only twenty-four and they had had hopes of sending him home soon. She had a feeling that he would not last more than a few hours – and his family lived too far away to get here in time. Emily would sit with him until the last.

* * *

Frances looked uneasily at the clock. She seemed to be doing this more and more often of late, her life dominated by the slow moving hands that ticked away the seconds of her life. A harsh laugh escaped her, for such fanciful thoughts were foreign to her and were brought on by her feeling of impending doom.

Marcus was late home again. She couldn't complain, because as far as she knew he was keeping his promise not to drink. He had even given up having a glass of wine with his dinner, because he said it always made him want something more – something stronger. These past few months he had been coming home later and later, but it was because he had to drive long distances. Frances wasn't happy about him being away so much, but he seemed happier now that he was his own boss.

She had learned not to cook anything that wouldn't keep when he was out on one of his runs. She usually made pies that would warm up quickly, or did something on toast when he came in, though often he would say that he had eaten at a cafe somewhere.

She heard the front door bell ring and sighed with relief. That must be Marcus at last! He had probably forgotten his key. She went through the hall and opened the door, but the smile died on her lips as she saw that it was a policeman standing there. Her heart jerked wildly and her knees felt as if they had suddenly turned to jelly.

'Is it my husband?' she asked fearfully. 'Has there been an accident?'

'Are you Mrs Marcus Danby?' the officer asked and frowned as she nodded, too frightened to speak. 'I'm not here about your husband, madam. I understand that Connor Searles is your brother?'

'Yes, he is.' Frances felt the fear draining away to be replaced by anger. 'What has he done? I hope he isn't in trouble, officer?'

'Yes, well, I am afraid he may well be,' the policeman told her. 'We've got him and another lad in the cells at Ely. It seems that they took one of the punts out of the boatyard without paying for the hire.'

'A lot of the lads do that if they can get away with it,' Frances said, for she knew that Henry and Clay had done it when they were youths, and plenty of other kids did it too. 'Surely you didn't have to lock my brother up for that? It was only a lark.'

'A bit more than that, madam. The boat was damaged and the

owner says he wants to press charges. He has had enough of the kids thinking they can just take his property when they feel like it.'

'Damaged? How badly?'

'I think it was substantial,' the officer said. 'Anyway, would you like to come and see Connor this evening? We prefer that a parent or relative should be there before he is charged.'

'I have a young child in bed and my husband isn't home. I can't come out and leave my son alone. May I telephone my brother Daniel?' Frances asked, blessing Daniel for having had one fitted at his house.

'Yes, that might be best.' The officer frowned. 'Does he live in Stretton Village?'

'No. His house is further out in the fen – but he has a car and he has recently had the telephone connected.'

'You had better do that then, madam. Well, I'll get back to the station. I thought I would come in person as that lad needs someone to speak up for him.'

'Thank you for coming to tell me.'

Frances closed the door and went to the telephone, her finger working swiftly as she dialled her brother's house. It was Alice who answered it almost at once. Frances explained and asked if Daniel would go into Ely and sort things out with the police.

'He isn't home at the moment,' Alice said. 'But he shouldn't be too long.'

'I can't leave Charlie or I would go myself. Besides, Daniel ought to be there. If we don't do something they might take Connor to court this time.'

'I'll tell Dan as soon as he comes home,' Alice said. 'Don't worry, love. It isn't that serious. The boatyard owner may settle if we offer to pay for the damage.'

'Yes, well, it might do Connor good to be taught a lesson,'

Frances said. 'I can't cope with him, Alice. He needs someone to keep him in line – and the only one who might be able to do that is Daniel.'

Frances put the phone down before Alice could answer. Daniel seemed to have forgotten his promise to take his brother on when he got home. She had agreed to have him for the duration of the war, but she'd had more than enough of trying to keep him out of trouble.

She went upstairs as she heard a cry from Charlie. He must have heard voices and he probably thought that his father was home. A spasm of nerves clutched at her stomach. Why wasn't Marcus back? She prayed fervently that he hadn't had an accident.

Why did her life have to be so complicated? All she wanted was to be a wife and mother and not have to worry.

* * *

'Well, what did you think you were up to?' Daniel asked as he was driving his brother home later that night. 'Taking the punt was one thing. I've done it myself when I was a lad, and I know it seems a laugh – but sinking it was a bit much, wasn't it?'

'We didn't mean to do it,' Connor said, feeling ashamed. 'Honest, Dan, it wasn't all our fault. The other bloke was hopeless at steering the houseboat he'd hired. He ran into us – it was his fault the punt was so badly damaged, and we managed to get it back to the yard.'

'Where it sank within minutes,' Daniel said. He sighed, because he didn't want to make a big fuss over something he believed was a bit of fun gone wrong, but it had cost him twenty pounds to sort out the mess, money he could ill afford to waste. 'I paid him off, Connor, but you were lucky this time. It might have led to an appearance in court – and you don't want that, do you? What kind of a job do you think you will find then?'

'I don't know...' Connor looked at him awkwardly. 'I'm sorry, Dan. I know you couldn't afford to pay for the damage. I'll pay you back when I start to earn money.'

Daniel shook his head. 'It doesn't matter, just don't do it again. Have you made up your mind that you've finished with school?'

'Yes. I know Frances thinks I should stay on and take my higher exams – but I don't want to go to college, Dan. I want to work on a farm. I've wanted that ever since I was a lad and Dad took me with him to the yard.'

'Well, I might put those fields down to arable next year,' Daniel said. 'And there's a bit of land in the fen that I might be able to get cheap. We could buy some more pigs and perhaps a couple of cows.'

'Are you saying I could work for you?'

'Maybe in a while,' Daniel said. 'But I'm not ready just yet. We'll have to see what else we can find for you for a few months.'

'All right,' Connor said, though his expression was mutinous. 'But I'm not going back to school next week. I want to work same as my mates. And I'm fed up living with Frances and Marcus. I know she doesn't want me there.'

'Well, I'll take you back to mine for the night,' Daniel said. 'I'll ring her and let her know – and then we'll see.'

* * *

'I don't want him back here,' Frances said when Daniel rang her late that evening. She was still on edge because Marcus had just come in and gone straight to bed. She suspected that he might have been drinking heavily. 'It's your turn to have him, Daniel.'

'Yes, I know,' he said. 'I promised him I would. I'll have a word with Alice. We've got plenty of room here – and he can give me a hand with the pigs. I'm probably going to buy a bit more land here. It's going cheap and we can put up more sties.'

'I thought you wanted to be a mechanic, not a pig farmer?'

'It is what I want, but at the moment I'm having to do what I can to hold things together,' Daniel said. 'Most of what I had was in the farm, Frances. It wasn't just Henry that lost out.'

'I am well aware of that,' Frances said sharply. 'I was expecting something from the sale but it all went for nothing.'

'Yes, I'm afraid it did,' Daniel said. 'But you're all right, Fran. You and Marcus have no need to worry. Sam will never let his family starve.'

'Marcus has had a fight with his father,' Frances said. 'You know he bought a lorry of his own and is doing haulage work.'

'I thought all that would blow over,' Daniel said. 'Marcus is a fool if he doesn't make it up with his father. Sam may be a bit of a rogue in some ways, but he cares about his family. Marcus could be throwing a fortune away if he keeps this up.'

'You don't know Sam Danby at all,' Frances said, a little shudder running through her. 'You can come and fetch Connor's things when you are ready. I'll pack them for you. He hasn't got that much anyway.'

'Yes, all right,' Daniel said. 'But talk to Sam yourself, Frances. It doesn't make sense to throw away all the advantages that Marcus might have had working for his father.'

Frances put the receiver down with a little bang. She was relieved that Daniel had at last decided to do his bit for his brother. She had certainly done her share, and she couldn't put up with it any longer. She had enough worries of her own.

* * *

'Tell Connor I should like to see him,' Emily said when Daniel rang her the next day. 'I'm glad you're going to have him with you, Dan, because I know he wasn't happy at Frances's house. But before he settles down with you, I should like him to come on a visit here. It might give him some ideas about what he wants to do with his life.'

'I think he is pretty set in his mind what he wants to do,' Daniel said. 'He would like to work with me. I've told him I might put those fields down to arable instead of letting them for grazing next year – and I might get some more pigs. He could find some odd jobs elsewhere. There's always someone wanting extra labour for the potato harvest, riddling and threshing. I daresay we shall manage.'

'My offer of money is still there. Ask Connor if he will come for a holiday next week, Dan. I should like to have him here for a while. I've already spoken to Vane about it, and he's quite happy for Connor to visit. He is always telling me to ask my family to visit. You and Alice are welcome if you ever want to come and stay.'

'I'll tell Connor that you've asked,' Daniel agreed. 'I'm not sure what he will say, but I'll ask. As for coming down myself – I'd like that one day, but at the moment I don't have the time.'

'I'll send Connor some money for his fares and things,' Emily said. 'Give my love to Alice – and don't work yourself to death, Dan.'

'I'll try not to.'

Daniel was frowning as he replaced the receiver. He was committed to taking his brother on now, and he wouldn't go back on it. Buying the extra land and some livestock would take most of the money he had been saving towards his garage, but that would just have to go on hold for a couple of years. Connor needed a steady hand and he was the one to set him right, but it might be a good thing if he went on a visit to Emily.

She wasn't like Frances. She wouldn't nag him to do something he didn't want to do, and it might make him think about what he really intended to do with his life.

Daniel was whistling as he went outside to the back yard. It was only early September but though the sun was shining, the breeze was cool. He was working on a car he hoped to sell when it was finished, and he had taken on a couple of repair jobs for other people. One of them was a tractor, but that didn't matter – engines were all the same to Daniel. He'd worked on lorries for the army and he'd been pretty good at his job. One of these days he was going to buy that garage he wanted, but for the moment he couldn't complain.

He had a beautiful wife he loved and his son. Stuck in that damned camp, he had wondered if he would ever see Alice again. He was home now and even if money was sometimes difficult, he would get through somehow. The nightmares didn't come so often now and he was beginning to feel stronger. Come the end of the year he should be back to normal again – and then he would be after Clay for the money he still owed him.

'Go and stay with Emily?' Connor pulled a face as Daniel suggested the idea. 'Would I be staying at the big house?'

'Yes, I expect so,' Daniel told him. 'Apparently, Lord Vane says you will be very welcome.'

'Yeah, likely,' Connor said and grinned. He looked thoughtful. 'Emily is all right. I wouldn't mind seeing her. She doesn't come here much now, does she?'

'I think she is too busy with that home of hers. She says she wants to see you. I expect it is just for a couple of weeks – but you don't have to go if you don't want to, Connor. Your home is here now.'

'Yeah, Alice told me,' Connor said. 'She says she's pleased I'm going to live here, because it is a big house and seems empty when you're out sometimes.'

'I expect it does,' Daniel agreed. He had thought the house was a bit large and rather isolated from the start, but Alice had wanted it and it had been going cheap, perhaps because most people would rather live in the village than out in the fen these days. 'You'll be company for her sometimes.'

'Yeah,' Connor said. 'I reckon I'd like to go for that holiday, Dan. Just for a couple of weeks.'

'Right, that's it then. Emily is sending you some money for your fares, and I'll take you to the station,' Daniel said. 'I'll be teaching you to drive when you get back – and you can learn a bit about how to look after the engine as well. It is always best to know at least the basics, because you'll be wanting your own vehicle when you're seventeen.'

'Yeah?' Connor looked at him in surprise and dawning pleasure. 'Do you mean that, Dan?'

'I wouldn't say if I didn't,' Daniel told him. 'But I want no more of that nonsense. No more taking what doesn't belong to you, Connor.'

'I don't steal,' Connor said. 'I know Frances thinks I do, but I don't – it was just a lark borrowing the punt. We used to get into the pictures for nothing if we could – all the kids do it at the Majestic in Ely – but stealing is different.'

'Well, some folk wouldn't agree with you,' Daniel said. 'I'm not going to lecture you, Connor, but I expect you to do a decent job and I expect you to be honest with me. That's the deal.' He held out his hand and Connor took it. Daniel grinned and cuffed him across the head. 'You go and enjoy yourself with Emily.'

'Yeah, I will,' Connor said. 'You fetched most of my stuff from Frances's house, but I shall get my bike this afternoon – and I've promised to go to the youth club in Ely with Peter. I promise I won't do anything daft – and I shan't drink alcohol either.'

'I should hope not! You're not eighteen yet, you young devil.'

'Well, I've done it a few times,' Connor said, and he hesitated. 'But I think it's daft to drink too much the way Marcus does.'

'Marcus drinks?' It was the first Daniel had heard of it. He raised his eyebrows. 'Are you sure?'

'Yeah. I've heard them rowing about it a lot. He came home drunk a few times, and it made Frances angry. She worries about him – and about what people will say.'

'Yes, I expect she does. Poor old Fran,' Daniel said. 'I had no idea things were as bad as that. I shall have to pop in and see her another day.'

'Don't tell her I told you,' Connor said. 'She thinks I'm trouble as it is – but I couldn't stand living there after she got married. It was my home but she changed it all, and I felt like a lodger.'

'Yes, I understand,' Daniel agreed. He wouldn't have wanted to live in Frances's house either. It was too immaculate, too cold. He preferred the warmth and muddle of his own home. Alice wasn't above rearing a box of chicks in the kitchen when he brought them home from market. He could just imagine the look on Frances's face if he had suggested it to her. 'Well, I hope you will think of this house as your home in future.'

'Yeah.' Connor grinned at him. 'Alice told me – that means chopping wood and doing some dishes now and then.'

Daniel laughed, because he could see that his brother was happy with the idea that he was going to have some chores about the house.

'Women,' he said and winked at his brother. 'We're all under petticoat rule from the cradle to the grave – and don't you forget it!'

Connor laughed and went off to find some work to do at the back of the house. Daniel didn't need to tell him that the shed needed painting with creosote, because he had seen it for himself, and he wanted to make himself useful about the place. He thought it was going to be much better living with Daniel and Alice, but he was looking forward to his visit with Emily. She had always been his favourite sister and he missed her when she didn't visit.

* * *

Emily met her brother at the station. He had brought one small suitcase with him, which made her smile. He would need more clothes than he'd brought with him, but that didn't matter, because she intended to buy him a few things anyway. He looked quite grown up now and it was time he had a decent suit for Sundays and some good tweeds.

'Did you have a nice journey?' she asked and kissed his cheek. Connor went bright red and rubbed at the mark her lipstick had made with his hand. 'Too grown up for that now?' she asked, a twinkle in her eye. 'You'll change your tune soon enough, Connor.'

'Kissing is for softies,' he replied, though he didn't believe it. Alice was always kissing Dan, and Connor wondered what it would be like to sleep with a woman. He hadn't had a proper girlfriend yet, though he'd slipped his hand up a girl's knickers at the fair in Ely once. She hadn't minded, though she had pretended to at the time. She might have let him do more if he'd had the courage to ask her.

'Well, I beg your pardon, sir!' she said. Emily's teasing laughter made him grin, because he was pleased to see her. 'I hadn't realised that you were Mr Tough Guy!'

'Well, you'd better get used to it,' Connor said and flexed his muscles. Emily realised that he was almost a man now, with a man's strength – and rather good looking. 'Are you sure Lord Vane doesn't mind me coming to stay?'

'I think he is pleased,' Emily replied with a smile. 'Vane says this is my home and I must ask whoever I like – but you're the one I wanted to see, Connor.'

Connor tipped his head to one side. He looked so much like Dan at a younger age that Emily's heart caught. He was going to be a heartbreaker when he was older, and all the girls would be after him. She was thankful that there was no war to claim him, praying that it would never happen again in her lifetime.

'Why? Are you mad at me for what I did? Frances was as mad as fire because the police went to her house. She said I had humiliated her.'

'Frances says things she doesn't mean,' Emily said. 'You haven't humiliated anyone from what I hear – but it was a bit silly, Connor. You don't want to be known as a troublemaker, love. The police might get their hooks into you, and you could go down for some silly thing you didn't really mean to do.'

'Yeah, I know. Dan says it's time I grew up. I'm going to be working for him – and doing odd jobs for other people. Peter's father says I can help them with the harvesting and the potatoes.'

'You are sure that farming is what you want to do? You wouldn't rather drive a delivery van or something of the sort?'

'I wouldn't mind doing that,' Connor said. 'Frances was talking daft – she said I could be a bank clerk or a doctor or something like that if I tried, but I couldn't, Emily. I should hate being inside all the time. I need to be out in the open.'

'What about when it's freezing cold?' Emily teased as she drove them away from the railway station. 'You might change your mind then.'

'I want to be like Dad,' Connor said, and something in his face made Emily's heart contract with pain. Connor had never quite got over his father's unexpected death from an infection. 'One day I'm going to own lots of land. I'll buy back all the fields Henry lost and I'll have a herd of prize cattle. I shall employ a lot of men to work for me and drive about in a Daimler like Sam Danby.'

'Yes, perhaps you will,' Emily smiled and glanced at him, seeing the pride in his face. Dan had spoken of his own humiliation when the farm was sold, but no one had asked Connor what he thought about it. He must have felt it as much as any of them. It was hardly surprising that his unhappiness had spilled over into youthful pranks. 'Well, I'm not going to try and change your mind, love. There's nothing wrong with being a farmer. Henry was a wonderful farmer. Don't let anyone ever tell you anything different. He had a lot of debt to cope with and times were bad. You will do things differently.'

'I can count and write as well as anybody,' Connor told her, a hint of defiance in his voice. 'I know how to keep books and how to write letters – and I can read books if I want. I like working with my hands, Emily. I don't need to go to college for that, do I?'

'No, you don't,' his sister agreed. She looked at him affectionately. She was going to spend some money on him this holiday, and she would send him home with a few pounds in his pocket – but one day she might be able to give him the money he needed to start a farm of his own. 'You must do whatever makes you happy, Connor. The only thing you have to remember is to play fair with others – do what you would like to have done to you, love. If you can look yourself in the eye when you shave, you won't go far wrong.'

Emily wished that she had followed her own advice. She had not wanted to lie to Vane about her child, but she had hesitated and then it was too late. Sometimes she felt like telling Vane the truth, but so far she hadn't found the courage.

* * *

Connor kicked at a stone as he walked through the grounds of Vanbrough House. He was wearing a pair of wide-legged grey flannels that Emily had insisted on buying for him, and he knew that they were fashionable but he felt a bit of an idiot. He was on his way down to the home, because Emily was at work this morning and he didn't like hanging around the house when she was out. Vane was all right, but he didn't much like Amelia. She smiled at him, but the smile didn't reach her eyes.

Emily had spent a lot of time taking him out in her car. They had gone into Winchester and he'd enjoyed that, also the various football and rugby matches that she had taken him to see. He hadn't cared for the shopping much, but Emily had insisted he must have some clothes now he had left school, and he supposed she was right, though he felt like a softie.

He could see some of the men moving about in the gardens of the convalescent home. They were walking slowly or being pushed in wheelchairs, and Connor felt slightly awkward. He wasn't sure how to talk to these men, because he was aware that they had done and seen terrible things – and he was a little in awe of them. Dan had never talked much of his experiences in the army, and Connor didn't like to ask – but he was curious about what it felt like to go to war.

As he approached the small group, one of the men in a

wheelchair called out to him, beckoning him forward. Connor approached hesitantly, wondering what to say to a stranger who had lost his legs and would never walk again.

'Did you want me?' he asked. 'Is there something I can do?'

'We're going to have a wheelchair race,' the man said. 'I'm Roger – and I think you're Emily Vane's brother, aren't you?'

'Connor. I'm staying with her for a couple of weeks.'

'Good.' Roger grinned at him. 'You can push me round the lawn for a start just to get the hang of it. My driver has gone home for the weekend, lucky blighter – but you'll do if you're game?'

'Yeah.' Connor grinned at him, the last vestige of shyness gone. 'Yeah, I'd like that, sir. I'll have to have a practice first or I shall let you down.'

'Nonsense,' Roger said in a rallying tone. 'A strong lad like you will have no problem. We're up against Nurse Rose and she is a terrier, but the others aren't much competition. Get me over to the lawn and I'll soon have you driving like a veteran.'

* * *

After the race, Connor couldn't believe they had won. His strength and enthusiasm had finally told over Nurse Rose, who had been breathing heavily by the time they had been round the building twice. She had been laughing as she came up to him, congratulating him on the victory.

'It's beginner's luck, of course,' she teased, 'but you did well, Connor. I think we should all go and celebrate with a cup of tea and some orange squash.'

Connor smiled and agreed, feeling pleased with himself, but he looked down at Roger as he touched his arm and winked.

'We'll have a drop of something better than squash in my

room,' he said and grinned. 'We have to celebrate properly, Connor. That's the first time I've managed to beat Nurse Rose.'

Connor sensed that Roger fancied the nurse, who was young and pretty, and his throat felt tight as he wondered if his new friend would ever be able to have a normal relationship with a woman. He thought it must be hell to be stuck in a chair like that without hope.

'Yeah, sure,' he said easily, hiding his emotion. 'Do you mind me asking what service you were in?'

'Flight Officer Ransom!' Roger saluted smartly. 'Shot down over the coast and damned lucky to be alive. I should have died when the kite went down. Anything is better than that, Connor – and don't forget it. Live for the moment, lad! Once you're in one of those bloody boxes, you're done for. I'm alive and I live every day to the full.'

'Yeah,' Connor said. 'Right. See what you mean. Nurse Rose is a smasher, isn't she?'

'We're all a little in love with her,' Roger told him. 'Most of us are in love with your sister too – but she is untouchable. Some of the nurses aren't, if you see what I mean?' He winked at Connor. 'I might be half a man but I've still got all my tackle. I can manage a crafty one now and then – and one or two of them aren't above obliging me. Unfortunately, Nurse Rose isn't one of them – but we live in hope.'

Connor laughed. Roger was a bit of a devil despite the loss of his legs and he admired him, liked him a lot. He wheeled the chair into the house, taking his directions from his passenger. It was interesting to get to know someone like Roger, and he was beginning to understand why Emily didn't have time to visit her family often.

* * *

Emily stretched her shoulders as she left the home the following morning. She had been with one of the patients for most of the night, and it had ended badly. She had held his hand towards the end, but he'd suffered despite all they had done to ease him and she was feeling the grief of his death.

As she walked up to the house, she saw Connor coming towards her. He was grinning and she saw that he had a football in his hand. She knew that the men had been planning a wheelchair football match that day, though she doubted that most of them would feel much like it after last night. The screams of the dying man must have been heard all over the home.

'Are you going to see someone?' Emily asked, because she had a feeling she knew who Connor was hoping to meet.

'Roger asked me to bring this,' Connor said. 'We're going to have a football match. I'm not sure how we do it, but he will show me. He's great, Emily. He told me loads of stuff about his life yesterday. He went through hell when his plane came down and yet he is so cheerful. I really like him.'

Emily reached out and laid a restraining hand on his arm. 'I don't think the match will go ahead,' she told him. 'Perhaps another day – but not this morning.'

'Why? We had a great time with the race yesterday and it isn't raining.'

'Someone died last night,' Emily told him. She drew a deep breath, because she knew this was going to shock and perhaps hurt him. 'I'm sorry, Connor. I am afraid it was Roger...'

'Roger?' Connor stared at her in disbelief. 'No, I don't believe it. You must have it wrong. Roger couldn't have died. He was full of it yesterday.'

'That's how it goes sometimes,' Emily told him, a catch in her voice. 'We thought, hoped, he was getting better. We even had hope that he might go home soon – but it wasn't to be.'

'Why did he die?' Connor felt his throat close. 'Was it because of the race yesterday? Was it too much for him?'

'I don't think so. The change came very suddenly last night.'

'What do you mean?'

'He was in a lot of pain towards the end,' Emily said, because there was no point in lying to him. 'He was healing outwardly, but his liver was failing because of an internal injury. We had hoped that the medication might help, but something went wrong and...' She shook her head. 'I'm not sure the doctors truly know why, Connor. It's something that happens at times, to patients who have suffered severe trauma. We get a lot of successes, and when we can send someone home it all seems wonderful – but this is the other side of the coin. Some of the men are never going to leave here alive.'

Connor nodded. He could feel something hurting in his chest and he wanted to weep, but he couldn't in front of his sister. He walked away from her, bouncing the football because he needed something to relieve the tension. He could hardly believe that Roger was dead. He was such a brave man, so full of life, determined to make the most of what he had – and it was damned unfair!

It was like his father all over again, Connor thought, his teeth grinding in frustration. He wanted to hit out at something, to take out his frustration and anger on something... Anything.

'Make the most of life,' a voice seemed to say in his head. 'Use every day because life is sweet. Once you're in those bloody boxes, you're done for.'

Connor blinked back his tears. Roger hadn't deserved to die like that, but there was nothing he could have done to change things. Behaving like an idiot and inflicting damage on someone else's property wouldn't bring Roger back.

He decided he would go back to the home anyway. Maybe the

men wouldn't feel like playing football, but there might be something he could do to help. He could write letters for those who couldn't see, and he could fetch things from the village – anything they wanted. It hurt like hell to think of Roger being put into one of those damned boxes, but he would never forget him.

* * *

Connor left the house by one of the side entrances, feeling that he couldn't stand being cooped up indoors any longer. He was restless, disturbed by Roger's death and unable to make small talk with Vane's wife. Amelia was all right in tiny doses, but he didn't know how Emily could bear to live in the same house as her.

He walked for a few minutes, lost in thought, and then he stopped, fished a packet of cigarettes from his jacket pocket and lit one. He drew the smoke into his lungs before blowing little circles, because it helped to settle the swirling emotions inside him. Life was so damned unfair!

'I've always wanted to do that,' a voice said out of the gloom. 'Have you got a cigarette to spare?'

Connor recognised the voice, although he couldn't see her clearly at first. She walked towards him and now he could see that she had changed out of her uniform into a skirt and red twinset, her hair swinging loose on her shoulders. In her uniform she was pretty stunning, but that twinset outlined her breasts in a way that made Connor aware of a fierce urge somewhere deep down inside.

'Yes, of course,' he said in a gruff voice that didn't sound like his own. He took the packet from his pocket and offered it to her, his throat constricting with desire as she selected a thin white tube and inserted it between lips that had been painted to match the colour of her cardigan. 'I'll light it for you, Rose.' He flicked the lighter he had recently bought, pleased with himself because his hand was steady even though he was shaking inside.

'Thank you,' Rose said and smiled up at him. 'Did you feel the need for air too?'

'Yeah.' It was all Connor could do to keep from groaning. He had never felt this way before. He wanted her so badly that it made his groin ache, but he knew that she would never look at him. Roger had told him that Rose wasn't one of the nurses who sometimes obliged him. 'Yeah, I can't stand being cooped up too long.'

Rose came nearer. The scent of her perfume was tantalising, wafting under his nose and making him even more aware of his need. She was standing too close now. What the hell did she think she was doing?

Rose put one hand on his shoulder, a little smile on her lips as she looked into his eyes. 'Why don't you kiss me?' she asked. 'You want to, don't you?'

Connor swallowed hard. 'I didn't think you would...' he began, but the words were lost as she moved in even closer, her lips seeking his softly. He felt the shudders run through him, and he slid an arm around her, holding her tight against his body, his hungry mouth devouring hers. Rose wriggled and he let go, feeling uncertain, but she was still smiling.

'Steady, my love,' she whispered, a gleam in her eye. 'You're not eating me. Let me show you how to give pleasure. Open your mouth a little.' Connor stood as if mesmerised as she put her lips to his again, teasing them with the tip of her tongue, and then plunging inside his mouth to explore its warmth. 'That's better,' she whispered, giving them both a moment to breathe. 'Just do what I do and we'll progress from there.'

Her hand moved over his chest, sliding down his body until

she found the hardness of his erection, fondling him gently over his trousers in a way that he had previously only dreamed of, making him groan because it was so good. He put out a tentative hand, caressing her breast, enjoying the feel of its pertness, the peaked nipples tight against the wool, because she wasn't wearing anything underneath. He experienced a thrill of pleasure that made him gasp.

'Would you like to make love to me, Connor?' Rose asked. 'Go all the way?'

'Yeah,' he growled. 'Damn it, I don't know how. You'll have to teach me, Rose. The same as kissing...'

'Yes, I know,' she said, and her eyes were filled with soft laughter, as though she were enjoying the situation. 'I'm your first, aren't I?' Connor nodded, torn between need and embarrassment. 'That's all the better,' Rose said. 'Don't be shy and don't worry about it, Connor. I like you and I'll show you how to make this good for us both.'

'But where?' Connor asked. 'And why me?'

'Too many questions,' Rose said, touching a finger to her lips. 'Just take what's offered, Connor. Sometimes you can wait too long and then it is too late.'

'Yeah,' he said, and suddenly he knew. He knew why it was him, and why it was now, but it didn't matter. Rose needed him as much as he needed her, and it was going to be fine.

* * *

Emily drove Connor to the station. He was wearing the grey flannels she had bought him and a tweed jacket. He looked so grown up and serious that it almost broke her heart.

'I'm wishing I didn't have to part with you,' she said. 'You've been so good helping out, Connor. Vane says he would be happy to give you a job on the estate if you wanted it.'

'That's decent of him,' Connor said and leaned forward to kiss her cheek. 'I've enjoyed being here, Emily – but I want to get home. I'm not cut out for the kind of thing Vane has offered me. Yes, he did mention that he might take me on. He said I could work in the estate office, learn about the management of a place like this, but I told him I had plans for the future. He wanted to know more about it. I explained that I want to buy back the land that was Dad's and I think he understood. He said it was good to be loyal to your father – and he wished me well.'

'Yes, he would. I'm proud of you,' Emily said, looking at him affectionately. 'I've really enjoyed having you here, getting to know you better. You'll get your farm one day, Connor. I know you will.'

There was something different about him this morning, though she wasn't sure what had made that difference. It was almost as if he had become a man, leaving his childhood behind him.

'If I don't, I'll make the most of what I do,' he said, and then grinned. 'But I shall get the farm back, Emily. Sam Danby bought most of the fields. I'll buy them back from him – and I'll buy more land. I'll build up everything Dad had and more.'

Emily nodded. She wanted to hug him, but she knew that this new wisdom was very fragile. He had learned some good lessons on his visit here, but he was still a young lad. He had a lot of living and learning to do – but she believed that he would get his land one day.

She stood back and watched as he got into the train, waving to him as it chugged slowly out of the station. Her eyes were wet with tears and she stood watching for a long time, until it had disappeared out of sight. Connor had brought back a lot of memories.

6

'Oh, hello,' Frances said as she opened her door to Daniel one morning in October. 'I was just about to put the kettle on – if you have time to stop for a cup?'

'I can stop for half an hour,' he said. 'I wanted to talk to you, Frances – make sure you're all right.'

'Of course I am. What have you heard?' Frances looked annoyed. 'That's the trouble with this village. People talk too much.'

Daniel followed her into the kitchen. It smelled of baking, but there was no sign of any mess. Frances had obviously tidied everything away. He thought of Alice's cluttered kitchen and smiled inwardly. He knew what he preferred. He wouldn't want to live in this perfect order all the time.

'I saw Marcus in Ely the other day. He had been drinking, Fran. He came out of the pub and got into his lorry. I'm not sure he was fit to drive it. What is wrong with him? Have you quarrelled?'

'We argue most of the time,' Frances said. She moved the kettle on to the range, her back to him. 'But it isn't that – something is eating away at him inside. I don't know what is wrong, because he won't tell me.'

'Is it that bust up with his father?'

'That may be a part of it.'

'Couldn't he make it up? Sam would take him back. He told me that Marcus only has to ask.'

'You really have no idea what that means.' Frances sat at the table, her face set in stone. 'Sam wants him to crawl back, and he won't – and I don't want him to either. I would rather have less money in my purse.'

'But you can't agree with Marcus drinking so much?'

'No, of course I don't,' Frances said. 'It has changed him and I hate it. I live in fear of him being killed in an accident – but there's nothing I can do. If I say anything he flies into a temper.'

'He hasn't hit you?' Daniel looked angry, prepared to defend her.

'No, he hasn't been violent to me or Charlie,' Frances said. 'When he hasn't been drinking, he's the same as he used to be – but he is drinking more often lately. I think he did try to stop but he couldn't.'

'Can't you stop him? Tell him you will walk out on him if he continues.'

'Where would I go?' she asked. 'I've got hardly any money of my own. It's not fair, Dan. Margaret had thousands when Dad died and neither Emily nor I got a penny.'

'It was all in the farm,' Daniel told her. 'You know that, Frances. We expected that we would get an income when things picked up, but none of us did. I'm sorry. It may have been better to have sold all the land then, but we agreed to keep it and hope that it would come right eventually.'

'No one asked me,' Frances said. 'You and Henry arranged it

all between you. If you had asked me, I should have done what Clay did and taken my share out.'

'It was mostly left between Dad's sons,' Daniel told her. 'But I agree that you should have had something – though both you and Emily had a small trust fund as I remember it.'

'Only a couple of thousand,' Frances told him. 'I spent most of that ages ago. I was expecting more when you came back and settled everything.'

'Well, I'm sorry it didn't work out that way,' Daniel said. 'You don't think I liked what happened, do you? I asked the bank for more time. If I'd had a chance to get things straight I might have saved something, but they wouldn't listen.'

'How is it that Mary has the house?' Frances asked. 'Surely it should have been shared between us?'

'Emily bought it for her,' Daniel said, feeling disgusted that she should ask. 'Mary is on her own now, Frances. She needs something to fall back on. You and Marcus are hardly short of money – and you could have more if he went to work for his father.'

'Yes, I know.' Frances looked a bit ashamed. 'I didn't realise that Emily had bought the house for Mary. But you shouldn't tell me that I could walk out on Marcus. I have a son to support and no way to do it, because I've never worked.'

'No, you haven't, have you?' Daniel frowned, because he hadn't realised how helpless Frances was until this moment. 'You're not like Emily. She went into the fire service.'

'And I got married. It was all I wanted to do, Daniel. I thought it was going to be wonderful, and it would have been if the war hadn't come along.'

'Yes, I know.' Daniel looked grim. 'I would offer to help if I could, Frances, but at the moment I am stretched to the limit. Emily might help if you asked her.'

'Yes, I suppose she might,' Frances said, but didn't look happy with the idea. 'I shall have to stick it out, Daniel. Anyway, I don't want to leave Marcus. I still love him – at least, I do when he isn't drunk.' She lifted her eyes to her brother's. 'He might listen to you if you spoke to him. I don't know what to say any more.'

'I doubt he would listen to me, Fran,' Daniel said. 'We've never mixed much. He went to a private school and I went locally – he always thought himself a cut above me. I daresay he was right.'

'That's nonsense,' Frances said. 'I had private schooling and you could have done too if you'd wanted to go to boarding school.'

'I should have hated that,' Daniel said. 'Dad asked where I wanted to go – and then I won a scholarship to grammar school and that was it. I did well enough.'

'I wish Connor would take his exams. I am sure he could win a scholarship too if he tried.'

'It isn't for Connor,' Daniel said. 'He's going to be working with me. It is what he wants, Fran.'

She shrugged her shoulders. 'He is your responsibility now. I have enough to think about.'

'Yes, perhaps you do,' Daniel said. 'I don't think I'll stop for that tea, Frances. I'll speak to Marcus if I see him, but I think he may resent it.'

He left her standing in the kitchen. Frances was right; she had been entitled to something from the farm, but they had agreed that she would get an income. The war had put paid to that and there was nothing he could do about it. She would just have to put up with her husband's drinking and hope that he would pull himself out of it.

Daniel thought he understood. They all carried memories that would be better left behind.

* * *

After her brother had gone, Frances fetched her son in from the garden. He was well wrapped up because it was cold out. She put on a thick tweed coat and a silk headscarf. She had some shopping to do and then she would visit her mother-in-law. She hadn't liked Rosalind Danby much when she was first married, but now they got on reasonably well. At least she was someone to talk to, and Frances didn't have many real friends in the village. Like her brother, most of the women had gone to the local school; they thought Frances was a snob because she had gone to boarding school and lived in a big house, and perhaps in a way she was.

* * *

'I wish Marcus would come and see me more often,' Rosalind Danby said. She had been nursing her grandson on her lap, but Frances was ready to leave. She had stayed for nearly three hours and that was as long as these visits ever lasted. Sometimes Rosalind wished that she could have Charlie for a whole day, but Frances was very jealous of her son's affections. 'Ask him to pop in on Sunday, will you?'

'I'll ask him,' Frances said, 'but I can't promise anything. Marcus is very busy these days.'

'Is something wrong?' Rosalind asked. She had sensed it for a while now, but no one told her anything. Sam seemed to think she was an imbecile, treating her as though she didn't see or hear things – but she knew a lot more about him than he realised. 'Marcus isn't in any trouble, is he?'

Frances hesitated, and then shook her head. 'No, of course

not. I shall have to go now or I shan't have his tea ready when he comes home.'

'Yes, of course,' Rosalind agreed. She never tried to keep her daughter-in-law longer than she wanted, because she was afraid that Frances would simply stop bringing the boy to visit. Charlie was the only good thing in Rosalind's life and she didn't want to lose the small privilege she had been granted. 'You will come again next week, dear?'

'Yes, I expect so,' Frances said. 'Come on, Charlie. Mummy wants to go home. Kiss Grandma goodbye.'

Charlie obligingly enveloped his grandmother in his arms, delivering a kiss sticky with jam and chocolate. He liked coming to his grandmother's house, because she spoiled him – and she had a big garden. At the end of the garden were hutches with rabbits that Charlie liked to stroke when he was allowed. No one had told him that the rabbits were there because people ate them.

'Come along then.' Frances took his hand and led him outside. She was saying a lingering farewell to Rosalind when Sam drew up in his car.

'Just leaving, Frances?' he asked and smiled at her. 'Why don't I take you in the car?'

He asked the same question every week. Frances had tried leaving earlier, but he seemed to have the knack of turning up at the right moment every time.

'Thanks, but it is quite pleasant this afternoon,' Frances said. She tried to hold on to Charlie, but he had wriggled from her grasp, running to his grandfather, who swung him aloft. She watched helplessly as Sam tucked the boy into the car, knowing that she had no choice. 'Well, if you insist.' She got into the car, taking Charlie on her lap. 'Bye, Rosalind. See you next week.'

Sam turned his head to grin at her. 'Well, isn't this nice?' he asked. 'Just the three of us – the way I like it.'

'Marcus will be home for his meal soon.'

'Will he?' Sam looked at her, the smile settling into a grim line on his mouth. 'If I know anything, that idiot of a son of mine will be out half the night. He was caught driving under the influence last week, Frannie. Did he tell you that?' Frances shook her head. 'No, I didn't think so. He will be lucky if he doesn't lose his licence. Then what is he going to do? Tell him to come and see me, will you? It's time we put an end to this nonsense between us. He's my son and it's time he started to behave like a Danby!'

* * *

Frances was thoughtful as she entered the house. Perhaps it was time that Marcus made up the breach between him and his father. Whatever it was that was eating away at him, it was never going to get settled until he faced up to it.

Frances busied herself with giving Charlie a bath and putting him to bed. She sometimes thought that this was the best part of her day. His soft body smelled delightfully of soap and talcum powder, and she always cuddled him before putting him into his bed. That evening he wanted a story and she read to him from his favourite book for half an hour before going down to the kitchen. It was just seven o'clock when Marcus came in, looking tired and drained.

'You're home early for once,' Frances said.

'Something wrong with that?'

'No, of course not. I'm pleased you're home. You must know that I worry when you're late.'

'You shouldn't. I'm well insured. You'll be better off as a widow, Frances.'

'Don't you dare say that to me!' She was angry now. 'I don't deserve that, Marcus. You know I love you.'

'Do you?' He ran his fingers through his hair. 'If you do, you must be a sucker for punishment. Haven't you realised that I'm finished? No good to anyone...'

'You shouldn't say such things.' Frances rounded on him. 'Your son is in bed upstairs. Surely you care about what happens to him?'

'He has you – and my mother. He'll be all right. My father will probably leave him all his money. As long as he doesn't find out where it came from, he'll be fine.'

'What are you talking about? You hint at things but you never say what you mean. Rosalind was asking when you were going to see her. I think she believes that I stop you visiting – though how she imagines I have any influence with you, I don't know. Oh, and your father says it's time you came to your senses and went back to work for him.'

Marcus stared at her, something flickering in his eyes. 'I suppose you agree with him?'

'No – yes, perhaps,' Frances said, feeling frustrated. She couldn't get through to him these days. 'Something is wrong with you, Marcus. I have no idea what it is, because you never tell me anything. But if it has something to do with your father, perhaps you should sort it out with him. I know I've had enough of your drinking and your temper.'

Marcus was silent for a moment, then: 'I told you I was no good to anyone,' he said and moved towards the back door, clearly intending to leave.

'You're not going out again?' Frances asked sharply. He didn't look at her as he turned the door handle. 'Marcus! Where are you going?'

'I'm going to sort things out, like you said. Don't wait up for me, Fran. I shall probably be late.'

'Marcus, come back. Surely it can wait until tomorrow.'

She stared at the door as he slammed it behind him. She could hear him starting the car and she wanted to run after him, to tell him she was sorry and beg him to come back, but her feet wouldn't move. She sank down on to a chair as she saw the flash of headlights, clutching at herself in despair.

'Marcus, come back. I didn't mean it...'

What was happening to them? She hadn't meant to quarrel with him that evening. Tears stung her eyes because she wanted to go back and start again. She wanted Marcus to be the way he was before the war, before the drinking became a problem. She felt cold and shivery, a tingling sensation at the nape of her neck. What did he mean by saying he was going to sort things out? Was he going to have another row with his father?

She wished she could believe that he was prepared to mend the breach with Sam, but she knew it wasn't going to happen. She had no idea why she had even suggested it, though he had made her angry. Suddenly, she wished very much that she hadn't said anything about it.

She had an awful feeling that Marcus was going out to get drunk. Oh, why had she said anything about his father at all? She was on her husband's side, and she ought to have made that clear.

She felt the tears stinging her eyes. It was going to be another long evening alone, and she didn't know how she could bear it.

* * *

Alice replaced the telephone receiver and frowned as she went out to the back yard to find Daniel. The call had been from

Frances, who was in a bit of a state because Marcus hadn't come home all night. She knew that things weren't right between them, but she hadn't wanted to say anything because Frances might think she was interfering. Now it seemed that the situation had reached a crisis and her sister-in-law was desperate.

She paused to feel the late autumn sunshine on her face, thinking how lucky she was to be married to Daniel, because she knew he would never behave the way Marcus was now. Marcus had done his bit in the war, but in Alice's opinion, he had been lucky. At least he hadn't been shut up in a prisoner of war camp for months on end, and Frances hadn't had to wonder if her husband was still alive.

Daniel came out of the barn, where he had been working on one of his second-hand cars. 'Is it time for docky already?' he asked and glanced at his watch.

'No, not yet,' Alice said. 'Frances just telephoned me. Marcus hasn't been home all night and she is worried about him.'

'That man doesn't know when he's well off,' Daniel said. 'To be honest, I don't have much sympathy with him. Sam is a bit of a rough diamond, but he was willing to give Marcus a free hand with running the lorries. Marcus turned him down and went off to find a job elsewhere – but he couldn't hold it down, and he won't make a success of what he's doing now.'

'Marcus used to be charming,' Alice said, looking thoughtful. 'I don't know why he changed – but I feel for Frances. It can't be very pleasant for her if her husband drinks too much.' She looked at him with a worried frown. 'You would never do that, would you?'

'Not in a million years,' Daniel told her. He reached out to draw Alice close, bending his head to kiss her softly on the lips. 'I know how lucky I am, love. All I want is to work hard and make a good life for you and Danny.'

'We already have a good life,' Alice said, nestling her head against his shoulder. 'I don't care about having a lot of money, Dan. I have all I want right here in this house.'

Daniel smiled. 'What did I do to get so lucky?' he asked.

'You fell in love with me,' Alice said, but avoided his seeking mouth. 'No, not now, Dan. Frances needs you. I promised that you would go and see her straightaway.'

'I'm not sure what I can do,' Daniel said, 'but I suppose I shall have to show willing. Marcus will probably turn up five minutes after I get there – but I'll see if I can have a word with him when he comes in. I may go into Ely and pick up a few bits I need for the car afterwards, so don't bother cooking anything until this evening.'

* * *

Frances ran to look out of the window as she heard a car engine outside. She was disappointed to see that it was her brother, though pleased that he had come to help her.

Daniel knocked at the back door and then entered. He raised his eyebrows at her. 'Has he turned up yet?'

'No. I'm really worried,' Frances said and bit her lip. 'We had a row last night and Marcus went off in a temper.'

'He probably got drunk and is still sleeping it off somewhere, Frances. You may be worrying for nothing.' He glanced at the range where a kettle was simmering. 'Any chance of a cup of tea?'

'Yes, of course,' Frances agreed and moved the kettle on to the heat. 'What do I do, Dan? Should I telephone the police?'

'You haven't done that yet?'

'I was afraid of making a fuss. Marcus might be angry...'

The kettle had started to boil. Frances was pouring water into a large blue-and-white teapot when they heard a car stopping outside. Daniel went to the window and looked out. He sucked in his breath, which made Frances run to look out. She gasped in shock as she saw a police officer get out and come towards the door.

'You speak to him, Dan,' she said, her voice breathy with fear. 'Don't let it be bad news.' She sat down in a rocking chair by the range, her legs trembling. 'Please don't let it be Marcus...'

She could hear Daniel talking to the police officer, but they were talking in low voices, and Frances was blocking out what they were saying. She didn't want to know, and yet when Daniel closed the door and turned to look at her, she knew instinctively.

'He's dead, isn't he? Was it a car accident?'

'Yes.' Daniel walked towards her. 'I'm sorry, Fran. His car went off the road into a ditch and caught fire. He must have been unconscious and—' He stopped, his throat catching with emotion. He hadn't had a great deal of time for Marcus of late, but this was a wretched business. 'It's rotten luck – to go all through the war and then...'

Frances was just staring into space. She looked stunned, as if she couldn't believe what he was saying. And yet she had known before he told her.

'I'll take care of all the details,' Daniel was saying, his voice seeming to come from a distance. 'I've agreed to go into the police station this afternoon and do whatever is necessary. When they release his body it may be best if he doesn't come here.'

'I don't want him here,' Frances said and stood up. Her face looked frozen and her voice was cold. 'Just do whatever you think best. I don't want to know.'

'Frances...' Daniel moved towards her, intending to put his arms about her, but she moved away, turning her back on him. 'No, I'm all right. I don't want that.'

'Don't hold it inside, Fran,' Daniel said softly. 'It is better if you cry.'

'I don't feel like crying,' Frances said and turned to look at him. 'I'm angry. He just threw it all away. We could have had so much – and he chose to drink himself silly. I don't know why, because he didn't tell me. He didn't tell me anything. If he had cared for Charlie or me he wouldn't have done it.'

Daniel stared at her awkwardly. There was no sense in mouthing words of comfort that meant nothing when he agreed with what she was saying. If Marcus had cared for his family, he would have taken more care, left the drinking alone.

'I expect he had his reasons. It can't have been easy day after day, going up there to be shot at, never knowing if he was going to be alive by nightfall.'

'The war has been over for months – and plenty of other men have bad memories. You don't go drinking to forget.'

'No, I don't,' Daniel agreed. 'I have nightmares sometimes – but I don't give in to them. I try to forget, because I want to make things right for Alice.'

'That's what I mean.' Frances looked angry and distressed. 'If Marcus had loved me, he would have got through it somehow – the way you do.' She frowned. 'I don't think it was just the war, but I'm not certain what the trouble was, because he never told me.'

'You know I'm sorry, Fran.'

'I'm glad you were here.' She gave a little shudder. 'You will do everything? I can't face... I won't look at him. I can't!'

'I've told you, I'll see to things,' Daniel said. 'But I don't like to leave you here alone. Shall I take you to Alice?'

Frances hesitated, and then shook her head. 'No, thank you, not yet. Perhaps tonight – if I could stay with you until after...'

She closed her eyes for a moment. 'Thank you for being here, Dan – but I think I should like to be alone for a while.'

'I'll fetch you later,' Daniel told her. 'Get a few things together for you and Charlie – and I'll call and tell Sam the news.'

'Yes, thank you,' Frances said. 'I don't think I could bear that.'

Daniel approached her hesitantly. He kissed her cheek. She didn't react, and he thought she was unnaturally calm. He would have preferred tears, but Frances was holding them inside – perhaps until she was alone.

* * *

Frances sat down after Daniel had left. She could hear her son playing in the garden with his dog, and she knew that in a few minutes she was going to have to fetch him in and give him something to eat. It was probably time to feed the dog too, but for the moment she couldn't motivate herself to do anything.

Somewhere inside she was hurting so badly that she couldn't bear it, but she was refusing to let go, refusing to allow the pain through. If she blocked it out, perhaps it would go away. Perhaps she would wake up and find that this was all a terrible dream. Marcus couldn't be dead. It wasn't possible. She had dreaded that he would be shot down all through the war, but he had come back to her.

But the real Marcus had never come back. She had lost him months ago, Frances realised, feeling angry again. If he'd loved her and Charlie, he would have stopped drinking. He would have made a success of his life. She didn't care so much about the money. He would have built up his own business slowly if only he had stopped drinking.

'Damn you, Marcus,' Frances said softly. It was easier to be angry with him for letting her down. Much easier than allowing the dreadful thought into her mind that she had driven Marcus to his death. If she hadn't quarrelled with him, he might still be alive.

* * *

Sam saw the colour fade from his wife's face as he told her the news that afternoon. Rosalind had been shopping in Ely when Daniel Searles came to the house, walking in with her parcels about ten minutes after he left. Her eyes looked strange, as if she couldn't see properly, and he thought she was going to faint. Sam was feeling sick himself, but also angry – angry because Marcus had thrown everything he had offered him back in his face.

He'd been foolish enough to put some of the property into his name, never thinking about the consequences if Marcus discovered what was going on in those houses. Sam had never expected him to bother about where the money came from, but he had and he'd thrown a fit when he discovered the truth. Sam had thought he would calm down eventually and talk things through – but instead of that, the fool had thrown his life away.

'You're lying!' Rosalind's voice was a thin screech. 'You're trying to hurt me. Marcus isn't dead, he can't be.' Her face was working with emotion, her hands clenching at her sides. 'Damn you, Sam! I hate you.' She suddenly flew at him, her hands crooked like claws as she went for his face, hysterical in her grief. 'It's your fault. He discovered what you are and it destroyed him.'

'Don't be such a damned fool,' Sam said, catching her wrists, holding her as she struggled against him. He was solidly built and she had no chance as he forced her back, shoving her so that she fell on to the sofa. She half lay there, staring at him, her eyes bleak now as the pain began to sink in. 'He took after your family – no guts or back-bone. If he'd been sensible we could have sorted things out. Besides, it was your own fault, Rosalind. You told him there was something odd going on and he poked his nose in where he had no right.'

'It's you and your filthy business,' Rosalind muttered through her tears. Her nose was running, her cheeks mottled with red. Never pretty, she looked ugly, and older than her years. 'I hate you, Sam Danby – and one day I shall pay you back for what you've done.'

'Don't be stupid, woman,' Sam growled. 'I've kept you and that useless son of mine in luxury for years. If you hate me so much, why don't you walk out of that door?'

Rosalind lifted her head. 'It was my father's money that gave you your start, Sam, and don't you forget it. I daresay you would like to be rid of me, but I shan't make it easy for you.'

'Don't be daft, woman,' Sam said and turned his back on the sight of her. She made him want to hit out, irritated him with her moral tone and her belief that she was so superior. He walked out before he was tempted to use his fists on her. He couldn't deny that her money had got him started, but he'd built up a few thousand pounds into a huge fortune.

But what for? The question hammered at his brain as he left the house. All his life he had schemed and worked, building up his empire to pass on to his son and grandchildren when he died. Now Marcus was dead and he had just the one grandson, Charlie.

A look of determination came over his face. His thick neck was red and a dark vein stood out at his temple. Charlie was all that mattered now – and Frances. His throat tightened at the thought of her. She was never very far from his thoughts these days. He wasn't sure why, because she had made her feelings quite plain. She didn't like him much, but he wanted her – and he mostly got what he wanted in the end.

He decided that he would go to see her, comfort her a bit. He wouldn't try any of his usual games, because she would knock him back, and he would deserve it. No, he'd be the grieving father and offer to help her, build up her confidence. She was going to need him now, and he would be there for her. Now that Marcus had gone, she would turn to him. He would be patient. He could wait for what he wanted.

He smiled as he got into his car. Losing Marcus was a disappointment, but he still had Charlie and if he played his cards right, he would have Frances too.

* * *

Alice turned as the kitchen door opened. Frances walked in carrying Charlie in her arms, Daniel just behind her. One look at her face, at the suppressed pain in her eyes, made Alice's heart bleed for her sister-in-law.

'Dearest Fran,' she said and went to her. She put her arms about her and Charlie, laying her head against Frances's shoulder. 'I'm so sorry, love, so sorry.'

Frances made no response. The pain was in her eyes but she was putting on a brave face, holding it inside.

'Thanks for having me, Alice,' she said in a calm, flat tone. 'I couldn't bear to stay there alone tonight. I'll be all right in a few days.'

'You can stop as long as you like,' Alice said. 'You know we are always pleased to have you.'

'Yes, you're both very good.' Frances put Charlie down. He ran off to join Danny, who was playing with a kitten at the far end of the long kitchen. 'Sam came to see me while Dan was in Ely. He has told me I don't need to worry about money. I think he was a bit annoyed that I had asked Dan to see to things for me, but he didn't make a fuss. He was kind, generous.'

'You sound surprised,' Alice said. 'I should think he is devastated. I would expect him to do everything he can for you. After all, Charlie is his only grandchild.'

'Yes...' Frances looked thoughtful. 'He was much nicer than I expected. Sometimes...' She shook her head. 'It doesn't matter. I telephoned Emily. She says she will come down for—' Frances sat down at the kitchen table. Her hands were trembling. She gripped them in her lap. Her thoughts were disjointed, jumbled up in her head. 'I'm sorry. I feel a bit odd.'

'Well, of course you do,' Alice said. She glanced at Charlie, who seemed quite content playing with his cousin and the kitten. 'Does he know?'

'I've told him that Daddy isn't coming home,' Frances said in that calm, flat tone. 'But I don't think he understood. He was more upset because Sam took his dog away with him, but I didn't think I should bring it here – and Sam said he would bring it back as soon as I decided to come home.'

'We've got plenty of animals here to amuse him,' Alice said, smiling as she saw the children turn their attention to the train set Daniel had set up for his son. 'Charlie will be all right with us, Frances, but he is bound to start asking questions one of these days.'

'Yes, I expect so,' Frances said, but there was no spark in her. She was devoid of any emotion, though Alice guessed that it was simmering inside her, kept down by the barrier she had built to deaden the pain.

'Shall I make a cup of tea?' Alice asked. It was difficult to know what to say to Frances. She appeared so much in control, but Alice sensed that underneath there was a well of pent-up emotion that was going to boil over sooner or later.

'Yes, thank you,' Frances said. Her eyes travelled around the huge, old-fashioned kitchen with its pine dressers and black-leaded cooking range. Alice had bunches of herbs hanging from a wooden bar overhead, and her copper pans were burnished brightly on their rack. Danny's toys were scattered all over the floor at one end, and a dog had just come in from the yard, its paws making muddy prints on the floor. It settled in front of the fire, sure of its place. 'This is very nice. Where did you get all that blue-and-white china?'

'I collect it,' Alice said. 'Mum gave me that big meat plate and the tureens, but I bought some of it from the fair on Midsummer Common in Cambridge. I went in on the train once and they were auctioning it off a few bits at a time. It was fun, because they toss bits in the air and keep lowering the price until someone bids for it. I bought a basketful for a pound.'

'Oh...' Frances seemed shocked, and Alice knew she must be thinking of her bone china dinner service at home. 'You were lucky.'

'Well, it isn't china,' Alice said. 'It's only earthenware, Fran, but I like it.'

'It's nice,' Frances said. 'It looks comfortable, homely.'

'Thank you.' Alice beamed because she took that as a compliment. She was well aware that her kitchen wasn't neat and ordered like Frances's, but it was comfortable. She kept her front room pristine, but they only used that at Christmas and sometimes on a Sunday if her parents came to dinner. 'I'm always so busy, and Dan is in and out all day, Connor too. It would be difficult to keep us all tidy.'

'It is a home,' Frances said. 'Our kitchen used to be like this once – but I had it all changed.'

'You're more modern than us,' Alice said. 'Very smart. If I

lived in the village I wouldn't mind something like you have – but here the animals and the boots bring in mud all the time.'

'Doesn't that drive you mad?'

'No, I don't bother,' Alice said and laughed. 'It all gets scrubbed off first thing in the morning – but then they start bringing it in again.'

'I think I should hate that,' Frances said. 'But Marcus never brought in any mud.' She choked back a sob, her eyes wet with tears all of a sudden. 'I can't believe...' The tears were flowing now, running down her cheeks and into her mouth. 'Alice, I don't want Charlie to see...'

'I'll take you upstairs to your room,' Alice said. 'You can have a lie down before supper, love.' She led the way out of the kitchen and up the stairs. She opened the door of a large bedroom, which was furnished with a double bed covered by a white candlewick bedspread, a washstand, wardrobe and dressing table, and two mahogany chests of drawers that didn't match. 'You have a good cry, Fran. I'll leave you to rest – unless you want to talk?'

'No. I would rather be alone for a few minutes. I'll come down soon. I am sorry.' Frances gave a muffled sob. 'I've been shutting it out, trying not to cry.'

'You'll feel better if you let it out,' Alice said. 'If you want me – or Dan – we're just downstairs.'

'Yes, I know, thanks.'

Alice closed the bedroom door, standing just outside for a moment. Frances was crying now, sobbing as if her heart were breaking – which it probably was, Alice thought. Frances had been very much in love when she married Marcus. It hadn't just been the money, though some people thought it, but Alice wasn't one of them.

She went back downstairs to the warmth and comfort of her

kitchen. Daniel was making the tea. He looked at her, his eyebrows raised.

'She's having a cry,' Alice said. 'She will be all right in a while, Dan. We'll have a cup of tea, but I think we should leave her alone for a few minutes.'

Alone in the bedroom that wasn't hers, Frances sobbed, her body shaking with the force of her emotion. She had held it back all day, but Alice's sympathy had overset her. Finding herself a guest of her sister-in-law had suddenly brought it home to her. Marcus was dead and her life was never going to be the same again.

* * *

'Surely you won't take Robert to a funeral?' Amelia asked. 'Everyone will be under a shadow – and a small child will just be in the way.'

'Robert could never be in the way in Alice's home,' Emily said, holding her temper on a thin string. Anyone would think she had to ask permission to take her son away from Vanbrough. 'My family will expect to see him. Besides, I want him with me, Amelia. He is my son. I think you tend to forget that sometimes.'

'I don't know what you mean, Emily,' Amelia said, looking at her huffily. 'Of course I know Robert is your son. I am well aware who his mother is – and his father.'

'Just what are you trying to say?' Emily glared at her. 'If this is a threat, Amelia, you might as well say it at once.'

'Of course it isn't a threat,' Amelia said, a wary expression in her eyes. 'I was merely suggesting that it might be better if you left Robert here with us while you visit your family.'

'I am going to take him with me,' Emily said. 'I do not wish to quarrel with you, Amelia – but Robert is mine and I shall do what I think best for my son. Excuse me, I have something to do before I leave.'

She walked from the room. There were a few things she needed to sort out at the home before she went down to Cambridgeshire. She was feeling angry and slightly uneasy. There had been an underlying threat in Amelia's words. Perhaps it was her own fault for allowing the situation to drag on. It might be better if she confessed the truth to Vane – but not now. She couldn't cope with that at the moment. All she really had time to think about was Frances.

It was so awful, Marcus dead in a car accident! Daniel had told her it was pretty horrific. Marcus had been badly burned and died on the way to hospital. Emily wasn't sure if her sister knew all the facts about the accident, because Daniel had told her that the police seemed to think it had been quite deliberate. Not an accident at all, but suicide. She hoped that wasn't the case, because it would probably all come out at the inquest, and that would be very upsetting for Frances.

Frances had always been the lucky one. When she was young, it had seemed that she always got whatever she wanted of life – but now it had all gone wrong for her. Emily wasn't sure how her sister would cope. Frances was inclined to be nervy, short-tempered and easily upset. She had relied on Marcus to look after most things, at least as far as business and money were concerned. Marcus must have left her some money, and perhaps a life insurance – though if a verdict of suicide was given, she probably wouldn't get a penny of that.

Oh, why did things have to be so horrible? Emily had been thinking about Terry ever since she heard the news. The pain of his death had been so bad that she hadn't been able to face it for a long time. She could imagine what her sister was feeling now, and her heart ached for Frances. She couldn't wait to leave here, because she wanted to see her, to hold her and comfort her.

7

Frances let herself into the house. She hadn't taken anything suitable for the funeral when she left with Daniel the previous night. She felt a chill strike her as she walked in, because the kitchen range was out and she had never let that go out before. A shiver ran through her, because alone in this house, she felt misery building inside her. All she wanted to do was to get out of here as fast as she could!

She left the door unlocked as she went quickly through the kitchen and up the stairs to her room. She had packed her case and was about to leave when she heard something – a door banging.

Frances went out to the landing and looked down. As she did so, the kitchen door opened and someone came out into the hall. Her heart caught with fright and then she saw that it was Sam.

'You gave me a fright,' she said as she came down the stairs. 'I was just getting a few things together.'

'I saw the door open and thought I had better investigate,' Sam said. 'Someone might have broken in. What are you doing here? I thought you were staying with Daniel?'

'I am staying with him. I told you, I need a few things, clothes for the funeral.' Frances stared at him, the tears starting to form in her eyes. The grief and guilt were choking her and she couldn't hold it in. 'Why did he have to do it? The police say it was deliberate. Why?'

'Frannie...' Sam moved towards her, catching her in his arms. For a moment, she was too distressed to move away and she let him hold her. 'My God, you're so warm and soft, and you smell wonderful,' Sam muttered, pressing his mouth against her neck. 'I've always wanted to hold you and touch you, Fran.'

'No!' Frances pushed him away in revulsion. 'Don't you dare to touch me like that! I hate you!' She was sobbing but angry too, her disgust showing in her eyes.

Perhaps it was the disgust that drove Sam past the edge of reason. He grabbed hold of her again, pressing her against the wall, his knee between her legs, clawing her skirts up above her waist. Frances struggled but it was no use. He was too strong for her and she couldn't escape as his hand moved up her thigh, touching her, his finger pushing up inside her. She could feel the heat of his erection as he pressed himself against her and she knew what was coming next. With a great effort, she shoved hard against his shoulders, bringing one knee up sharply. Sam gasped in pain and staggered back.

'Damn you!' he muttered, doubling over. 'What did you want to do that for? It was just a bit of fun.'

'To you, perhaps.' Frances spat the words at him. 'You were going to force me if you could, Sam, and don't deny it. You can think yourself lucky if I don't tell Rosalind what a brute you are.'

'I'm sorry,' Sam said. 'I didn't mean it to happen that way, Fran. You know I care for you. If you give me a chance, I'll look after you.'

'Just get out of this house,' Frances said. 'And don't come back until you're invited. I shan't say anything for the moment, because it isn't the time – but I might.'

'I shouldn't have done it,' Sam said. 'I'm sorry, Fran. I'll make it up to you. I'll give you this house just to show you how sorry I am.'

'The house was a wedding present, but you never signed it over,' Frances said. 'Just get out, Sam, and leave me alone.'

He looked at her for a moment and then turned and left her, slamming the front door as he went out. Frances stood where she was for a moment, feeling as if she might faint. After a minute or two she went into the sitting room and poured herself the last of the whisky from a bottle Marcus had left on the sideboard. She tossed it back in one go, feeling it sting her throat. The memory of Sam's hateful touch would linger in her mind for a long time, but she was lucky it hadn't been worse. She shuddered as she looked about her. She certainly didn't want to live in this house ever again, whether Sam gave it to her or not.

She pulled the kitchen door shut behind her, glad that she would be staying with Alice and Daniel until the funeral was over – and Emily would be here soon. She blinked back her tears. She couldn't let Sam make her weak. She had to be strong. She had to find a new life for herself and Charlie somehow.

* * *

'I don't know what to do,' Frances said. Emily had her arm about her and they were alone, walking in the lane that led from the fen into Stretton Village. It was quite warm for the time of year, though the breeze was cool. 'Sam scares me. I fought him off the other day but...' She held back a sob. 'He apologised and said he would give me the house, but I don't want to be beholden to him, Emily.'

'Wait and see how you're situated after the will is read,' Emily advised. 'If you can afford it you might want to move away somewhere.'

'But where?' Frances frowned as she looked at her. 'I wouldn't know where to go. I've never lived anywhere but here. I shouldn't know anyone.'

'You would soon make friends,' Emily said. 'Anyway, you will have time to think about it, because when tomorrow is over I am going to take you and Charlie home with me. You can stop for as long as you like, and it will give you some breathing space. When you know how things stand you will be able to decide what you want to do, love.'

'Yes, I suppose so,' Frances said. Her smile was a little forced as she looked at Emily. 'I wasn't sure you would come – after the way I spoke to you at Henry's funeral.'

'Well, you were right in a way,' Emily said. 'It's true that I've been wrapped up in the home for a long time, but that may be coming to an end soon.'

'What do you mean?'

'They are talking about closing us down,' Emily said. 'We don't have anywhere near so many patients now. We've been able to send some of them home; they will never be quite normal but they can make some sort of a life for themselves. I'm not sure what will happen to those that remain. At Vanbrough we have made them feel as if they are at home, but if they get put into a state institution...' She shook her head. 'We could keep the home open as an entirely private venture, but it would be expensive, because most of the patients couldn't afford to pay. A couple of families might, but that wouldn't cover the running costs. Vane has been paying a lot of the cost anyway, but he did receive a subsidy from the government to help with the nursing staff. I'm not sure if he will be prepared to carry on.'

'What will you do if he decides to close it down?'

'I'm not sure. Vane will want me to stay on, of course – but I don't know if it is the right thing.' Emily was thoughtful. She had believed she was settled at Vanbrough, but just recently Amelia had been trying to take Robert over rather too often for her liking. 'Like you, Fran, I don't know what I should do if I left. I don't think I would come back here – perhaps the seaside. I might try my hand at running a small hotel.'

'You wouldn't?' Frances saw the look on her face and nodded. 'I suppose it wouldn't be much different from running the home.'

'Easier, I would imagine. We shouldn't have so many problems with the nursing staff. We are losing one of our best nurses. Rose is getting married. I think she is having a baby, though she hasn't said as much. I shall be sorry to lose her, especially the way things are. I don't feel like taking on someone new at the moment.'

'It must be difficult for you.' Frances gave her a natural smile. 'You've made me feel better, Emily. It was so awful when Dan told me. I can't bear to think of...' She drew a sobbing breath. 'But it must have been the same for you when Terry was killed, and you've managed, haven't you?'

'After a fashion,' Emily said. 'It hasn't been easy, Fran, don't think that – it never is when you love someone. For a long time I was like a zombie, walking about in a daze. I don't know how I got through the first few months, but having Robert helped. I had to eat because of my baby, and when he was born I knew that I had to find a way to live again. I have – but that doesn't mean I've forgotten Terry, and it still hurts.'

Frances nodded. 'We had a row that night. Marcus went off in a temper because of something I said to him. Do you think...?'

Emily put an arm about her waist, giving her a little squeeze.

'No, I don't, Fran. Something was eating at Marcus. You told me so yourself. He should have faced up to whatever it was, found a way of dealing with it – but it wasn't just because of a little quarrel with you. So don't go blaming yourself.'

'I have been,' Frances admitted. 'I keep thinking that if I hadn't gone on at him he might still be alive.'

'And it might have happened next week or next month. If Marcus was drinking too much, he could have had an accident at any time, love. Don't take all the blame on your shoulders, please.'

'I'll try not to,' Frances said and shivered. 'I shall be glad when tomorrow is over. I hate funerals, Emily.'

'Yes, I'm not keen on them,' her sister admitted. 'But Dan and I will be with you. Alice's mum is going to look after Robert and Danny, so Alice will be there too. I expect Dorothy and Mary will come if they can. We'll be there to support you – and, as I said, I'm taking you back with me afterwards.'

'Yes, thank you,' Frances said. 'I should like to visit you. See it all for myself. I'm not sure what I'm going to do next. As you said, it depends on my situation – but I might go away.'

* * *

Afterwards, Frances thought that she could never have faced the funeral if Emily hadn't been there by her side. Dan was there too, but her brother seemed to get on well with Sam, and somehow that made her uneasy. She wanted to distance herself from her father-in-law, but he hovered around her, offering his assistance when all she wanted was for him to leave her alone. She could see the calculating look in his eyes, as if he was wondering whether or not she was going to show him up to his wife. It was what he deserved, but Frances couldn't see much sense in it. Rosalind probably wouldn't believe her – she might even think that Frances had invited his abuse.

Rosalind nodded to her once but didn't speak. Her eyes were dark with misery, and Frances sensed that at the moment she was raw with grief, hating everyone because her son was dead. Frances had sensed that Rosalind blamed her for the change in Marcus, which was quite unfair. She hadn't made him drink, and she certainly hadn't tried to stop him visiting his mother. He had made his own choice.

The service seemed to drag on and on interminably. The church was packed out, quite a few people standing outside. Frances thought it was probably in deference to Sam Danby, though she received a lot of sympathetic looks as she walked into the church.

Sam stood up and told the congregation how proud he had always been of his son. Marcus had been captain of the school cricket team. He had done well at college and might have gone on to an academic career if it hadn't been for the war. He had served his country well and received several mentions and commendations.

Frances stuck her fingernails into the palms of her hands. She wanted to scream at him to stop acting as if butter wouldn't melt in his mouth and tell them the truth. Only she wasn't sure what the truth was – except that the drinking had got much worse after Marcus discovered something about his father's business affairs.

She sat dry-eyed throughout the service, because her weeping had been done in private and she wasn't going to make a show of herself in public. The raw grief had been changing over the past few days, settling into an ache in her breast and a deep-seated anger. Marcus had been selfish and careless, throwing his life away in a drunken rage. If he had cared for her and Charlie, he would have stopped drinking and settled down at his job.

She pasted a look of calm on her face when they left the graveyard after the internment. She would be glad to get away from all this, to go off with Emily and not have to see people she knew for a while.

The family solicitor had attended the funeral. Alice had invited him back to her house for the usual sandwiches and a sherry, and Frances knew he would tell her about her financial situation later that afternoon. She hoped he would say that there was a little money, because she might take Emily's advice and move away from the village.

* * *

'Are you sure you have everything you need for a few weeks, Fran?' Emily asked as they all packed into her car. 'Hold on to the dog, Charlie. He is excited because he is happy to be with you again.' As if to confirm her words, the dog yelped and wriggled free, but she caught it almost at once and shut the back door of the car on Nanny, the two small boys and the dog. 'I'm sorry, Nanny,' she said as she got into the driving seat and glanced over her shoulder. 'Are you all right there?'

'Yes, madam, don't you worry about me,' Nanny said stoutly. 'We shall all be fine, though we may need to stop a little more often to go walkies.'

'Yes, I see what you mean.' Emily smiled ruefully. It was difficult enough keeping one small boy clean and dry for the journey; two boys and a dog would be more difficult. 'Well, are we all ready?' She looked at her sister, who was sitting by her side in front. 'You all right, Fran?'

'Yes, I'm fine,' Frances said and smiled at her. 'I feel much better now that *it* is all over.'

'Good,' Emily said. 'Off we go then.'

She was thoughtful as she set off. Frances hadn't told her exactly what the lawyer had said, but Emily gathered that her sister might be better off financially than she had imagined.

* * *

Emily was busy that morning so Frances walked as far as the lake on her own. There was a touch of frost in the air, because they were well into November now, but Frances had a thick coat and a silk headscarf to keep out the cold. It was very peaceful here; such a beautiful house, and the grounds were wonderful. It wasn't really surprising that her sister enjoyed living here. She wouldn't have minded it herself, but not as a permanent house guest. Not while Amelia ruled the roost here.

Frances sighed. She understood what Emily meant when she said that Amelia sometimes tried to take over Robert. She'd done it a few times with Charlie, but Frances didn't mind because she was going home in a few days. She wouldn't have stood for it if she were in Emily's shoes!

Frances was trying to decide what she ought to do next. She had come to terms with her loss in this glorious place, and although the anger was still there, it was under control. It appeared that Sam had put a block of apartments into Marcus's name after the war, at least a half share, and half still remaining with Sam. Marcus hadn't told her anything about them, but that wasn't unusual. He had made a will during the war leaving everything to her and hadn't bothered to change it after Charlie was born.

The lawyer had told Frances she was free to do as she

pleased with her half share of the property in London. Apart from that, Marcus had only left a thousand pounds, which wasn't very much. The house she was living in had never been transferred to Marcus, even though it was supposed to be a wedding gift.

'The London property is run by your father-in-law,' Mr Sanderson had informed her. 'Properly, you ought to ask him to buy your shares, but you could sell elsewhere if you chose – though I wouldn't recommend that course of action. I am sure Mr Danby will be more than happy to buy them from you, though of course you could take the income instead. I imagine that must be substantial. I think your husband must have waived it for the time being, but any such agreement would be at an end now.'

'What do you mean by waived it?' Frances had asked. 'Are you saying that Marcus didn't choose to take his share of the income?'

'Well, there is no record of him ever having received any money from the property,' the lawyer said. 'So I imagine he was leaving it to be reinvested.'

Frances hadn't disagreed with him, but she thought it was unlikely. If Marcus hadn't drawn on the income it was because he wouldn't take his father's money. She knew that at one time he had hoped to manage the London property, but something had happened that made him quarrel with his father.

Marcus had never told her, and she had decided that she would try to find out what had caused all the trouble, and it seemed that the London property might be a good place to start.

* * *

'Are you sure you won't stay longer?' Emily asked as her sister came downstairs with her cases packed a few days later. 'You know you are welcome to stay as long as you want. You could even stay until after Christmas if you like?'

'Yes, I know that,' Frances said and smiled at her. 'But if I don't go back now it will just get worse. I have to face up to things, Emily. I have to decide what to do with my life from now on.'

'Have you any ideas?'

'Well, yes, I might,' Frances said. 'It all depends on how much I can get for my share of the property in London. If Sam offers me enough I might buy a little bed and breakfast place at the sea, not too far from here so that we can see each other sometimes. And I'm going to learn to drive. I ought to have done it years ago.'

'It comes in handy,' Emily said and kissed her cheek. 'I think you are being very positive, love. If you wait until the weekend I could drive you home.'

'No, I've decided to go on the train,' Frances said. 'I'm going to break my journey in London and have a look at that block of apartments. I want to know if Sam is offering me a fair price for my share or not, because he might try to get them back cheap. He never put the house into our names, even though it was a wedding gift.'

'I wouldn't trust that man farther than I could throw him,' Emily said. 'Be careful of him, love. If you're in any doubt, come to me – or ask Dan to sort him out for you.'

'Dan thinks he's a bit of a rogue but they get on all right,' Frances said. 'If I told him what Sam Danby was really like – what he tried to do to me that day at the house – he wouldn't believe me. That's why I'm going to take my money and leave, Emily. It wasn't so bad after Marcus came back when the war ended, but...' She shook her head. 'I don't like Sam, and I'm going to get away as soon as I can. If I stay there's no telling what he might do next.'

'Good for you,' her sister said and kissed her cheek. 'I'm glad you're so positive, Frances. Just remember that I am on the end of the phone and I'll always help if I can.'

'Thanks,' Frances said and gave her a quick hug. 'I feel a lot better now. Being here with you has made me see there's more to life than I ever dreamed. All you need is a bit of money and you can do anything.'

'Well, I'm not sure that's completely true,' Emily said. 'But you're certainly entitled to your share of that property and you want to tell your lawyer to make sure that you get it.'

'Yes, I shall, when I know what it is worth,' Frances agreed. She didn't add that she was curious to see just what it was about these flats that had made Marcus have a terrible row with his father.

* * *

Frances stood outside the block of apartments. It was bitterly cold now and the pavements were icy beneath her feet. She was conscious of a feeling of disappointment, because this side of the river had a lot of industrial stuff going on and they weren't exactly the luxury apartments she had been hoping to find. In fact they looked a bit rundown, even seedy, and she was surprised that Sam bothered to come up to London as often as he did. Surely they couldn't be that valuable?

She had employed a professional nanny to take care of Charlie and the dog for the morning, thinking that she might be quite a while, but now that she was here she didn't feel like going inside. She lingered at the entrance door, looking at the names above the bells. It was a moment or two before she realised that they were all a bit peculiar... and all girls' names. She read the names out to herself: Candy, Blondie, Sugar Susie, and Mary, Mary Quite Contrary. There was a frown on her face as she tried to make sense of it. And then a man came and stood beside her. He pushed the bell with the name Candy on it and waited. After a few minutes, a girl with bleached yellow hair, wearing what looked like a pink silk dressing gown, came down and let him in. She shot a look at Frances but didn't say anything as she disappeared up the stairs with the man following her.

Frances moved to a position across the street to watch. In the next half an hour, six men came and rang the various bells, and six different girls came down to let them in. At first she thought it was her imagination, but she continued to watch and a steady stream of men rang and were admitted to the building at regular intervals. She had almost decided to leave when the door of the building opened and a girl came out wearing a bright red suit and high heels. She walked straight across the road to Frances, a challenging look in her eyes.

'Have you seen enough? Or are you after a bleedin' job?'

'What kind of a job?' Frances asked, feeling the sickness swirl in her stomach. Her feet were frozen and she was sure her nose had turned red. All she wanted was to be somewhere warm, but a stubborn need to know had kept her standing here, watching. She was fairly certain she knew what was going on, but she didn't want to believe it.

'Don't give me that,' the girl said. 'Are you after a job or one of them bleedin' do-gooders that keep tryin' to save our souls?' Her eyes narrowed, her red mouth thinning with dislike. 'You ain't with the bleedin' coppers, are you?'

'No, I'm not,' Frances said, her mouth dry. 'How much do you get paid for doing... your job?'

'Not as much as it's bleedin' worth,' the girl retorted. 'The bloke what owns these flats takes a cut – and with the rent, that's more than half we make. If I had my way I'd find somewhere else, but it ain't much different on the street. You need protection and you have to pay for that, see.'

'Oh...' Frances felt a little faint. 'You're sure it is the man who owns the flats, not someone else?'

'He comes up to town regular to collect his money, and to have a bit of fun himself. Sam isn't so bad, but I don't reckon it's fair takin' all that money off us girls.' She narrowed her gaze. 'So did you want a job then? I've got a spare room in my flat. We all let the rooms to friends to get a bit extra what Sam don't know about if we can.'

'Thanks for asking,' Frances said. 'I'll think about it.'

'Don't wait too long then. I shan't have a spare room long. There's plenty of girls on the streets glad to get in somewhere like this. Sam makes sure we don't get any trouble and that's why we pay him.'

Frances walked away without answering. She was sickened by what she had discovered. How could Sam Danby do something like that? It wouldn't have been so bad if he had just let the flats to the girls, but to take a cut of what they earned, and to sleep with them himself!

It was so nasty that she didn't want to believe it, and yet she knew that Marcus must have found out about this himself. She could imagine how he had felt, discovering that the money, which had sent him to a good school and paid for his food and clothes as a child, had come from prostitution. Marcus would have hated that so much. He was like his mother. He thought himself a gentleman and above such things. He would have been shocked and angry with his father.

Frances knew she had discovered the reason for the quarrel with Sam. Marcus had already been addicted to heavy drinking when he came back from the war. Something like this must have knocked his pride, made him ashamed, forcing him to find solace in strong drink.

He had refused to take an income from the property. He hadn't even told Frances about the gift of a half share in the apartment block. It was quite possible that he would never have taken his share, but Frances was made of stronger stuff. She was angry that Sam Danby should pretend to be such a righteous man, a pillar of the community, when all the time he was involved in something like this. He had tried to rape her and he was involved in running what amounted to a brothel.

He should be ashamed of himself! Well, he could pay her for her share of the property – and he could pay her for what she knew too. It was his fault that Marcus had begun to drink more and more heavily. He had to pay for what he had done to Marcus and to her!

* * *

'What are you doing?' Emily asked as she walked into the nursery and saw that Amelia was giving Robert a sticky pink bun with a glass of milk. 'Where is Nanny? She gives Robert his tea – and I don't like him having things like that, Amelia.'

'It won't hurt for once,' Amelia said. 'We went shopping in the village and Robbie asked for a bun, didn't you, darling? Tell Mummy it's nice.'

Robert took a bite and pulled a face, putting it down on the nursery table. 'It's too sweet,' he said. 'Nanny gives me nice buns.'

'He meant home-made fruit buns without all that icing,' Emily said. 'I'll get Nanny to bring you one, Robert.' She glanced at Amelia. 'Where is she, by the way?'

'Oh, she wanted an hour or two off so I said it was all right,' Amelia replied and wiped a sticky mark from Robert's chin. He shook his head and threw the bun at her. It landed on her silk blouse and she gave a little cry of annoyance, because grease stains were so difficult to get out of such a fine material. 'You naughty boy! Amelia won't take you to see the swans tomorrow if you throw things at her.'

'Robert, you shouldn't do that; it isn't nice,' Emily said. 'Say sorry to Amelia please.'

He mumbled something reluctantly. Emily hesitated. She wanted words with Amelia, but now wasn't the time.

'I came to take you to see the swans and ducks,' she told her son and picked him up. 'Nanny might give you one of her buns when we come back – if you are good.' She shot a look at Amelia over her shoulder as she went out. 'I shall speak to you later.'

* * *

Emily was feeling angry when she returned to the house. Amelia had gone too far, giving Nanny time off without asking her and feeding Robert sugary buns. She had put up with Amelia's behaviour long enough and she was going to have it out with her.

She left Robert with Nanny, who had returned and was apologetic for going off without speaking to Emily. 'I think I ought to have asked you, madam,' Nanny said when she saw Emily. 'Lady Vane said it was all right – but strictly speaking she isn't my employer.'

'No, she isn't,' Emily said. 'I would prefer that you refer to me another time, but we shall say no more about it.'

She wasn't going to say anything more to Nanny, but she had every intention of having it out with Amelia. It was time that they talked properly about this situation, instead of hinting at each other.

Amelia was sitting in the back parlour reading an Agatha

Christie mystery when Emily walked in. She looked up, a slightly wary expression in her eyes as she put her book down.

'Vane is back,' she said a little hastily. 'I've ordered a tray of tea in a few minutes.'

'Fine,' Emily said and closed the door. 'Amelia, I didn't want to say much in front of Robert – but I would rather you did not give Nanny orders or time off without reference to me. And I like him to have a healthy diet, not too much sugar, if you please – it is bad for his teeth. When I took him to the dentist he said there was some decay and it was best to be careful.'

'You make too much fuss over small things,' Amelia said. 'Anyone would think I had done something dreadful.'

'No, you haven't done anything wicked,' Emily said. 'But please remember that I am Robert's mother and I like to know what is going on as far as he is concerned.'

'You are becoming impossible,' Amelia said, an angry spark in her eyes. 'Anyone would think you ruled the roost around here. Please remember that I am Lady Vane, and as long as my husband is alive I decide what goes on here.'

'I do not interfere with the house,' Emily told her. 'I am aware that I should be hopeless at doing what you do, Amelia – but Robert is my son. And I have the right to decide what is best for him.'

'But who was his father?' Amelia said, clearly very annoyed now. 'Supposing I tell Vane the truth... How long do you think it will be before he kicks you out? And your precious son? Think about that!' Amelia got to her feet and flounced out of the room.

Emily went over to the French windows, looking out at the magnificent view. She would miss this place if she left, but perhaps it might be for the best to get it over with now. She still had a little money, not enough for the hotel she had in mind, but enough to manage until she found herself a job somewhere. It would ease her conscience, because Daniel was right. She had done something very wrong when she allowed Vane to believe that the boy was his grandson.

She turned as the door opened and Lord Vane came in. He smiled at her and her heart caught, because she had become very fond of him, and she didn't want to hurt him. However, she could not live with the threat of exposure hanging over her.

'How are you, my dear?' he asked and looked round. 'Amelia not here? I thought we were going to have tea?'

'I am afraid Amelia left because we had a little argument.'

'Oh dear, I am so sorry. Should I inquire why?'

'I'm afraid it was my fault. Amelia gave Nanny time off without asking me and... Just little things. I got cross and we had a tiff.'

'Yes, I see.' Vane sighed. 'I have noticed that Amelia is a little possessive over Robert. She must remember that she is not his mother, however much she might wish it to be so.'

'I shouldn't have made a fuss,' Emily said, because she felt a bit silly now. 'I am sorry I upset Amelia.'

'Not at all, my dear. I have thought you remarkably patient. I shall have a word with her.' His gaze narrowed as he saw her expression. 'Something else on your mind?'

'Yes, there is.' Emily took a deep breath. She had to do it because she couldn't continue the lie. 'It's something I ought to have told you a long time back. I didn't want to hurt you then and I don't now, but perhaps you ought to be told.'

'If it concerns Robert, I prefer that you leave things as they are,' Vane said. 'I may already know what you wish to tell me, Emily. I am not quite a fool, my dear, but still I prefer things to be as they were. In the eyes of the world Robert is my grandson, and that is the way I wish it to remain. I am hoping that you will continue to live here and allow us to share Robert – providing that Amelia remembers she is not his mother?'

'Oh, Vane...' Emily's throat caught with tears because he was such a dear man. 'Forgive me. I've been making a fuss about nothing.'

'I doubt that, Emily. Amelia has it within her to become obsessive about the boy. She so wanted to give me a child and it wasn't possible – but we have our heir, don't we?'

Emily looked into his eyes. They were so gentle but also clear and knowing, and she could do no other than smile and nod. 'If that is what you want. I certainly don't want to leave this house, Vane – but I couldn't go on living a lie. At least, I couldn't keep it from you.'

'Then we shall forget this conversation ever took place,' he said. 'And now I want to talk to you about the home. You know that the government wants to finish their involvement. We cannot continue to run it as it is, of course. However, most of the inmates still in residence have nowhere to go and I am thinking that we should let them make the place their home. We shall have a greatly reduced staff, of course, and no further admissions – but I see no reason why the present occupants shouldn't finish their lives in comfort and peace. I doubt many of them have more than a few years to live.'

'We would need to keep at least two of the nursing staff, and some others,' Emily said, 'but I am sure the local doctor would come in if necessary – and there are only five guests left.'

'Yes, we will call them guests,' Vane said and nodded his satisfaction. 'I shall make you a monthly allowance to cover the expenses, and I hope you will keep within its limits as much as possible, Emily – but you may come to me if you find it too difficult.'

'I am sure I shall manage,' she said. 'You need not continue to pay me. I have enough for my personal needs.'

'I am going to set up a trust fund for you instead of the salary you have received,' Vane told her. 'You will have the income for as long as I live. Afterwards, it will be up to you if you wish to take the capital.'

'Oh, Vane,' Emily said, and her throat felt constricted with emotion. 'I am not sure that I deserve such kindness.'

'Oh, yes,' he said and smiled at her. 'I am perfectly certain that you do, Emily. I know what kind of a man my son was – and I regret the pain he must have caused you. But I cannot regret that he brought you into our lives. I think the past few years would have been rather empty had you not been a part of our family, my dear – and you know that I love Robert dearly?'

'Yes, I do,' Emily agreed. 'He loves you too, but you know that, of course. I think Amelia will be here in a moment. Please be gentle with her, Vane. It may have been as much my fault as hers.'

She left the room, going upstairs just as Amelia came through the hall and entered the parlour. It felt as if a huge weight had lifted from her shoulders. Vane had always known the truth, but he wanted Robert to be his heir. She didn't have to feel guilty and she could stay on, just as the last few guests at the convalescent home were going to be allowed to stay on for as long as they needed a place to live.

Somehow she felt better about Amelia. Now that Vane knew the truth, she wouldn't feel constantly threatened. Amelia might still try to take over, but that wouldn't matter now. And Emily would try to be more tolerant in her turn. It was best if they could all be friends and live together in harmony.

* * *

Frances glanced nervously at the clock. She was expecting Sam to call at any moment, and she was torn between excitement and terror, because she knew that what she was planning was dangerous. Sam wouldn't like what she had to say to him, but she was determined that he wasn't going to get away with his nasty little secret any longer. She was pretty certain that it was the discovery that his father was the owner of flats that were used for prostitution which had driven Marcus to the edge, making his drinking worse. And there was what Sam had done to her. He had to pay for that!

She had sent Charlie off for the afternoon. One of his friends from the nursery school that he was now attending two mornings a week was having a birthday party. Muriel had taken him for her, and Frances would collect him later – after she had spoken to Sam.

She tensed as she heard his car draw up outside, her nails curling into the palms of her hands. Taking a deep breath, she went to answer the door, giving him a cool nod as she asked him inside. She walked through to the formal drawing room, her back very straight, and then she turned to look at him.

'No, please don't sit down, Sam,' she said. 'I didn't ask you here for tea. I have something to say to you, and then I want you to leave.'

Sam's eyes narrowed warily, remembering the last time he was here. He had made a stupid mistake that day. He wasn't sure what was coming now. Frances had never been exactly welcoming, but now she was angry – aggressive in a way he'd never known her to be previously.

'What is wrong?' he asked. 'Something on your mind, Frannie? You're not still upset because of my little bit of fun?'

'My name is Frances. I would be grateful if you would remember it, please.' She lifted her head proudly. 'And no, it isn't just that you tried to rape me two days before my husband's funeral, though that was bad enough. On my way home from Emily's I stopped off in London. I went to look at that apartment building, the one that you gave half of to Marcus... The one where all the prostitutes live.'

'That's nothing to do with me, Frances,' Sam said, his eyes narrowing. 'An agent lets it for me. I didn't know anything about it until recently, and I'm planning to move them all out soon. I may sell it if I can.'

'Don't lie to me, Sam,' Frances said, her expression one of disgust and dislike. 'I spoke to one of the girls. She wanted to know if I was looking for a room and a job – and she mentioned you by name. Apparently, you take forty per cent of their earnings as well as the rent.'

'That's a lie!' Sam growled and glared at her. 'It's only that bitch's word against mine – and who would believe a whore?'

'I would,' Frances said. 'Perhaps I couldn't prove it in court, but a few whispers here and there and you might find yourself getting some odd looks. A letter to the local newspaper might spark an investigation that the police would be interested in – and you would certainly be asked to resign from the parish council.'

'You witch!' Sam muttered and moved closer, a threatening look in his eyes. 'What do you want in order to keep your mouth shut?'

'I think my share of that building is probably worth ten thousand pounds. I want twenty thousand.'

'You mercenary little bitch!' Sam said, and a nerve throbbed at his temples. 'I never suspected what you were really like. I thought you were a nice decent girl, Frances, but underneath you are as hard as nails. No wonder Marcus drunk himself into an early grave.'

'You know why Marcus drank too much,' Frances said, her face pale. She clenched her hands at her sides. 'He got into the habit during the war and then he couldn't stand it when he found out about your nasty little secret. He just went to pieces. Well, I'm different. The price just went up. As well as the twenty thousand, I want three thousand a year for life.'

'You are treading on dangerous ground, Frances.' Sam moved closer, a menacing look in his eyes. 'I was going to give you two thousand a year anyway. You can have that and ten thousand for your share of the property, but that's all.'

'I want twenty thousand pounds and three thousand a year,' Frances said. She looked at him proudly, refusing to show fear, though she was trembling inside. 'If you don't pay I shall go to the police – and even if they can't prove anything it will cause trouble for you, Sam. You won't like that.'

His eyes flashed with temper and he grabbed hold of her arm, his fingers digging into her flesh so that she almost cried out. 'And you won't like what I'll do to you if you open your mouth. I'll give you fifteen thousand and two thousand a year.'

'I want the twenty thousand, Sam.' Frances raised her head proudly. 'And three thousand a year. I think you owe me that. I've kept quiet about what you did – but I could tell Rosalind. She might think it was cause for divorce.'

His eyes dropped before hers. 'I'll admit I shouldn't have done what I did – but it doesn't have to be this way, Frances. Be nice to me and I'll be nice to you. You might end up with a lot more than twenty thousand.'

'No, thank you,' she said. 'As soon as I have my money I'm going to move away from here. To be honest, I can't stand you, Sam. It was bad enough before you did what you did – but now I don't want to have to see you at all.'

'What about Charlie?' Sam demanded. 'He's my grandson and I'm entitled to see him sometimes.'

'I shan't stop you coming down to visit now and then,' Frances said. 'You can bring Rosalind and stay at the guest house that I am going to buy with the money you are going to pay me, Sam.'

Sam's eyes narrowed. 'There's more than one way to skin a cat,' he said. 'You think you've won, and maybe you have for the time being – but watch out, Frances. I'm not a man to take things lying down. I'll make you pay for this, believe me.'

Frances stood quite still until he had left, and then she went into the kitchen and found the cooking sherry. She poured herself a large glass and drank it down quickly.

Sam scared her because there was such violence in him. She hated being in this house, because it was too big without Marcus. She wanted to take Charlie and run away, but she had to wait for her money. Sam had caved in at the end, but she still wasn't sure he would pay up.

Frances poured another glass of sherry, sipping it more slowly this time. She didn't want to get into a bad habit the way Marcus had, but there was no doubt that it steadied her nerves. She just hoped that Sam would pay her so that she could leave soon.

Perhaps she ought to have taken the ten thousand and the income he'd been prepared to pay. He wouldn't have been angry then, and she might have got her money quickly. As it was, he might make her wait. She felt a bit regretful, but she had been so angry with him – and he deserved to be punished for what he had done.

* * *

Sam was furious as he drove home. Frances knew too much, and he was aware that she could make a lot of trouble for him if he didn't give her what she wanted. He was damned if he would cave into her blackmail. If there were any way out, he wouldn't pay her a penny. He'd been a damned fool to put one half of the property into Marcus's name. If he hadn't done that she wouldn't be entitled to anything – and she wouldn't have known a damn thing about his business.

He might have to pay her the ten thousand but he wasn't going to be blackmailed into giving her the twenty she wanted. He had planned to give her an income, see that she was all right, but now he had changed his mind. And yet, if she tried she could ruin him. He cursed Marcus for being such a soft fool. If he'd only accepted where a lot of the money had come from – the apartments were only a part of his empire of vice and corruption. Marcus had pushed his nose in too far, discovering the seedy gambling clubs and other things, but Frances only knew about the apartments.

He would have to play her along for the moment. He might have to sell that apartment block. He knew someone who would give him more than Frances had demanded. He would pocket the difference, pay her ten thousand up front and make her wait for the rest. She might go away and forget about it... And if she didn't, well, he might just have to arrange something else for that little madam.

* * *

'I suppose I should say I am sorry,' Amelia said as Emily walked into the small back parlour the next morning. It was a room they both liked, though there were others that they could use if they chose, but it had a particularly lovely view of the gardens. 'I must say it wasn't very nice of you to go to Vane behind my back.'

'It wasn't like that,' Emily said defensively. 'Vane asked where you were and I said we had had a tiff. And then I told him the truth about Robert – but he already knew.'

'Of course he did.' Amelia's eyes snapped with scorn. 'Did you imagine that he was a fool?'

'No, of course not.' Emily looked at her unhappily. 'I suppose I just felt guilty for letting him believe it – but I should have known. I'm glad I talked to him. It means that I have no need to feel that I am lying to him, and if you can accept it, Amelia, I want to stay on here.'

'Well, of course,' Amelia said. 'Vane would be upset if you went. He loves Robert, as I do.' She looked a little ashamed. 'I know I do things I shouldn't sometimes, but I feel as if Robert belongs to me. He is the son I wanted to give Vane.'

'I know that,' Emily said. 'And I am quite happy for you to take him out for walks and things, Amelia – but please not too many sweets and cakes for the sake of his teeth. And Nanny is my employee, even if I am a guest here.'

'All right,' Amelia said and shrugged. 'I suppose we have to learn to get along together. I was thinking of starting Robert on a pony next spring – if you agree? Vane told me to buy something suitable and either he or I will supervise, but one of the grooms is very good with teaching children. He works at a riding school at the weekends.'

'I should like to talk to him and see the pony before Robert does,' Emily said. 'But my brothers learned when they were about his age. I know you are good with horses, Amelia – and I think you will want to take good care of him.'

'You know I would never do anything to harm Robert. You must know that, Emily?'

'Yes, I do,' she said and smiled. 'I hope we can forget that silly tiff we had and be friends again?'

'Yes, of course. We have to,' Amelia said. 'It is what Vane wants – and the least we can do is get on for his sake.'

'Yes, I know,' Emily said. 'He is all right, isn't he? No sign of any more trouble with his heart?'

'He seems fine,' Amelia said. 'But I don't want to upset him.'

'No, of course. We mustn't do that,' Emily agreed. She was thoughtful as she left the house and walked down to the home. She was very fond of Vane and it wouldn't be the same if anything happened to him.

8

'I saw Frances this morning in Ely,' Alice said when her husband met her in the village main street. She had been into town and returned on the bus with her shopping, but Daniel had come to meet her to save her the long walk along fen droves. 'She said she might be moving away soon, perhaps after Christmas. Apparently, Marcus left her some property. Sam is selling it for her and she is going to invest in a guest house by the sea – somewhere down where Emily lives, she thinks.'

'Sam won't think much to that,' Daniel said with a frown. 'He dotes on Charlie – and so does Rosalind, come to that. I wonder why Frances wants to go off like that? She won't know anyone and it is going to be hard running a place like that on her own.'

'Well, it's what she wants,' Alice said, looking doubtful. 'I suppose she will employ girls to help her – but the business side will be down to her and I'm not sure that she will find it easy.'

'I shouldn't think she has a clue,' Daniel said. 'Marcus always looked after the money side.' He glanced at his wife as he drove through the High Street. It was clear of traffic, just a tractor chugging a little way ahead of him and a young boy on a pony. 'Do you think I should talk to her? See if she really knows what she is doing?'

'It might be a good idea,' Alice said. 'She had two bottles of sherry in her basket...' She shook her head. 'I expect she just needs it for cooking. After all, it is nearly Christmas.'

'I shouldn't have thought she was doing that sort of cooking these days. How many sherry trifles can one person eat? She wouldn't give them to Charlie, would she?'

'No, I shouldn't think so,' Alice said. 'She said Muriel was looking after Charlie this morning. Apparently, he has a bit of a cold.'

'Most children get them at this time of the year,' Daniel said. 'It's December, Alice. Danny had a bit of a cough last week. Frances fusses too much.'

'I suppose Charlie is all she has to think about these days,' Alice said. 'I hadn't seen her for ages, Dan, and she looked a bit strained. Do you think I should ask her to come to dinner on Sunday?'

'It wouldn't hurt,' he said and smiled at her. 'Connor won't be here. He and some of his friends are going to London for a week. They are switching the Christmas lights on again this year, and they want to go to some of the shows.'

'Really?' Alice was surprised. 'Can he afford it? I thought he was broke last week.'

'Well, I gave him a few pounds when I sold that car I had been working on,' Daniel told her. 'He doesn't earn a lot but he works hard – and it will do him good to get away and enjoy himself.'

'Yes, I expect so,' Alice said. 'He has settled down a lot since he came back from staying with Emily, hasn't he?'

'We had a talk the other day,' Daniel said. 'I think it upset him when he thought I had been killed, and then I was in that camp...

We talked about that and he seems to understand. I think he has grown up a lot these past months.'

'I agree,' Alice said. 'He's happier living with us, Dan. He never did get on well with Frances.'

'Well, like I said, he won't be here this weekend. Have Frances to dinner and it will give us a chance to talk. I am sure she must be lonely, but I don't like to think of her going off somewhere on her own. I suppose I ought to pop in and see her more often, but I don't get a lot of time these days.'

'Of course you don't,' Alice said. 'She told me she has taken a couple of driving lessons. I was surprised after the way...'

'After what happened to Marcus?' Daniel nodded. 'Yes, it surprises me a little – but I think it is a good thing. If she could drive she could come and visit you. Perhaps I ought to teach you, Alice? Would you like to learn?'

'I'm not sure,' Alice said. 'I'll think about it, Dan. I don't really get much time, though it would be a help when I wanted to do my shopping. You wouldn't have to meet me off the bus.'

'But I like meeting you,' he said and drew the van into their yard. He grinned at her and aimed a kiss at her cheek. 'I'd better go and see if Connor has fed the pigs yet. Any chance of a cuppa in twenty minutes?'

'Yes, of course,' Alice said. 'I bought some fresh cream in Ely and I shall be filling that sponge I baked this morning before I went out.'

'Make it fifteen minutes,' Daniel said and grinned at her as he set off across the yard.

Alice was smiling as she went into the house. She had felt a bit bothered about Frances when she saw her that morning. She would ring her later that evening and ask her to dinner. They were all so busy with their own lives, but it really was time that she made an effort as far as her sister-in-law was concerned.

* * *

Daniel drew his van into the drive of Clay's house in Chatteris. He could see that his brother had had new guttering put up and the windows had all been painted. It looked as if Clay was doing all right for himself, and it was about time he paid him some more of the money he owed him.

Clay was out in the back yard chopping wood. He came towards his brother, still carrying the axe he had been using.

'What are you doing here?' he asked, his tone aggressive.

'You know very well why I'm here,' Daniel said. 'I paid Margaret two thousand pounds to keep you out of trouble, and so far you've given me five hundred. I want the rest of it, Clay – and you can put that axe down. Unless you're willing to do murder rather than pay up?'

Clay flushed an angry red. 'Damn you! You know very well I wasn't threatening you. I told you I hadn't got much to spare.'

'This house looks as if you've spent money on it, and I happen to know you've just bought a new tractor and there's a new barn on your land. All I'm asking for is what you owe me.'

'Clay...' Dorothy had come out into the yard. 'Aren't you going to ask Daniel in for a cup of tea? It's ages since we saw him.'

Clay looked at him, and then called out to his wife, 'He can't stay. He has to get back for Alice.' He turned to Daniel again. 'All right, I can find four hundred next week – and that's it, Dan. I'm not going to pay you a penny more. It's take it or leave it this time.'

'Right, I want seven hundred and we'll call it quits,' Daniel said. 'There's a bit of land going I want. If I get it I shan't ask for the rest.'

'All right, damn you,' Clay said. 'I'll bring the money to you.

Don't come here. Dorothy will want to know why, and if she finds out, you'll whistle for the money.'

'All I want is that seven hundred,' Daniel said. 'It's in your interest to pay up, Clay.'

'When I have, we're finished,' Clay said. 'I don't want to see you again.'

Daniel shrugged. 'Suits me,' he said and turned his back. At the gate, he looked over his shoulder. Clay was still standing there watching him. 'Next week without fail.'

He got into the van and drove off. The extra land would make things easier. He hadn't really been able to afford to give Connor that twenty pounds for his holiday, but he had wanted to see the lad happy, and his friends were going. Connor hadn't asked, but he'd known he wanted to go with the others.

Daniel owed Sam Danby a hundred pounds for some feed and an old tractor and trailer that he'd bought from him. If Clay paid up, he could settle his debt – and next time he wouldn't take anything on tick, even if Sam pressed him. He wasn't sure why, but it had made him uncomfortable owing the money to Frances's father-in-law. He wouldn't do it again.

Frances opened the door to her mother-in-law. She was a little surprised, because it wasn't often that Rosalind came to visit her. It was annoying that she should choose this day to start visiting, because Charlie hadn't been well that morning and Muriel hadn't come in, so the house wasn't as pristine as usual.

'You didn't let me know you were coming,' Frances said, leading the way into the sitting room. 'Charlie has a cold. He is in bed at the moment.' As if right on cue, her son let out a wail of distress. 'Excuse me, I must go to him. I'll put the kettle on when I come back.'

She ran up the stairs, because Charlie had been sick twice that morning already, and she didn't want to have to change the bed again. However, when she got there, she discovered it was too late. He had been violently sick on the sheets she had put on fresh less than an hour ago.

'Oh, Charlie...' She sighed. 'Why didn't you call me? I changed those sheets only half an hour ago. Well, I can't do them again just yet. I'll just clear up the mess and—' She sensed something behind her and turned to see Rosalind watching her from the door. She was annoyed that her mother-in-law had followed her upstairs, but there wasn't much she could say. 'I'll be down in a minute, Rosalind. Charlie has been sick again. I'll just clear up and come down.'

'Aren't you going to change his sheets?'

'This is the second clean set this morning,' Frances said. 'He will have to put up with it for a little while. I'll do them later.'

'I'll give you a hand,' Rosalind offered. 'We can't have you left in this nasty mess, can we, Charlie?'

Charlie shook his head wanly at his grandmother. He was feeling dreadfully ill and his mother seemed cross. 'Charlie feel sick,' he said and promptly threw up again just as Frances was bending over him, splashing the bile on to her dress and the floor.

'Oh, Charlie,' Frances said, distressed but sounding annoyed because she was under pressure. 'Whatever is the matter with you today?'

'That is what I should like to know,' Rosalind said, laying a hand on his forehead. 'He feels hot and damp, Frances. Have you telephoned for the doctor yet?'

'No.' Frances frowned as she admitted it. 'I thought it was just a bilious attack. I was going to see how he was and then phone this afternoon if he was no better.'

'I think I should ring for him now,' Rosalind said. 'I'll leave you to put the clean sheets on, Frances. I do think the doctor ought to see Charlie immediately.'

'Yes, all right,' Frances agreed. 'He might come out more quickly for you than me, Rosalind. I'll clean Charlie up – and give him some water to rinse his mouth.'

Frances stripped the bed and changed Charlie's pyjamas. She gave him a glass of water to rinse his mouth and he drank a little afterwards. She placed her hand on his forehead. It was true that he did feel a little over-warm. She kissed his cheek, settling him back against the pillows as Rosalind came back, turning to look at her once more.

'Did they say how long the doctor would be?' Frances asked, feeling anxious now.

'He is out on a call, but they will give him the message when he gets back,' Rosalind said. She gathered the dirty linen up in her arms. 'I'll take these down and put them in the copper for you. Muriel will see to them when she comes in, I expect.'

'Yes, she couldn't manage it today,' Frances said. 'I think I'll sit with Charlie for a while if you don't mind?'

'Please don't worry about me,' Rosalind told her with a smile. 'I'll make a cup of tea and bring it upstairs. Charlie needs his mother with him at a time like this.'

'Thank you,' Frances replied, thinking that it was the first time she had ever felt close to her mother-in-law. 'You have been very kind. I am glad you came, Rosalind.'

'Well, I don't expect to make a habit of it,' Rosalind said. 'I wanted to ask you if you will come to us for Christmas Day, and to talk to you because Sam said you might move – but now isn't the time. It will keep for another day.'

'Yes, of course,' Frances said. She thought that if Rosalind had always been this approachable, they might have been friends long ago.

Rosalind went downstairs. Frances sat by the bed stroking Charlie's head. She thought that he felt a little cooler now and he certainly seemed to have settled. He was lying with his eyes closed, breathing easily.

By the time Rosalind returned with a tray of tea, Frances was ready to leave him. She went to the door of the room, a finger to her lips.

'I think it will be best if we leave him to sleep,' she said. 'That last bout of sickness seems to have got rid of whatever it was in his stomach. I am glad you telephoned the doctor, though. I shall feel better if he has a look at Charlie.'

'Yes, of course,' Rosalind said. 'Children often have fevers and sickness and most of the time they come to nothing – but just now and then it can be more serious, Frances. It is always a good idea to either call the doctor or take him to the surgery if he is sick, because you never know.'

'Yes, of course,' Frances said. She was almost sure now that it had all been a storm in a teacup, but she smiled at her mother-in-law. 'I wouldn't think of neglecting him, Rosalind.'

'No, I am sure you wouldn't,' Rosalind said. 'After all, he is all you have now – isn't he?'

'Yes...' Frances looked at her. 'How are you feeling now? I know you were terribly upset over Marcus.'

'Yes, of course, as you must have been, Frances.'

'I still can't believe he isn't coming back.' She took the tray from the older woman and carried it down to her parlour. 'I listen for his car and I catch myself thinking that he will be home soon.'

'Yes, I know what you mean,' Rosalind said. 'I saw a car like his the other day and my heart stopped. For a moment I thought it was Marcus.'

Rosalind had tears in her eyes. Frances hesitated and then went to put her arms about her. 'I'm so sorry,' she said. 'I didn't stop him visiting you, believe me. I think he was afraid that he might meet his father and—' She broke off, wondering how much her mother-in-law knew about Sam.

'Marcus quarrelled with him over the London property,' Rosalind said. 'Neither of them would tell me exactly why, but I've suspected something for a long time. Sam is doing something illegal, isn't he?'

'Marcus didn't tell me,' Frances said. 'I know he was angry and upset – but he didn't tell me why.' She wasn't going to tell Rosalind what she knew, because it was one of her holds over Sam. He obviously wouldn't want his wife to know what went on at that apartment block!

'You don't have to tell me anything,' Rosalind said. 'I'm not a fool, Frances, and I know that you have discovered something. Sam is furious with you. He doesn't tell me much, but little things slip out. It was another reason I came to see you. Be careful. He can be ruthless. You can push him so far and then he becomes dangerous.'

Frances turned away, avoiding her eyes. 'I am not afraid of Sam. I've told him that I want enough money to set me up in business at the sea somewhere, and I need some spare capital until I can make it pay. I don't think it is too much after...' She broke off because she couldn't tell Rosalind all of it.

'I know he is a brute,' Rosalind said. 'Believe me, I would have left him long ago if it hadn't been for Marcus – and the money. Sam wouldn't tell you, but my money started him. I don't see why I shouldn't have my share of it. If he would let me have the house and an income I would be satisfied for him to go off to London and never come back – but he won't do that, you see. He enjoys being Sam Danby. He is a big fish in a little pool and people look up to him here. In London he would be nobody – just a small-time crook, I imagine.'

Frances heard the bitterness in her voice. 'I didn't know you felt like this, Rosalind.'

'I don't tell everyone – but we shouldn't have secrets, Frances. We need each other. Apart we are vulnerable, but together we are much stronger. I am not your enemy, and Charlie means everything to me. If I promise that Sam will leave you alone in future, would you stay here – please?'

'Perhaps.' Frances was thoughtful. 'Sam is my main reason for leaving. I don't trust him, Rosalind. He scares me – and I've made him angry.'

'He won't harm you as long as you don't push him too far,' Rosalind said. 'But he dotes on Charlie and I think he might try to stop you taking him away from here.'

'He couldn't stop me if I chose to leave.'

'Perhaps not – but be careful,' Rosalind said. 'May I pop up and look at Charlie one more time before I go?'

'Yes, of course,' Frances said. 'I'll come with you.'

She followed Rosalind up the stairs. Charlie was sleeping when they looked in. Rosalind smiled at her as they half-closed the door behind them.

'He seems a lot better,' Rosalind said. 'But I should call the doctor again if he doesn't come soon. You can't be too careful, Frances.'

'Yes, I shall,' Frances said. 'Thank you.' She leaned forward, giving Rosalind a kiss on the cheek. 'Even if I go away, I shall always be pleased to have you come and stay with us. And I'll come for lunch on Christmas Day, but I shan't stay for the evening.'

'Oh good, I am so pleased, and I shall come and visit you when you get settled,' Rosalind said. 'I'll let you get on with your work, dear. Don't forget to keep an eye on Charlie.'

'Of course,' Frances said. 'I was worried when he was so sick earlier, but he does seem easier now.'

She saw Rosalind to the door, and then went into the back scullery. There were three sets of bed linen that needed to be washed, and then she would have to change her own dress. She was glad that Rosalind had called on her, but she wasn't going to give in and let Sam win over the money. Why should she? He deserved to pay for what he had done to Marcus – and to her.

'I telephoned Frances,' Alice told Daniel when he came in for his docky that morning. 'I asked her to lunch on Sunday but she wasn't sure she would be able to make it.'

'Is she being stand-offish or what?' Daniel asked as he went to the large sink to wash his hands under the cold tap. 'I thought she would be pleased to come. She hasn't got much else to do, after all.'

'She says that Charlie isn't well,' Alice said. 'Actually, she sounded quite worried. He has been sick several times this morning. He settled for a while when Rosalind Danby was there, but now he is feeling very hot and feverish. Frances has telephoned for the doctor again – Rosalind phoned the first time – but he is still out on a call.'

'Frances fusses too much,' Daniel said. 'Danny had a bilious attack last week. You took him to the doctor yourself and he was soon over it.'

'Danny was just a little bit sick,' Alice said, looking anxious. 'I've got a funny feeling about this, Dan. Do you think you should go up there? If he is really ill it might be best to call for an ambulance.'

'Surely you don't think it is that serious?'

'I don't know,' Alice admitted. 'But Frances doesn't have anyone else, does she? I know she is very worried and I sense something. I can't tell you why, but I think this could be serious.'

'All right,' Daniel said, because Alice was usually a good judge of things like this. 'I'll go and see what I can do – but I should think it is just Frances fussing.'

'Oh, Charlie,' Frances said, taking him into her arms because he wouldn't stop crying. 'What is the matter, darling? Mummy can't do anything. The doctor is coming soon.' But she had already telephoned twice herself and been told that he was still out on his rounds.

Hearing the front doorbell, Frances lay Charlie back on the pillows and ran downstairs. His desperate crying was breaking her heart and she prayed that the doctor had arrived. She was torn between relief and disappointment as she saw her brother.

'Daniel,' she said on a sob. 'Did Alice tell you to come? I don't know what to do. He just won't stop crying.'

'Has he been sick again?'

'Not since earlier – but he is so hot, and he seems odd.'

'What do you mean, odd?' Daniel asked, moving towards the stairs. He could hear Charlie start to scream. 'It sounds to me as if he is in pain.' Frances followed him as he ran up the stairs. He was bending over Charlie, lifting him from his bed. 'He is burning up! This child needs a doctor, fast!'

'I've been ringing the surgery all morning,' Frances said. 'The doctor is out on an emergency call.' She caught another sob as Charlie screamed again. 'What can I do?'

'Give me a blanket to wrap him in and get your coat,' Daniel said. 'I don't think we should wait for the doctor to come back, Frances. I'm going to take you straight through to the hospital in Cambridge.'

'Addenbrooks?' Frances stared at him in alarm. 'Do you think...?'

'Yes, I do,' Daniel said. 'It is a good thing Alice telephoned you herself. Were you just going to sit here and wait? Surely you could see how ill he was?'

Frances flinched at the anger in his voice. 'But he wasn't this ill,' she said, defending herself. 'Both Rosalind and I thought he was resting when we looked in earlier. And we had sent for the doctor.'

'You ought to have asked for the doctor the first time he was sick,' Daniel said, and then glanced at her white face. 'But I'm not blaming you. Alice says that I worry too much over Danny – but children die too easily.'

'Don't!' Frances begged. 'Please don't even think it!'

Daniel looked at her over her son's head. 'I think you had better start praying,' he said. 'Get in the car and I'll put Charlie on your lap. We haven't much time to waste.'

* * *

The drive to the hospital was one of the worst times of her life, Frances would think afterwards. Charlie was crying all the time at first, and then, quite suddenly, his head fell back and his body went rigid as he went into a spasm, jerking and twitching like a puppet on a string.

'Something is happening!' Frances said, glancing at her

brother. 'He is having a fit, I think! How much longer to the hospital?'

'Not long now,' Daniel said, his mouth set into a grim line. 'Just hold him, Frances, there's not much more you can do until we get him there. You could try blowing into his mouth if he stops breathing.'

'No, he's still breathing,' she said, 'but he has gone a funny colour. He looks strange, Dan. Oh, God! I don't want him to die. He mustn't die!'

'Don't panic,' Daniel said. 'We're almost there.' He drew the car to a halt in the front courtyard of the hospital, jumping out to open the door for Frances. 'Take him in. I'll find somewhere to park and come in. Don't worry, I'll find you wherever you are.'

Frances thanked him, rushing into the hospital through the main door, Charlie in her arms. He had gone very still now and she was terrified. She saw a nurse walking along one of the green-painted corridors and rushed up to her.

'My baby is ill,' Frances babbled. 'He was sick and I called the doctor but he didn't come. My brother brought me in.'

'He did the right thing, by the look of it,' the nurse said. 'Come with me. This child is very ill. He needs to see a doctor immediately.'

'Will he be all right?' Frances asked, feeling frantic.

'I can't tell you that,' the nurse said. 'You need to talk to the doctor, but you should never have left it this late. The boy looks as if he is in an advanced stage of the illness, whatever it is.'

'But he wasn't really ill at first,' Frances said. Her throat felt constricted and she was close to tears. 'I thought it was just a little bilious attack.'

She was almost running to keep up with the nurse, who took her through several seemingly endless corridors to a small ward.

She could see that there were other children in cots and a staff of two nurses and a doctor in a long white coat.

'Here, give him to me,' the nurse said. 'Sit over there outside the door. We need to give this child treatment immediately, and you will be in the way.'

'But what are you going to do? What is wrong with him?'

'He has become dehydrated because of being constantly sick,' the nurse said. 'We have to redress that first and then we'll see. Please leave this to us, Mrs...?'

'Frances Danby,' Frances said, feeling lost and bewildered. 'But I want to be with him. His name is Charlie – Charlie Danby.'

'Just sit there and wait,' the nurse said, and she went off with the boy in her arms, calling to one of the staff as she walked. 'Doctor, this child needs your immediate attention...'

Frances stood at the entrance to the ward, looking through the glass top of the door. She was terrified, her nerves stretched to breaking point as she watched the nurse and doctor talking. Charlie was being taken through a door at the far end of the ward. She went back inside, catching the arm of a passing nurse.

'Where have they taken him? Where have they taken my baby?' she asked desperately. 'I want to see Charlie.'

'Calm down,' the nurse said, a sharp note in her voice. 'They have taken him into the intensive care ward next door, because he needs immediate attention. You can't go with him as you would be in the way. Please go and sit down and we'll contact you as soon as we know if he is responding.'

'If? Do you mean he might die?' Frances asked, her voice rising shrilly. 'He can't die! He mustn't die! He's all I've got.'

'There's no point in you getting hysterical,' the nurse told her coldly. 'I haven't time to deal with hysterics at the moment. I have patients to look after. Go and wait in the corridor as you were asked and someone will come to you soon.'

Frances wanted to scream and shout, but she sensed it was useless. They had no sympathy with her, because they thought she had neglected Charlie, bringing him in at the last moment.

She sat on one of the hard seats in the corridor outside the ward. The walls were painted in a dark green glossy paint to waist height and a muddy-coloured cream from there to the ceiling. She supposed it made them easier to clean, but they looked dismal and cold, and everywhere smelled strongly of carbolic.

She seemed to have been sitting there for ages when she saw Daniel coming towards her down the corridor. She got up and ran to him, relieved that he had found her at last.

'They took him away from me,' she said. 'They won't let me see him. I am sure they blame me because he is so ill.'

'Calm down, Frances,' Daniel said, frowning. 'Of course they don't blame you. Charlie has some kind of a fever. They may think you should have got help sooner – but if you called the doctor there was nothing more you could have done yourself.'

'Perhaps I should have called for an ambulance or got a taxi before you came?' Frances put a hand to her face and sighed. She was on edge, her nerves stretched to breaking point because she was so worried. 'I didn't know what to do, Dan. At first I didn't think he was very ill, just had a little tummy upset, and then Rosalind thought we should phone for the doctor but he was out. Before she went home he was sleeping. We both thought he was better. I looked in later and he was whimpering so I picked him up and gave him a cuddle, and then I rang for the doctor again. Charlie was sick again soon after, and I phoned again, but they said the doctor was still out on his rounds. I was wondering what to do when Alice called me, and then you came. I didn't neglect him, Dan. I swear I didn't.'

'No, of course not,' he said and put an arm about her waist. 'Usually you fuss too much over little things, but this time he seems really ill. Just sit down for a moment and I'll go and talk to the nurses and find out what is happening.'

Frances sat down. She was a little calmer now that her brother was here, but she still felt uneasy. It was bad enough having her child so ill, but it made things even worse to see condemnation in the eyes of the nurses. She sensed that they thought she had neglected her child, but it wasn't true. She loved Charlie so much. Without him her life would have little meaning. She couldn't bear even to think about it.

Dan had been gone a long time. Frances stood up and walked to the door of the ward. She couldn't see her brother and she was tempted to go back into the ward to find him, but then a door opened a little further down the corridor and he came out and began to walk towards her. She got up and went to meet him, her heart racing.

'How is he? What is happening?'

Daniel put out a hand to touch her arm. 'They've put him on a drip of some kind, Frances, but they are very worried about him. They seem to think it may be some kind of a brain fever.'

'What do you mean?' Frances felt a thrill of horror. 'I don't know what that means.'

'I'm not sure that they do at the moment,' Daniel said. 'They are refusing to put a name to his condition; they just say he is very ill and will need to stay here at least overnight and perhaps for a few days.'

'Stay here?' Frances felt an icy chill trickle down her spine. 'But I can't leave him here. He's only a baby. He will want his mummy.' She felt close to panic. What was happening to her child? 'I don't understand...'

'The doctor is coming to talk to you in a few minutes. We'll sit and wait for him, Frances. He won't be long.'

'I don't feel like waiting,' Frances said. 'I want to see Charlie.'

Daniel held her arm, preventing her from going into the ward. 'I need to see him, Dan. I can't leave him here alone.'

'Here comes the doctor,' Daniel said, giving her a warning look. 'Be calm and sensible, Fran. There's no sense in making a scene.'

Frances was beyond listening to him. She broke from his grasp and ran up to the doctor, grabbing at his arm. 'Where is my baby? I want to see him! Is he all right?'

'Charlie is very far from all right,' the doctor told her sternly. His large hand pried hers from the sleeve of his coat. 'Try to be calm, Mrs Danby. We are doing all we can for your son, but I am afraid he is very sick. I am not sure that he will pull through this, though we shall do all we can for him. It would have been better if we could have seen him much earlier.'

'But he wasn't ill until this morning,' Frances said. 'I rang the doctor but he didn't come, so my brother brought us here.'

'I understand from your brother that he has had a little chill and a bit of a fever for a few days?'

'Well, yes, he was a bit grizzly, but not really ill,' Frances said. 'Even this morning I thought it was just a bilious attack.'

'It is always best to take children to the doctor straightaway,' he said. 'Had you done so, we should have stood a better chance of fighting this illness.'

'What is it?' Frances asked, thoroughly frightened. 'I've never seen anything like the fit he had on the way here.'

'We have to do certain tests...' The doctor was hesitant. 'It may be a condition called meningitis, but we can't be sure yet.'

'I've never heard of that,' Frances said. 'He had the German measles the other year but he wasn't as bad as this. I don't understand it.'

'If it is meningitis I am afraid it is rather more serious. We shall just have to pray that it is merely a fever, Mrs Danby.' His stern features relaxed into a slightly less disapproving look. 'You may see him for a few minutes, but then I think it best if your brother takes you home. We don't like parents on the ward because it gets in the way of our work. You may visit him tomorrow afternoon between two and three – or in the evening between seven and eight.'

'Just one hour?' Frances was disbelieving. 'But he will want his mummy. He will be so upset when I'm not there to cuddle him.'

'At the moment he is in a coma,' the doctor told her. 'Charlie will not know if you are there or not, Mrs Danby. If he comes out of it you may be able to spend a little more time with him.'

Frances stared as he walked back towards the ward he had come from, following at a little distance, her heart racing. As she went into the ward and saw her son lying in a cot with high sides, a needle and saline drip attached to his arm, she felt as if she would weep. Her throat was tight with pain as she bent over him, touching his pale face. He stirred slightly and his eyelids fluttered but did not open. She stroked his face and then his arm, taking his tiny hand in hers and soothing it with her fingers. He looked so small and so vulnerable, and it was breaking her heart to see him like this. Her baby.

'Charlie,' she whispered, tears trickling down her cheeks. 'I love you so much, so very much. Don't die, my darling. Please don't die. I can't bear to lose you too.' She had already lost her husband; surely she wasn't going to lose her child like this?

'He will be well cared for,' a nurse said, coming up to her and touching her arm. 'Sister Norton says that you have to leave now. I shall give you a telephone number to ring – and I shall need all your details. Are you on the telephone at home?'

'Yes. I'll write it all down for you.' Frances took a pad she was offered from the nurse and wrote her name, address and telephone number. 'I've written his name down too. We call him Charlie.'

'Good, that is what we needed. Give us a call later and we'll tell you how Charlie is.' The nurse gave Frances a sympathetic look. 'I know it must feel awful to leave him here, but you can't do anything to help, you know.'

'I suppose not.' Frances looked at her, relieved to see a friendly face at last. 'I love him so much and he is all I have.'

'Your husband?'

'He was killed in a car accident a few months ago.'

'Oh, you poor thing,' the nurse said. 'My name is Shirley and I lost my fiancé in the war, so I know how you feel. Look – can I get you a cup of tea?'

'No, thank you.' Frances took out her handkerchief and wiped her eyes. 'I'd better go or your superior will be cross. If you could give me that number to ring?' She took the small piece of paper Nurse Shirley offered and slipped it into her coat pocket. 'Thank you. Goodbye.'

Frances went out into the corridor. Daniel was speaking to a doctor but he saw her and came towards her almost at once.

'All right?' he asked.

'No, not really,' Frances said. 'But they won't let me stay so there's nothing we can do here. I can telephone and come to visit tomorrow afternoon or in the evening.'

'I can't come in the afternoon,' Daniel said. 'But I could bring you over in the evening.'

'I'll get a bus and come over in the morning,' Frances said. 'I shall stop all day so that I see him twice. I might try to find a room in Cambridge if he is going to be here more than one day.'

'Yes, that's a good idea,' Daniel said. 'I'll take you home now, Fran – unless you would like to come and stay with us?'

'No, I'd better stay at home tonight. I gave the nurse my own number and she says they will ring me if anything...' She choked back a sob. 'It isn't going to happen. He will be all right. He has to be.'

Frances was silent for most of the journey home. She didn't feel like talking, because she was too upset and scared. Leaving Charlie lying in that hospital bed had been like tearing her heart from her chest, and she wanted to ask Daniel to turn round and take her straight back. How could they send her away when her little boy was so ill? They were cruel and uncaring, and she should never have left him in that awful place.

'There was nothing more you could do, Fran,' Daniel said, glancing at her white face. 'If we hadn't taken him in he would almost certainly have died.'

'I know,' she whispered, her throat aching. 'But I hated leaving him. He looked so defenceless and small.'

'I know – but they will look after him. You'll be bringing him home in a few days.'

'I hope so.' Frances was praying that her brother was right, but she had a horrible cold feeling spreading over her, and a fear that she would never see her son alive again.

Daniel asked if she would like him to come in when they drew up outside her house. 'I can stop for a while, if you like?' he offered. 'Or you can change your mind and come to us?'

'Thanks for all you've done,' she said and gave him a wan smile. 'But I would rather stay here. I've a few jobs to do and I can telephone the hospital soon.'

'All right – if you're sure?'

Frances nodded. She got out of the car and went up to the house, letting herself in at the front door. Charlie's dog was howling at the back door and she opened it to let him in, bending down to stroke him.

'I had better feed you,' she said, because she realised that she had forgotten all about the poor creature that morning.

For a few minutes she busied herself by giving the dog some food and water, and then let it out into the garden again. The house felt empty without her son and she almost wished that she had gone to stay with her brother. Daniel had been considerate, but even he had asked her why she had left it so long before getting her son to the doctor. It seemed that everyone thought she had neglected Charlie – and now she was beginning to blame herself.

She took off her coat, hanging it on a peg behind the kitchen door. Reaching for the kettle automatically, she stopped and turned to the dresser, taking out a bottle of sherry she had bought in Ely recently. She took down a large glass from the shelf of the pine cupboard and filled it to the brim.

Raising it to the empty room, she toasted her absent husband.

'Thank you for being there when I needed you, Marcus,' she said bitterly. 'I might as well follow your example and drown my sorrows in drink. I might as well be dead like you and...' Putting down the glass after one sip, she got to her feet and went out to the hall. She would ring the hospital and see if there was any change.

It took a while to get through, because the girl on the main switchboard was a long time transferring her, and the ward sister answered in a frosty tone that told Frances she wasn't pleased about being disturbed.

'There has been no change as yet, Mrs Danby. We don't expect it for some hours. I am afraid you'll just have to be patient.' Frances thanked her and replaced the receiver. Clearly, she was being warned not to ring again before the evening. What on earth was she going to do with herself until then?

Frances realised that she had no real friends. There was no one she could call who she wanted to be with her – except Emily, and she was too far away. She supposed that she would have to tell Rosalind at some point during the day, but she didn't feel like it just at this moment. She walked back to the kitchen and picked up her glass. She was filled with a cold dread, and the certainty that she was going to lose her son.

* * *

Rosalind Danby replaced the telephone receiver and went back into the sitting room. Her husband had just got up to pour himself a glass of beer and he looked at her expectantly.

'What is wrong? You look upset.'

'I am worried,' Rosalind told him. 'I visited Frances this morning and Charlie was being sick. I telephoned the doctor but he was out and Charlie seemed a little better when I left to come home, but that was Frances on the telephone. Apparently her brother took her and Charlie to Addenbrooks a couple of hours later and they've kept him in. She says that he is very ill.'

'Good grief! Why didn't she let us know before this? I could have taken you over to see him. It's too late now.'

'Apparently, the doctor told her no visitors until tomorrow afternoon. She says that she is going to catch a bus in the morning and stay there all day. I said that you would take both of us in the car – you will, won't you?'

'Yes, of course,' Sam said and frowned. 'What did she say?'

'She just mumbled something about wanting to be alone and rang off,' Rosalind said. 'She sounded quite odd – I suppose she had been crying but her voice was a little slurred, I thought.'

'Do you think I should go round and see her? Do you want to talk to her?'

'She said she wanted to be alone, Sam. I don't think that we should interfere with her if she doesn't want us.'

His gaze narrowed. 'You said you telephoned the doctor? Why hadn't Frances done it herself?'

'She thought it was just a little bilious attack – and he had settled down before I left. I thought he would be over it by now.'

'I've a good mind to telephone the hospital myself.'

'Frances said she rang an hour ago and they told her there was no change – whatever that means.'

'Damn it, I shall ring myself,' Sam said and went out into the hall. He returned a few minutes later looking concerned. 'They say he is on the danger list, Rosalind. Apparently it is some kind of brain fever – at least that is what they are saying.'

'What do you mean?'

'The nurse I spoke to hinted that a fall or a bang on the head might have started the trouble off. She almost seemed to say that it might have been Frances who caused it, or that she had neglected to have him seen by a doctor in time.'

'That is ridiculous,' Rosalind said. 'Frances loves that child. She would never do anything to hurt him – and we both thought he was getting better.'

'You told me yourself that *you* rang for the doctor.'

'Because I was worried when he was sick, but I didn't think he was really ill, Sam. You can't think she neglected him, because if she asked her brother to take her into the hospital she must have been out of her mind with worry.'

'If she had gone to the hospital sooner it might not have got to this stage. They seem very concerned about him, and I don't like what you were telling me about the way she sounded. I think I shall go round and see her.'

'I don't think you should,' Rosalind said, but he ignored her and walked out of the room. A few minutes later she heard the sound of his car starting and saw the flash of headlamps. She frowned and then went to telephone Frances to let her know that Sam was on his way, but the line was engaged.

Frances stared at the receiver. For a moment or two she just nursed it in her hand, numbed with disbelief. It couldn't be true. It just couldn't be true... Not dead... Not Charlie. Her beautiful, bright little boy had just died at the hospital. The doctor's words echoed in her head without her understanding them.

'We thought it might have been a blow to the head, Mrs Danby, but the tests have just come back and it seems that it was meningitis after all. We are so very sorry, but he was too far gone when he got here – there was simply nothing we could do.'

'Nothing you could do?' Frances blinked. 'What are you saying?'

'I am afraid your son died a few minutes ago.'

'But I rang and they told me—'

'It was just after that, Mrs Danby. Your father-in-law phoned half an hour after you, and when the night sister went to look at him afterwards... I'm very sorry. If you would like to make arrangements for Charlie's body to be collected tomorrow morning that will be quite in order.'

'His body...' Frances couldn't finish the sentence.

She replaced the receiver, walking into the sitting room in a daze. She felt ill and dizzy, and it wasn't just because she had drunk half a bottle of sherry, though that wasn't helping things. She couldn't believe what was happening to her. Charlie was dead. What was it the doctor had said? They had thought a blow to the head might have caused his illness, but now they knew it was meningitis, that fatal sickness she had never heard of until today. Did they think she had hurt Charlie? Was that why they had all looked at her so strangely at the hospital?

Frances sat down suddenly. Her legs had gone to jelly as she realised that the nurse who had rushed Charlie to the doctor had imagined that she had hurt him. How could she have thought such a thing? Frances had never raised a hand to her son in her life; even when he screamed and threw things on the floor, she had just told him to be a good boy, and now he was dead.

She was aware that a car had stopped outside the house. She heard someone knock at the back door but she didn't get up to answer it. A moment or so later it was thrust open, because she hadn't locked it after she let the dog out. She stared at Sam with dull eyes as he came in, feeling so numbed that she didn't even care he had entered her house without an invitation.

'Charlie just died,' she told him. 'They thought it might have been a bang to the head – but now the doctor says it was meningitis. I didn't know that it could happen—'

'What do you mean, meningitis?' Sam demanded, because he had never heard of the illness either. 'They told me it was brain fever – caused by a blow to his head. What did you do to him, Frances? Did he cry and upset you – was that it?' Sam picked up the sherry glass, looking at the half empty bottle. 'How long has this been going on?'

'What do you mean?' Frances asked. She was too numb to answer him properly. 'Go away, Sam. Didn't you hear what I said? Charlie is dead.' She put her elbows on the table, burying her face in her hands as the tears started to fall.

'I really cared about you, Frances,' Sam said. 'After Marcus threw his life away I would have been good to you if you hadn't tried to blackmail me – but I shan't forgive you for this. You killed my grandson. He was all I had in the world – and you have to pay for that.'

'Go away,' Frances said, refusing to look at him. 'What does it matter now? I don't care what you think or do. Charlie is dead. I have nothing to live for now.'

Frances sat at the table long after he had gone. She hadn't killed Charlie. It wasn't her fault he had died. Perhaps she ought to have taken him to the doctor sooner, but she had thought it was just a chill – and then a bilious attack. Only it wasn't just a chill or some minor sickness. It was a terrible illness that had taken her son's life. Nothing mattered any more. She didn't know or care what Sam had in mind for her. She wasn't even interested in the money. Charlie was dead and she was all alone.

At this moment, she didn't much care if she lived or died.

9

'That is terrible news,' Emily said when Daniel rang her the next morning. 'Frances must be so upset. I can't believe it could have happened so quickly. Just a few hours...'

'Frances told Alice that he'd had a chill for a few days, and then he started being very sick. She told us she was worried and Alice wanted me to go over there, so I did. When I saw Charlie I took him straight into the hospital – they seemed to think it might be some kind of physical abuse at first. One of the doctors asked me if Frances had a temper and if she shouted at Charlie a lot. I told him that she was a very good mother and had never smacked him to my knowledge – and they seem to accept it was meningitis now.'

'Frances would never have hurt her son,' Emily said immediately. 'Oh, I wish I was there. She must feel so alone. I shall come down tomorrow, but I have something on today – and I've tried telephoning her but I can't get through.'

'She probably isn't answering,' Daniel said. 'I went to see her this morning and she seems to be in a bit of a daze. She said Sam had threatened her because he thought she had killed Charlie, but she must have that wrong. I rang Rosalind and told her exactly what the hospital said – and I picked up the death certificate myself so I know it's right. Frances didn't want me to have Charlie taken to the house, because she couldn't bear to see the coffin so I've arranged for a Chapel of Rest.'

'She probably can't bear to face up to what has happened,' Emily said. 'I know she was a bit strange when Marcus died – but Charlie is different. I would have wanted him brought home if it were—' She broke off, a little sob in her voice. 'When I think of that lovely little boy, Dan – and he was all Frances had. Go up and see her, ask her if she will come to you. She shouldn't be alone in that house.'

'I don't think she will come,' Daniel said. 'I did ask but she said she wanted to stay there – and she had been drinking sherry.'

'Are you sure?' Emily asked. 'Surely she wouldn't – not in the morning.'

'Alice said she had two bottles in her bag the other day in Ely. It made me wonder for a moment if she had, but then I realised that she wouldn't hurt Charlie. Even if she has been lonely and miserable since Marcus died, she wouldn't take it out on her son.'

'Of course she wouldn't,' Emily retorted. 'Don't even think it, Dan. Frances might have a few drinks, but we can all do that when we're upset – but she would never hurt Charlie. Look, I'm coming down tomorrow. I shall see if she will come back with me like she did last time – but somehow that was different. She still had Charlie then.' She caught back a sob. 'I can't bear to think of it, Dan. It is heartbreaking to lose a child.'

Emily replaced the telephone. She turned to see Amelia watching her. Her eyes were stinging with tears as she told her that Frances's son had died in hospital.

'She must be so terribly upset,' Emily said. 'I have to go to her,

Amelia. I shall try to bring her home with me if she will come, but I don't think I should take Robert to another funeral. It is nearly Christmas and he has parties to go to. Besides, I don't want him upset. Will you help Nanny look after him for me? I shan't be gone more than a few days. I shall certainly be back for the Christmas party here – and at the home.'

'Of course I will,' Amelia said. 'If you are sure you trust me to take care of him?' There was a hint of resentment in her voice.

'I know you love him,' Emily said. 'Robert would be bound to wonder where his cousin was and I don't want to tell him that Charlie is dead, not yet. So I think I should leave him here this time.'

'He will be quite safe here with us,' Amelia said and smiled oddly. 'You've had nothing but tragedy in your family recently. This is the third death, isn't it?'

'Yes. I just hope it will be the last for a long time,' Emily said. 'It's getting so as I'm almost afraid to pick up the telephone.'

* * *

Emily glanced at her sister as the little coffin was carried outside to the churchyard after the service was finished. Frances hadn't shed a tear, but her black-gloved hands were trembling so much that she almost dropped her prayer book, and she was very pale.

'It will soon be over,' Emily said, laying a hand on her arm. Frances moved forward, almost as if she were saying that she didn't want to be touched. She had been cold and silent ever since Emily arrived, refusing to be held or comforted. She was very different to the way she had been after Marcus died, and Emily was worried about her. She felt that she was keeping it all inside and that the feelings she was denying would burst out when she could no longer bear it.

She followed the little procession round to the churchyard. Rosalind Danby was weeping into a large white handkerchief. Dressed all in black, she was wearing a fox fur about her shoulders, her hat a dark soft felt. Sam Danby stood at her side, his expression one of anger and even hatred as he looked at Frances. Emily was shocked. Surely he couldn't really blame her for what had happened to Charlie?

Emily saw Daniel and Alice together. Daniel had his arm about his wife, supporting her as she wept. Dorothy and Mary were standing together. Several of the village people had come to support the family, but nowhere near as many as had been there for Marcus's funeral. Emily noticed that one or two women directed an odd look at Frances, and she saw a couple of them with their heads together whispering.

That was the trouble with rumours. Once people got hold of a tale, they couldn't let it be, even if it wasn't true. Emily knew that there were rumours about how Charlie had died, and she wondered who had started them. Someone must dislike Frances a great deal to have started the rumour that it was her fault that her child had died.

She stood by Frances's side, fiercely protective of the sister she loved. Emily asked again as they left the church if Frances would come and stay with her. Alice had already offered several times, but Frances wouldn't leave her own house. She just said that she wanted to be left alone.

'Are you sure you don't want to come back with me?' Emily asked as they walked down the church path. 'It helped you the last time, Frances. Besides, it is almost Christmas. You can't be alone for that.'

'Last time was different,' Frances said. 'I still had Charlie then – now I don't. And I don't feel like celebrating Christmas. Why should I? I have nothing to be thankful for.'

'What are you going to do about the dog?'

'Alice's brother asked if he could have him. I told him to take it away. I don't want the brute in the house.'

'Oh, Frances. Toffee was a nice little dog.'

'Stupid name,' Frances said. 'I always called it "the dog" – and I told Alice I was going to have it put down. Her brother fetched it that night. I am glad, because I couldn't bear the sight of it.'

'Oh, Frances.' Emily looked at her with pity. This wasn't like Frances at all. 'Surely you wouldn't have had Charlie's dog put down?'

'Why not?' Frances looked at her bitterly. 'Some people think I killed my son – why not his dog?'

'No one who knows or cares for you thinks anything of the sort.'

'You might not – but Daniel suspected it at the start. He practically said that I had neglected Charlie.' Frances was so cold and removed from the situation, as if she didn't know or care that she had just left her son's funeral. 'I'm not coming to Alice's. I didn't want to ask anyone back, but she insisted it would look wrong – so she can play host and make everyone think what a lovely person she is. I'm going home – and I don't want you to come. When I'm ready I'll be in touch.'

'Frances...' Emily stared after her as she crossed the road and disappeared round the side of her house. 'Oh, Frances.'

'Leave her,' Daniel said, coming up to her. 'It's no use, Emily. Alice and I have both tried to talk to her, but we can't get through. She just shuts everyone out – and I'm sure she is drinking too much. Muriel told me she threw out three empty sherry bottles this week.'

'Why on earth does she want to ruin her health with drinking?' Emily frowned. 'After Marcus—' She broke off, shaking her head. 'It's just foolish.'

'Exactly. It's as if she is punishing herself. I think we must just leave her for the moment, Emily. If she won't let us help her there isn't much we can do.'

'I don't like to think of her alone in that house.'

'It is her choice. Alice has asked her to come to us for Christmas, and so have I. If she won't even come to you...' He shook his head. 'I'll come up and see her in a few days, but I owe it to Alice and Danny to celebrate Christmas. It is the first we've had together, and in our new house as well. I can't worry about Frances all the time, if she won't be sensible. Come on now, you're only wasting your time.'

'Yes, all right,' Emily said. 'I'll try talking to her in the morning before I go back.'

* * *

Frances could hear her front door bell ringing. She closed her eyes, willing whoever it was to go away. She had drunk a whole bottle of sherry the previous evening and her head ached. She didn't want to answer the door, and she didn't want to talk to anyone; all she wanted was to lie here until she died.

'Frances!' Emily was shouting through the letterbox. 'Let me in, please. I want to talk to you. I know you are there and I'm not going away until you let me in.'

Frances groaned and threw back the bedcovers. Her head swam as her feet touched the ground. She felt sick, and a hundred hammers were at work at her temples. She clung on to the stair rail as she walked down them, because otherwise she might have fallen. She had never felt this ill in her life!

'I was asleep,' she lied as she opened the door to her sister. 'Why all the fuss? I told you I would be in touch when I was ready.'

Emily looked at her and then went into the kitchen. She was shocked when she saw the state of it. Frances was usually so fussy about her house, but it looked as if nothing had been touched for days.

'Why hasn't Muriel cleared this mess up?' Emily asked as she filled a kettle. The range was low and she opened the door, raking the ashes to get a spark before putting on some wood and coke. 'I'll make you some coffee. It looks as if you need it.'

Frances looked at the empty bottle on the table and the dirty glass on the sink draining board. There were several cups and saucers but no plates. 'Muriel rang to say she wouldn't be in for a while. Her husband is ill or something. Maybe she doesn't want to come in, because she thinks I'm a murderer too.'

'Don't be silly, Fran. No one thinks that of you.'

'Sam does,' Frances said. 'He came round here after the funeral and told me he was going to make me pay for what I'd done to his grandson.'

'He is a nasty man,' Emily said. 'He's got it in for you because you wouldn't sleep with him.'

'I tried to blackmail him into giving me double what my share of the property is worth,' Frances said, shocking her sister. 'I know too many of his dirty little secrets – that's why he hates me. It isn't because of Charlie, though I suppose that made it worse.' She gave a sob. 'I don't care about him or the money. I would give it all away if I could have Charlie back again.' Her eyes were dark with grief. 'Do you think it was a punishment for what I tried to do? Is God punishing me because I am a bad woman?'

'That is the most ridiculous thing I ever heard! Of course you're not a bad woman, Fran. You loved Charlie.'

'I loved him so much,' Frances said, tears beginning to trickle down her cheeks. 'I wish I were dead. There's nothing left for me now, Emily. Nothing at all to live for.'

'You mustn't think like that,' Emily said, a cold trickle of ice at her nape. She shivered, because the despair in Frances's eyes was so awful to see, and there were no words of comfort she could offer. She had been expecting Robert when she was told of Terry's death. After a while it had brought her back from the brink. 'You have to try, Fran. You have to want to live for your own sake. I know the pain is unbearable now, but it will get better in time.'

'Will it?' Frances looked at her with empty eyes. 'I don't think I care enough to bother. I just want to die.'

Emily made coffee and put the cup in front of her sister. 'Do you have an aspirin or anything to take for the headache?'

'No, I never use them,' Frances said. 'I've never suffered with headaches in the past. It will go I expect.'

'Yes, it will pass – and you will start to feel better one day,' Emily said. 'Please change your mind and come with me, Fran. I know you would feel better if you stayed with me.'

'It just makes it worse when you come back to an empty house,' Frances said, picking up the cup and taking a sip of the strong coffee. 'And I had Charlie then. It just seems as if there is no point, Emily. I wish I were dead. There's nothing to live for now.'

'So you want Sam to win, do you?' Emily demanded, angry with her now. 'For goodness' sake, stop this, Frances, or you will be really ill.'

Frances shrugged. Emily wanted to take her by the shoulders and shake her, but she could see that nothing she could say would change the way her sister was feeling.

'I'm going to leave you now,' Emily said. 'But when you snap out of this I want you to get on a train and come to me. If Sam hasn't paid you what he owes you, we'll get a lawyer to sort him out – but the main thing is for you to leave this place.

You need to begin a new life, Fran, and you're not going to do it here.'

Frances stood up. She leaned forward and kissed Emily on the cheek. 'I know you are trying to help me and I'm grateful. I am truly, but at the moment I don't feel like thinking about the future. I can't think because it hurts too much – that's why I've been drinking, to numb the pain. I know it is stupid and I don't want to be like Marcus. I'll stop soon, but not just yet.'

'I care about you,' Emily said. 'Daniel and Alice care too, even if Dan did wonder why you hadn't taken Charlie to the doctor sooner – he really does, Frances, so don't pull a face. Your family knows you weren't to blame – and you have to stop blaming yourself for what happened to Charlie.'

'Perhaps.' Frances gave her a fleeting smile. 'You go, Emily. You have your son and a life waiting for you – and you can't help me. Not yet. One day I may ask for help, but that isn't today.'

'All right,' Emily said. 'I'll go but I am always there ready to help you, love. Remember that if you need me.'

'Yes, all right,' Frances said. She made an effort to seem cheerful as she went to the door with her sister. 'Thank you for coming – and I'll ring you when I feel better.'

Closing the door and locking it, Frances went back to the kitchen and sat down at the table. She looked at the coffee her sister had made her, and then got up and poured it down the sink. She stared out at the garden for a moment, and then went to the dresser and took out her last bottle of sherry. She also took a packet of aspirin from the dresser drawer. Muriel had left it there, because she often got what she called water wheels in her head.

Frances took the pills and the sherry to the table and sat down looking at them for a minute or two. She squeezed out all the pills, of which there were ten. Was that enough? It was all she had so they would have to do. She had no idea how many it would take to kill her, but she put them all in her mouth and took a long swig of the sherry to swallow them with. After that she drank some more sherry, and then some more. By the time the bottle was half-empty she was feeling sleepy. She slumped forward on her arms at the table and fell into a deep slumber.

'She must have done it shortly after you left her,' Daniel said when he telephoned Emily the following morning. 'Muriel went up there to see if she needed her and found her unconscious. They rushed her into the hospital and they tell me she is recovering. She probably didn't take enough aspirin to kill her, but the packet was empty. It couldn't have been a full one.'

'She told me she never took them,' Emily said, feeling her throat constrict with emotion. 'I don't think I can come back for a few days. We have so much going on here for Christmas. I must spend some time with Vane and Robert. Will you get Frances some flowers from me? I'll send her a card – and get down as soon as I can to see her.'

'Alice says she wants her to come here for a while, but I don't know if she will. I think she would be better off getting right away from the village. You can imagine the kind of tales that are flying around at the moment.'

'Yes, I can – and I imagine I know where they started too.'

'What do you mean?'

'Sam hates her, because he tried it on a few times and she told him to get lost. And she blackmailed him for twice what that property she had a share in was worth.'

'Blackmail? That would make him furious, but I don't know what you mean? He wouldn't have tried anything with his son's wife, surely? Sam is a bit of a tough case but he isn't that bad.'

'You don't really know him, Dan. Frances told me what he does at that London property. It knocked Marcus for six when he discovered that his father was running brothels, and perhaps worse for all we know. Frances believes that's why he started drinking so heavily.'

'I can't believe this,' Daniel said. 'I've known Sam Danby for years. I would have said he was a hard man in business, but fair.'

'Maybe he is when he is in Stretton. He likes to play the big man, the councillor with village affairs at heart – but underneath he is rotten, Dan. About as rotten as they come, and I think he is Frances's enemy. I've told her to be careful of him, but she doesn't seem to care at the moment.'

'I am finding this difficult to believe,' Daniel said. 'I don't doubt that Frances told you these things – but how could she know? Did Marcus tell her?'

'I think she went to the apartment block in London and spoke to one of the girls there. Apparently, she thought Frances was looking for a job – or a room to ply her trade.'

'Good grief,' Daniel said. 'The sly old dog! No one here knows anything about any of this, Emily.'

'No, well, they wouldn't,' Emily replied. 'You wouldn't expect him to broadcast it locally, would you?'

'No...' Daniel was thoughtful. 'I still can't quite believe it – but if it is true, Frances should be careful. Sam wouldn't take kindly to blackmail about a thing like that.'

'That is what I told her, but she didn't seem to care.'

'Well, she is in hospital for the moment. We must hope she is feeling better by the time they let her out. I suppose she could be in trouble for trying to commit suicide – it isn't exactly sensible behaviour, is it?'

'They might decide to keep her under supervision for a while, until she stops feeling suicidal,' Emily said. 'Poor Frances. I knew she was desperate, but I didn't think she would do something like this.'

'No, well, I shall take Alice to see her in a day or so and we'll see how she is then.'

'You will let me know?'

'Yes, of course,' Daniel said. 'I had better go now, because we are having an early lunch. We have some last-minute shopping to do for Danny. Oh, and Happy Christmas, Emily.'

'Happy Christmas to you, Alice and Danny. Give Frances my love when you see her.'

'Yes, of course.'

Daniel turned as Alice came to call him to the table. He was surprised and slightly disbelieving over Emily's revelations concerning Sam Danby. It might be true, but it just might be a mistake on Frances's part. He wasn't convinced himself, but of course you never could tell.

* * *

'You are worried about your sister,' Vane said, coming to stand by Emily's side as she stood near the window that evening. It was Christmas Eve and a huge tree stood at one end of the long room, decorated with glass balls and candles, a pile of gifts surrounding its base. Behind them the laughter and chatter was evidence that the party was a success. 'I am sure she will be all right, my dear. The hospital will look after her.'

'Yes, of course,' Emily said and smiled at him. 'I just keep thinking that it is Christmas and she is in hospital and all alone.'

'She has her family to care for her,' Vane said. 'You should ask her to come here, Emily. You know we have plenty of room and she would be very welcome.'

'Thank you,' Emily said. 'You are always so generous.' She

touched the choker of lustrous pink pearls at her throat. 'I wanted to thank you for my gift, Vane. They are lovely. I shall always treasure them.'

'I wanted to give you something special this year,' Vane said. 'I am glad you like them, my dear – but you haven't got a drink. May I pour you something?'

'Just lemonade, thank you,' Emily said. 'I need to be up early in the morning. We have a big day at the home tomorrow. Some of the patients who left us are coming for a reunion dinner with their relatives. It should be very pleasant.'

'You know that I would be willing to stand in for you if you wanted to go to your sister?'

'It wouldn't be fair because everyone is expecting me to be there,' Emily said. 'Besides, I want to be here when Robert opens his presents in the morning. He would be upset if I wasn't here. No, I am sure you're right. Frances will be well cared for in hospital and I shall go down and see her as soon as Christmas is over.'

* * *

Frances half opened her eyes to look at the three men standing by her hospital bed. She was feeling drowsy and not at all well, her mind still hazy after the effects of her attempt to end it all. She wasn't sure how long she had been in hospital, though she thought it must have been a few days. She vaguely remembered the nurses singing carols, but that seemed a long time ago.

'Mrs Frances Danby,' one of the men said to her. 'We would like to talk to you for a moment. Are you feeling well enough to answer some questions?'

Frances nodded. She didn't want to talk to anyone, especially doctors, but if she said yes to whatever they wanted to know perhaps they would go away and leave her alone.

'Yes,' she whispered.

'Why did you try to kill yourself, Mrs Danby? Was it because you felt guilty because of your son's death?'

'Yes,' Frances answered without really understanding the question. 'Charlie is dead... Don't want to live... Nothing to live for...'

'Do you feel responsible for his death?'

'Yes.' Tears trickled down Frances's cheeks. 'My baby... Too late. Too late...'

'She neglected him and then tried to kill herself because she knew it was her fault,' a voice she dimly recognised as Sam Danby's said harshly. 'What more do you need? She murdered my grandson and then tried to escape just retribution. She knew I would have the police look into the matter.'

'That isn't quite what she is saying,' another voice objected. 'I think she is still too ill to know what is happening – or what she is saying.'

'No, Dr Renton,' the first voice said. 'I agree with Mr Danby. She probably neglected her son because she was under strain after the death of her husband. And she tried to kill herself while the balance of her mind was disturbed. I think she would benefit from a period of incarceration in a mental institution. We should both sign the order, Dr Renton.'

'I'm not sure, sir,' the younger man said. 'This isn't a proper examination. We ought to do more tests, speak to her when she is fully conscious.'

'I daresay you have not experienced too many cases of severe melancholia before, Dr Renton. By virtue of my superior experience in these cases I must tell you that without the proper treatment Mrs Frances Danby will remain a danger not only to herself but also to others.'

'Yes, well, if you say so.' The younger man looked unhappy as he signed the paper thrust in front of him. 'But she should only be there for a temporary period. She looks ill and sad to me, rather than dangerous.'

'Yes, well, she will be under my care,' the first voice said. 'I shall do my best to help Mrs Danby recover her spirits – and when I consider that she is fit to be released I shall arrange it.'

The voices drifted away, becoming fainter until they ceased altogether. Frances opened her eyes and looked at the one man who remained by her bedside. The other two had gone now and she wasn't sure what they had wanted from her, but at least they had left her in peace. She looked at the man still standing by her bed, recognition that it was Sam Danby coming through the mists at last. She jerked up in bed as if suddenly aware of danger.

'What have you done?' she asked, coldness spreading through her. 'Who were those men? Why did you bring them here?'

'They have just committed you to a mental hospital, where you belong,' Sam said, a cruel sneer on his mouth. 'No one will believe your stories now, Frannie. You're mad, a victim of melancholia. That's why you neglected your son and then tried to kill yourself.'

'No! I didn't harm Charlie and I'm not mad.' Frances was filled with sudden terror and tried to sit up. 'I'm going home. You can't do this to me. I'll tell Rosalind and—'

'Nurse!' Sam called to the nurse approaching with a metal bowl in hand. 'She is becoming hysterical. You had better give her that medication now.'

'No!' Frances cried out in alarm as she saw the syringe the nurse was carrying. 'Don't believe him. I'm not mad. He's wicked and evil and he wants to put me away so that I can't tell anyone what he is.'

'Now then, Mrs Danby,' the nurse said kindly. 'You are under a terrible strain. You've been ill and you need help. Fortunately for you, Mr Danby brought in a private doctor to take care of you. Dr Marsham is just the right person to oversee your treatment. In a few months you may be well enough to go home again.'

'No...' Frances struggled but Sam held her down while the nurse plunged the needle into her arm. 'It's a lie!'

She fell back as the blackness claimed her. Unaware of anything that took place shortly afterwards, she did not know when she was put on to a stretcher and carried from the hospital ward, nor did she see the private ambulance waiting to take her away.

'They told us that Frances was suffering from acute melancholia and needed special treatment. It seems that she has been taken to a private hospital for the mentally ill,' Daniel said when he rang Emily that evening. 'We went in expecting to see her and were told she had gone. No one seemed to be quite sure where – except that it was a private clinic and the transfer had been arranged by a relative.'

'Oh, Dan,' Emily exclaimed. She was shocked and distressed by what he was saying. 'How could they do that? Frances isn't mad. I know she has been acting oddly for a while, but anyone would if they had been through what she has recently. I can't believe they've put her away. It must be to do with Sam. If she is in a private clinic, he arranged it, and he didn't do it for her benefit, believe me.'

'Are you saying he has had her locked away maliciously?'

'Yes,' Emily said in a firm tone. 'I don't know how or why but I know he did it and I intend to find out where he has taken her. I'm coming down there to ask a few questions – and if I find that he had her committed out of malice—'

'Just be careful,' Daniel said. 'If he did this – and I'm not convinced of it, because the sister at Addenbrooks told me two doctors signed the section form. I don't see how Sam could have forced them to sign if they didn't agree.'

'Can't you?' Emily was scornful. 'I can. Money is a great persuader, Dan.'

'You're saying he bribed them?'

'Well, how else would he get a doctor to commit a woman who is perfectly sane to a mental hospital? It's wicked! We can't let him get away with this, Dan. Can you imagine how Frances feels being shut up in a place like that? I can't bear the thought of it. I shall leave here in an hour or so – but I want to talk to Vane first. Sam Danby is a powerful man in his own little pond, but Vane can pull strings in places he has never heard of, and he will if I ask it of him.'

'You have to be sure that Sam actually did something wrong first.'

'Yes, I know,' Emily said. 'But I am going to be asking a lot of questions, Dan – and I don't intend to take no for an answer.'

'Well, just be careful, that's all,' Daniel told her. 'It might all be perfectly above board and what Frances told you might be something that a deluded mind would dream up.'

'Oh no,' Emily said. She was fierce in defence of her sister. 'Don't you dare say that, Dan – don't even think it. I spoke to Frances a few days ago and she was as sane as anyone I know – but very unhappy.'

'She tried to take her own life,' Daniel reminded her. 'The

doctors might have had good reason for thinking she was on the verge of a breakdown.'

'I know it was a stupid thing to do, and I know she shouldn't have done it,' Emily said. 'But she is my sister and I'm damned if I'm going to let Sam Danby get away with this!'

Emily was frustrated and angry when she replaced the receiver. How could Daniel even think that Frances might need to be shut away in a place like that? What she needed was love and care, not incarceration in a mental institution.

She turned her steps in the direction of Vane's study. He would be there now, working at his desk. She needed his advice because he would know exactly what she ought to do, and he had never let her down. She was comforted by the thought of him, knowing that she could rely on his strength.

Frances moaned, her head moving restlessly on the pillows. She had been dreaming such horrible things, but in a minute she would wake up and it would all be gone. Her eyelids flickered and she opened her eyes, staring up into the face of a stranger.

'Ah, so you are coming back to us,' the man said, his voice oddly familiar, though she was certain that she had never seen him before. 'I was beginning to think you might be lost in the fog.'

'Who are you?' Frances asked, becoming aware that she was very thirsty, and that her mouth tasted awful. 'Where am I? Have I been ill?'

'Don't you remember what happened to you?'

'No.' Frances wrinkled her brow because everything seemed hazy and far away. 'Have I been ill?'

'Yes, you have been ill. You are still ill, Mrs Danby. You are in a hospital – a special clinic where you can receive the treatment you need.'

'What kind of treatment?' Frances asked. 'My mouth is so dry. May I have some water please?'

'Yes, of course. A nurse will come in a while, but you must have your medication. Last time, you tried to refuse it.'

'Did I?' Frances stared at him. 'I can't remember.'

'It is often the case in disorders like your own. Do not concern yourself, Mrs Danby. In a few days we shall begin a course of electric shock treatment. It will make you feel even more confused for a while, but after that you will begin to remember the things you should remember.'

'No...' Frances wasn't sure what he was talking about, but she sensed it was unpleasant. 'I don't need that. I don't want to be made to forget.'

'You have been very unhappy. Trust me and I shall make the pain go away. You will feel calm and soon you will be content.'

He was asking her to trust him, but instinctively she knew that she must not let this man give her the treatment he said she needed. She did not know why she feared him, but deep down inside her she sensed that something was wrong. He meant to harm her, not to help her.

'No,' she said. 'I don't want to have your treatment. I want to go home. I want Emily. Tell her to come and get me. I want to be with my sister.'

'I am sorry but you cannot leave here until you are well again,' the man said. 'I had thought you might be sensible, Mrs Danby, but I can see that we shall have to keep you under seda-tion for a while longer – just until you are ready to do as you are told.'

'No, please don't give me that again,' Frances said as she saw him preparing the syringe, but he ignored her, and even though she tried to resist, as soon as the needle touched her arm she felt herself falling back into the darkness.

'I think we told your brother that Mrs Danby had gone to a private clinic for treatment,' Sister Norton told Emily when she invited her into her office that afternoon. 'I was not on duty that morning, but it must be in the relief nurse's notes. Ah yes, here it is.' She frowned as she read what her colleague had written. 'Mrs Danby was seen by two doctors who decided that she needed specialist treatment for melancholia. A relative was present at the time.'

'Who was that?' Emily asked.

'Mr Samuel Danby.' Sister Norton looked at her. 'Is there some problem?'

'Yes, I am afraid there may be. My brother and I are her nearest relatives and we were not consulted about having my sister sectioned. Indeed, neither of us would have agreed to it. The man who arranged this is her father-in-law.'

'Yes, that is slightly irregular,' Sister Norton agreed. She looked at the notes again. 'Dr Renton is on our staff but I don't know the other name. Dr Marsham must have been brought in privately by Mr Danby.'

'He had no right to do it,' Emily said. 'I should like to speak to Dr Renton – and I want to know where my sister has been taken.'

'I can arrange for you to speak to Dr Renton,' Sister Norton said. 'But I'm afraid these notes do not give the name of the clinic to which Mrs Danby has been transferred.'

'Then you had better arrange that interview immediately,' Emily said. 'My sister has been abducted without the permission of her family – and I am not prepared to let things stand as they are. Let me tell you that my father-in-law is Lord Vane and he knows the chairman of your board of governors. If my sister has been mistreated in any way, I intend to sue. This hospital had no right to allow Mr Danby to bring in his own doctor without the agreement of Mrs Danby's family.'

'Threats are unnecessary,' Sister Norton replied with dignity. 'Had I been on duty personally it would not have happened. It seems that the ward was in the charge of a staff nurse at the time and she was busy. I daresay she thought it was all right because Dr Renton was a member of our staff.'

'I should like to see him as soon as possible.'

'Could you return in an hour? I do not know whether he is on duty or not this afternoon.'

'Then perhaps you will find out,' Emily said, an edge to her voice. She drew herself up proudly, her manner implacable. 'Because I am going nowhere until someone explains to me exactly where my sister is – and why she was transferred without her brother's permission.'

Sister Norton looked at her face and saw the determination written there. It was obvious that Mrs Vane had every intention of making a fuss until she received the information she needed.

'Very well,' she said. 'I shall make a few telephone calls. If you would wait outside my office?'

'I think I would prefer to remain here. I don't think you can have anything to say on this subject that I may not hear.'

Sister Norton pulled a face but picked up her telephone and made a call. She replaced it almost at once and looked at Emily.

'Dr Renton is on his way down. I really do need to get on now – if you wouldn't mind?'

'Of course,' Emily said and smiled at her. 'Thank you for your help.'

She went out into the corridor and stood looking out of the

window. The hospital was situated on a main thoroughfare, but across the road was a row of cherry trees that would have looked delightful in the spring when the blossom was out.

'Mrs Vane.' Emily turned as a man's voice spoke to her. 'Sister Norton said that you wanted to talk to me?'

'If you are Dr Renton?' Her gaze went over him dubiously, because although tall, lean and attractive, he looked very young. 'Have you been qualified long?'

'No, actually just a couple of months,' he said, and there was a faint blush in his cheeks as if he were slightly embarrassed. 'How may I help you?'

'I understand that you were one of two doctors who certified my sister as being of unsound mind?'

'Are you speaking of Mrs Danby?' His brow creased in a frown. 'I was asked if I would be present at an examination. I understood her family wished her to undergo private treatment for extreme depression.'

'Her brother and I knew nothing about it,' Emily told him. 'The man who brought the other doctor in is her father-in-law – and he hates her. It is my belief that she has been abducted in order to cause her some harm.'

Dr Renton let out a low whistle. 'So that is why they picked on me. I did tell Dr Marsham that I didn't consider myself to have enough experience of melancholia disorders to give an opinion – but he insisted that all he needed was another signature.'

'Didn't you think that it seemed a little odd?'

'Yes, as a matter of fact I did. Actually I was reluctant to sign, because I felt Mrs Danby ought to have been given more time to recover her senses. However, in view of her suicide attempt I believed that she might be a danger to herself if allowed to simply return home. Dr Marsham told me that a quarter of all failed suicide attempts are superseded by a second successful attempt within a few weeks.'

'My sister had recently lost her husband and then her only son died in this very hospital. I think that explains why she tried to take her own life – but I shall not allow it to happen again. I want my sister released into my care and I give my pledge that she will not do it again.'

'In that case I would be willing to reverse my opinion, Mrs Vane. I would be quite willing to sign a release form for her – providing that she consents to live under your care until she is completely recovered.'

Emily smiled because she had been expecting a tussle of wills. Dr Renton was a surprise. She had expected an older man, someone more opinionated and autocratic. She rather liked this man's manner, which was open and honest. He hadn't tried to make excuses or bluster his way out of something potentially embarrassing.

'Thank you. I should be grateful for your help – but first I need to find out where they have taken my sister.'

'I am afraid I cannot tell you that,' Dr Renton said. 'Apparently, Marsham runs his own private clinic. It shouldn't be too difficult to discover where it is situated.'

'My father-in-law will help there,' Emily told him. 'Now that I have the name of the doctor who took her, it makes things easier. So if you would be kind enough to give me that release form? Do you need two signatures?'

'It should be enough that I have rescinded my consent,' he said. 'But if you need help getting her out I would be happy to accompany you, Mrs Vane. And, if Marsham tries to keep her, I could arrange for a colleague to examine her.'

'I think that Dr Marsham will believe himself fortunate to escape a prison sentence when Lord Vane has finished with him,'

Emily said. 'But I do thank you for your help – and I would be grateful if you could come with me to the clinic. Frances may need medical help.'

Dr Renton frowned at her. 'If you are correct in thinking that she is being mistreated, that is quite possible. And perhaps Dr Marsham should not escape a prison sentence for what he has done. I can only think that he had a reason for his action.'

'Sam Danby is a rich man,' Emily said with a twist of her mouth. 'I can't prove it, but I imagine Dr Marsham was paid for his services.'

He gave her a shocked look. 'I hope that you don't think I was paid for my part in this? I can assure you that had I known her family were not aware of what was happening I should never have agreed.'

'I suggest that you are more careful in future,' Emily said and then smiled when he looked upset. 'I do believe that you acted in what you imagined were Frances's best interests – but I am very afraid that they mean to harm her. She knows things about Mr Danby that he would not like to become common knowledge.'

'Electric shock treatment,' Dr Renton said thinking aloud. 'I've read about it, though I can't say I approve. It is supposed to help people who are suicidal and is sometimes used in cases of severe melancholia – but it can cause memory loss. One school of opinion believes that is a necessary side effect, but I am not inclined to that view. I think we need to be very careful when we are dealing with people. By destroying parts of their memory, we may deprive them of something very precious – even alter their personality.'

'My God!' Emily felt sick and angry. 'I had better telephone my father-in-law at once. If those devils do that to Frances...' She lifted her head. 'Frances thinks she doesn't want to live now, but I know how it feels to lose the people you love, and in time it gets better.'

Dr Renton nodded, looking at her thoughtfully. 'Come with me, Mrs Vane. I can show you where you can telephone in private.'

'Thank you,' Emily said. 'You are very kind.'

* * *

'If he is practising legally it should be easy enough to trace the clinic,' Vane said when she rang him. 'It's my advice that you take two doctors with you when you go to fetch Frances, my dear. Leave nothing to chance. If this rogue took money from Danby he is a menace to society. I shall see what can be done about getting him struck off the register. Of course he may already be working unlicensed. It sounds as if no one bothered to check his credentials at the hospital.'

'There was just a staff nurse on duty that morning, because Sister Norton was away ill. They may just have been lucky – and of course the nurse thought it was all right, because they drew one of the hospital doctors in with them.'

'He deserves a stiff reprimand!'

'Yes, perhaps,' Emily agreed. 'But he is quite newly qualified and I imagine he has learned his lesson. He says he was told that the family wanted Frances sectioned for her own safety – and he believed that Marsham was highly qualified in his field.'

'Perhaps he will check the information out in future,' Vane said gruffly. 'Thank goodness your brother discovered what had happened as quickly as he did. Hopefully, we shall sort this business out before too much damage has been done. I don't like the idea of her being given electric shock treatment, Emily. I've heard about that and it's not something I would approve for anyone I cared for.'

'I can't bear to think of her shut up in a place like that,' Emily said, her voice cracking with emotion. 'I'm going to be staying with Daniel and Alice until we know where she has been taken. I have a feeling the clinic may not be far away.'

'Not so sure about that,' Vane said. 'Didn't you say Danby had interests of a dubious nature in London? I imagine he may know a few shady characters from his dealings there.'

'Yes, perhaps,' Emily agreed. 'You will let me know as soon as you hear?'

'I have several sources that might know something,' Vane told her. 'Chin up, Emily. We'll find your sister for you – and when we do, one or two people are going to wish they had never become involved in this business, I promise you.'

Emily smiled as she replaced the receiver. Vane had sounded very angry, and she knew that was for her sake. She turned to discover that the young doctor was still watching her.

'I'm sorry,' she said. 'I must be keeping you from your work.'

'I have just about finished for the day,' he said. 'May I take you for a coffee? I think we should exchange telephone numbers – things like that?'

'Yes, of course,' Emily said. 'Vane said that we should need two doctors. You might know of someone who would help us?'

'Yes, I might,' he agreed. 'I have an elder brother who is also a GP. I am sure he would take some time off to accompany us – when you discover where she is?'

'Thank you. I shall be happy to pay for his time – and yours.'

'I don't think either of us would expect to be paid,' Dr Renton said. 'I feel responsible for what has happened to your sister – and my brother will tell me I am all kinds of a fool for not checking things out thoroughly before signing. However, he will be glad to help put things right.'

'Thank you,' Emily said. She gave him a smile that took his breath away. 'I'm not sure what I would have done if you hadn't been so understanding.'

'Oh, I think you would have persuaded me in the error of my ways,' he replied. 'My name is Paul and I am very pleased to be of service to you, Mrs Vane. I think your husband is a lucky man.'

'My husband died from injures sustained in the war,' Emily told him. 'No, please don't be shocked or upset. I am not distressed by what you said. You couldn't have known – and it was all a long time ago. I have a wonderful son and some good friends.'

'I am glad,' he said. 'I should be happy if perhaps I might be counted as one of those friends in the future?'

'We'll talk about that over coffee,' Emily said. 'Shall we go to the Copper Kettle? I have been before but I don't know what it is like these days.'

'Very busy,' Paul Renton said. 'I know somewhere much nicer – if you will trust me?'

'Oh yes,' Emily said. 'I think I can do that, Paul. My friends call me Emily.'

10

'I'm not sure I would trust him after what he did,' Alice said when Emily told them that she had had coffee with one of the doctors who had signed the committal papers for Frances. 'He is either dishonest or a fool.'

'No, I don't think he is either, actually,' Emily said. 'He wasn't careful enough and he knows that he made a mistake, but he is doing his best to put things right. He has promised to help me get Frances out once we know where she has been taken.'

'Daniel is furious with Sam Danby,' Alice said, looking worried. 'I think he borrowed some money from Sam once – or at least deferred payment for some foodstuffs for the pigs. I suppose he felt a bit obliged to him, and he didn't want to believe the things you told him.'

'I hope he believes me now?'

'Yes, of course. He was so angry when he went out. I hope he won't do anything stupid.'

'Like what?'

'I don't know,' Alice said, a worried expression on her pretty face. 'Dan is feeling a lot better these days. He wasn't strong when he first came home, but he is now – and he has such a temper when he is provoked.'

'You think he might go after Danby?'

'Yes, I do,' Alice said. 'I know what he did was wicked – and he needs to be punished – but I don't want Daniel to go to prison.'

'No, of course not,' Emily said. 'It is so unnecessary, Alice. Dan might give him a thrashing but he could end up in trouble himself. And once we have Frances safe, Vane is going to pull strings. We know that Danby has that apartment block in London. Vane thinks there may be other places and he has already put out some feelers. If we can prove what he has been doing, we can ruin him, and he may be the one going to prison. So tell Dan not to be a fool. Danby will be punished.'

'You're so sure of everything,' Alice said. 'It must be living in that big house and running that convalescent home all those years. You're not much older than me and yet you seem years—' Alice broke off and blushed. 'I didn't mean it like that. I meant you are more experienced.'

'Yes, perhaps I am,' Emily said. 'But sometimes I do feel as if I am older than my years.'

She smiled oddly, thinking how much she had enjoyed having a coffee with Paul Renton. He was probably about her age, but he too seemed younger. She imagined he thought her several years older than himself – and in some ways she was, because she had seen and done so much these past years. Sometimes she thought that the war had robbed her of her youth – but she wasn't unique. Too many men had died, and a lot of women had lost their husbands or sons. Emily wasn't the only one. She sighed and thrust the slightly regretful thoughts to the back of her mind. She had made up her mind after Terry died – she never wanted to fall in love again, because it hurt too much.

* * *

Daniel wasn't sure what had made him get on the train for London, but he was here and had been standing in front of the apartment block for the past hour, watching a succession of men ring the bell and be admitted by various girls.

It was all true, he realised. Everything that Emily had told him about the apartment block was right, because even though he had never used a prostitute himself, he recognised what was going on here. He hadn't taken his sister seriously, but faced with reality – some of the girls looked hardly more than fifteen – it sickened him. Sam Danby was no better than the pimps that plied their trade through girls walking the streets, except that he supplied them with a roof over their heads. He should damned well be ashamed of himself. Daniel certainly didn't think it was amusing now!

He turned and walked away, feeling disgusted with what he had seen. He had no doubt that Emily was right about Danby's motives – and he was going to pay for what he had done to Frances!

Seeing a red telephone kiosk, Daniel fished for some coins in his pocket, then went in and dialled his home number. After a few moments, Alice answered it.

'Is that you, Dan?' she asked when he spoke. 'Where are you? I was beginning to worry.'

'Sorry, love,' he said. 'I'm in London but I'll catch the next train back. Tell Emily I am sorry I doubted her – everything she said is true. Frances was right. He is running a brothel in those apartments – and I believe that he had her shut away so that she couldn't ruin his reputation. He made a big mistake, Alice. He is going to pay for what he has done, believe me.'

'Please don't do anything silly,' Alice begged. 'Emily has gone to fetch Frances back. Lord Vane telephoned her half an hour ago to tell her where Frances is being held. He is sending some people of his own there to sort this mess out. Emily is taking that doctor with her... Oh, you don't know, but he signed the papers and has now signed a release form. Apparently, the clinic is near Peterborough and Emily says that Frances will be with her when she comes back in a few hours' time. So please come home and forget about Sam. He isn't important.'

'I'm coming home on the next train,' Daniel said, his voice throbbing with suppressed anger. 'But I shan't forget what he has done, Alice. He isn't going to get away with this.' He replaced the receiver as his money ran out. As he walked away from the phone box, he was seething with anger. He was glad that Emily's father-in-law had traced Frances so quickly, and he knew that Emily would sort things out that end – but it was up to him to make certain that Sam got what was coming to him.

* * *

Frances had learned not to refuse medication. They had started giving her the drugs in tablet form now. She took the little container the nurse held out to her, put the two tablets into her mouth and drank from the glass of water she was given and then turned over on her side.

When she was certain that the nurse had gone, leaving her alone in the small room where she was being confined, she spat the tablets out from under her tongue and hid them under the mattress. She turned over on to her back, opening her eyes cautiously. Yes, she was alone. The nurse was one of the younger members of staff and she hadn't made Frances open her mouth to check that the drugs had gone.

Taking a deep breath, Frances sat up and waited for the dizziness to pass before putting a foot to the floor. She was still feeling unwell, because the drugs they had been giving her made her stomach ache and her throat was dry. She had been given some soup and a cup of tea earlier in the day, but she knew that it was only a matter of time before they started the electric shock treatment. She wasn't sure why they were still giving her sedatives to keep her quiet, because she had understood what was meant to happen to her. Dr Marsham was going to give her treatment that would make her lose her memory.

Frances didn't want to lose the past. She had grieved so terribly for Charlie – more than for Marcus, because he had wasted his life and she was still angry with him for leaving her. Charlie had been her adorable little boy, so full of life and the joy of living. She had wanted to end the misery and the pain, and so she'd taken those aspirin, but she hadn't had enough, because there were only a few left in the packet that Muriel had left in the drawer. If she'd really wanted to end it she should have gone out and bought at least two packets, Frances thought ruefully as she looked about her.

She certainly didn't want to stay here and become little more than a cabbage after Dr Marsham had finished with her. Her life might be empty but she wasn't prepared to be used in that way – and she had no intention of letting Sam Danby have the last laugh. It was her anger against Sam that had brought Frances back from the drug-induced fog that had made her so vulnerable at the hospital. He had destroyed Marcus and now he was trying to destroy her. Well, he wasn't going to get away with it.

Frances put her feet to the floor. She looked down at herself and saw that she was wearing a white starched hospital gown, similar to those used by patients undergoing an operation – but there were straps attached to the sleeves. She shuddered as she realised that they were long enough to go across her body and fasten at the back, which would make it impossible for her to free her arms if they were fastened.

Had someone neglected to restrain her as intended – or was that to come later when they took her down for the shock treatment? And why hadn't they already begun the treatment?

Frances moved softly on bare feet across to the window and looked out. She was too high up to get out that way, and from the look of the lock on the handle she would find it impossible to open. Yet somehow she had to get out of this place – and it looked as if she would have to leave through the door.

She crept towards it, her heart racing with fright. If someone saw her she would be brought straight back here and they would go back to using the needle on her. She breathed deeply as she turned the door handle and found that it opened easily. For a moment she stared at the opening, unable to believe that it hadn't been secured. She had been certain that she was locked in, but it seemed that either someone was being careless or they hadn't expected her to try and leave her room.

The corridor was dimly lit but a little further down she could see bright lights in one of the rooms. As she hesitated, the door opened and she heard voices.

'What are you going to do when they get here?' a man asked.

'Trust Marsham not to be here when he is needed,' a woman's voice said. 'What am I supposed to say to the police? I didn't bring the patient here. It's nothing to do with me.'

The door shut again, and Frances seized her opportunity, running past it as quickly as she could on bare feet that made no sound and disappearing round the corner before whoever it was could come out and discover her. She saw a staircase ahead of her; there was a metal handrail and the steps were of a dull grey marble. She held on to the rail and went down them, feeling the icy coldness strike into her. At the bottom of the stairs she saw a door and held her breath. Surely it had to be locked? She turned the handle, hoping she was wrong, but she knew even as she felt the resistance that it was a futile hope. A place like this was bound to have security measures, which made her wonder why her own door had not been locked. Had someone left it that way on purpose?

She couldn't go back, which meant that she had to go on. At the bottom of the stairs it was possible to go either to the left or the right. Frances hesitated, wondering which way to choose. She had no idea where she was going or how she was going to get out of the clinic, but hearing the voices of people approaching from the right, she realised that she had no choice and turned to the left.

She could see that there was an open space at the end of the corridor, and suddenly she heard the sound of something being wheeled. Two men were pushing a patient lying on a trolley and they came round the corner towards her. One of them gave a shout as he saw her, and Frances turned and fled. She had no choice but to go back the way she had come, but as she approached the stairs she saw a small group of people coming from the opposite direction.

'Stay where you are!' a man called from her left. 'You shouldn't be wandering about like that.'

Frances gave a cry of despair and put her foot on the bottom step in an effort to escape the way she had come. Even as she did so, she heard someone call her name and, turning, she saw a woman break from the little group to the right and come rushing towards her.

'Emily!' Frances cried with a sob of relief as she recognised her. Tears were streaming down her cheeks now as the fear she had suppressed overwhelmed her. 'Don't let them take me back.

They want to give treatment to make me forget. Please don't let them take me.'

'Of course I won't let them hurt you,' Emily said and grabbed hold of her, holding her tight. Frances was shaking, terror in her eyes as the clinic porter caught up to them. 'I'm taking you back to Vanbrough with me until you are better, dearest. I should never have left you alone in the first place.'

'You can't take a patient out without permission,' the porter asserted, having arrived in time to hear Emily's statement. 'She shouldn't be wandering about like that.' He reached out to take hold of Frances's shoulder.

'Kindly stand back and leave my sister alone,' Emily said in a voice of ice. 'I have two doctors with me and an order for her release. She should never have been brought here in the first place – and you, sir, are not a proper person to tell me what I should or should not do. What you can do is tell us where we can find Dr Marsham?'

The porter laughed harshly. 'That's what a good many more would like to know, madam. If you ask me, he's done a bunk – but if you want to see the person in charge you'd better go up those stairs and talk to Sister Rendle. I reckon she's about the only one who knows what is going on here.'

'Thank you,' Emily said. 'First, I want a blanket to wrap my sister in, and then I shall need a wheelchair, if you please. I am going to take my sister out to the car.' She turned to look at the two men accompanying her. 'I think I can leave the formalities to you, Dr Renton?'

'Yes, you certainly can,' the younger man replied. He looked apologetically at Frances. 'I am very sorry for what happened to you, Mrs Danby. Please go with your sister – we shall follow shortly.' Turning to the porter, he said, 'Fetch a wheelchair and a blanket immediately if you know what's good for you. This place may be officially closed down and heads are going to roll.'

'Nothing to do with me what goes on here, sir. I only take the poor devils where I'm told.' The porter looked at Emily. 'Hold on to her in case she faints. I'll be back in two minutes.'

Frances was still shaking. As the porter went off, she swayed and Dr Renton helped Emily to support her. He looked at her white face anxiously. Frances gave him a wan smile.

'It is all right,' she said. 'I'm just a little dizzy. They have been giving me drugs to keep me quiet ever since I got here. I fought them when they tried to give me medication and this time I didn't swallow the tablets. Dr Marsham said that once I had been treated I would forget all the things that had hurt me, but I don't want to forget Charlie. I love him and I want to remember all the good things.'

'Of course you will, dearest,' Emily told her with a sob in her voice. 'It will all seem better soon. I'll look after you, Frances. I promise you it will be better soon.'

The porter had returned with a chair and a blanket. He helped Emily settle Frances in it, wrapping the blanket around her shoulders and legs.

'Is there anything else I can do for you, madam?'

'You can help wheel Mrs Danby to the car we have waiting outside and get her settled,' Dr Renton said. 'I am going to speak to Sister Rendle and give her my authority to remove Mrs Danby.' He nodded and the two doctors walked on up the stairs.

The porter wheeled the chair down the corridor to the right of the stairs. He was silent for a moment and then he looked at Emily.

'We suspected something odd was going on,' he said after a moment. 'It was peculiar the way patients were kept sedated for so long – and some of the poor devils seemed worse after he treated them than they were before. Didn't seem to know what was going on.'

'You might be asked to repeat that in court,' Emily said. 'What is your name and how long have you worked here?'

'Eric Green, madam. I came here six months ago. It all seemed above board at first, but there was talk of money being short – and then things started to happen. Patients being brought here late at night in a drugged state... and other things.'

'Save it for the lawyers,' Emily advised. 'This is my car. I think Frances should come in the back with me. Dr Renton will drive us.' She smiled at Frances. 'It won't be long, dearest. We're going back to Alice's house for tonight, because I want Dr Renton to make sure you are fit to travel – and then I am taking you home with me.'

'Yes,' Frances said, tears beginning to trickle down her face. 'Take me home with you, Emily. I can't be alone yet. It hurts too much.' She gave a little sob.

'You won't be alone,' Emily said. 'I love you and I'm going to look after you until you are well again.' She smiled and kissed Frances as she sat beside her in the back of the car. 'Close your eyes and go to sleep. We shall soon be home.'

* * *

'She is sleeping now,' Emily said the next morning as she came downstairs to the kitchen where Alice and Daniel were sitting drinking a cup of tea. 'Dr Renton said that she might sleep for a long time once she felt safe. They gave her a lot of drugs to keep her quiet and it will be a while before that clears from her blood.'

'The devil they did!' Daniel was half on his feet, clearly furious. 'They might have killed her!'

'I think the idea was to make her more tractable,' Emily said and frowned. 'Paul says that electric shock treatment can be useful with some patients. If they are violent it can sometimes calm them, and it helps in various conditions – but it can leave a patient bewildered and forgetful, and that is what was planned for Frances. She would probably have been given far more than the regulated doses. Apparently, Dr Marsham was sacked from his last hospital for breaking the rules with similar treatments. He was working on a theory of his own that he believed might help schizophrenics and set up the clinic as a means of continuing his experiments. It seems that he may have gone too far in the treatment of some of his patients, and apparently the clinic was in financial trouble – and, Vane has learned, Sam Danby wasn't the first to pay him to keep a troublesome relative out of the way.'

'He deserves to be locked away for good!' Daniel said, his fists clenched. 'As for Danby...'

'I think Dr Marsham will be struck off the medical register,' Emily said. 'Vane is taking steps to ensure that he is barred from working in England. He may already have fled the country. Vane thinks he may have been tipped off that he was being investigated – and that's why he had disappeared. It was fortunate that he did decide to leave because he didn't have time to start giving Frances the treatment. As far as Sam Danby is concerned, I think you can be sure that he will be punished, Dan. Vane says that he has spoken to the chief constable at Cambridge – he knows him from his Masonic lodge meetings. Mr Danby will be thoroughly investigated.'

'Good, that is just what he deserves.' Daniel walked towards the kitchen door.

'Where are you going?' Alice asked with a worried frown.

'I have some work to do,' Dan said. 'Don't worry, love. I'm not

daft. If Emily says Danby will be caught and punished, I believe
her.'

'And if you believe that, you will believe anything,' Alice said
as her husband went out. 'He is going to find Sam Danby. I know
he is. He feels that he let Frances down – and he can't live with
that. He is going to find Sam and tell him what he thinks of him.'

'Let's hope that is all he does,' Emily said. 'It would be better
to leave Mr Danby to the police, but I know what Dan is like – he
won't be satisfied until he has given him a good hiding.'

'Yes, that is what I'm afraid of,' Alice said. 'I know he can do it
– but he will be in trouble himself then.'

'Let's hope he decides to be sensible,' Emily said. 'But neither
of us can stop him, Alice. He blames himself for what happened
to Frances and he won't be satisfied until he has done something
to set the balance straight.'

Daniel was seething as he walked out to his van. How could he
have been so stupid as to be deceived by Sam Danby? He had
never dreamed that a man who seemed to be so respectable
could do the things he had and get away with it. No one had even
suspected what he did in London – and Daniel hadn't believed
Frances when she'd hinted that Danby was making her life
miserable. He had found it difficult to take in when Emily said
that Sam had had Frances committed because he wanted to
punish her for attempting to blackmail him. But he knew the
truth now and he was bent on revenge.

It wasn't enough that Danby would be investigated. If he was
clever enough to keep his dirty dealings hidden all these years,
the police might not be able to pin anything on him. Marsham
might be in trouble if the authorities caught him, but whether he

would implicate Danby was another matter. And Sam would naturally plead innocent. He would say that he had tried to help his son's wife out of concern that she might try to kill herself again. A lot of people would believe him – Dan might have himself if he hadn't known the truth.

He wasn't going to get off that easily if Daniel could help it. He might get away with the rest of it – but he was going to pay for what he had done to Frances.

He knew where Sam was likely to be at this hour of the day, and if he wasn't there he would just keep on looking.

'Damn it, Marsham, you told me it would be perfectly safe!' Sam growled into the receiver at his home. 'You had her for a few days – why didn't you make sure she conveniently lost her memory?'

'She was difficult. I had to drug her sufficiently to make her more amenable before I could begin the shock treatment.'

'I paid good money and you haven't delivered. I hope they lock you up for good!' Sam slammed down the receiver and turned to see his wife watching him. 'What the hell are you staring at, woman?'

'You told me Frances was a danger to herself,' Rosalind said, an expression of disgust on her mouth. 'But you wanted to keep her quiet because she knew things about you that could cause you some trouble, didn't you, Sam?'

'Don't talk rubbish, woman. You have no idea what you are saying.'

'You think I'm stupid, don't you, Sam? Because I put up with your temper and your cheating ways, you imagine I'm just a doormat that you can wipe your feet on – but one of these days you will discover just how wrong you are.'

'Bloody woman!' Sam muttered, and he knocked her aside as he walked past and out of the front door. He got into his Rolls Royce and started the engine. It was time he was at his office. There were lorries to get off and loads to check. If those lazy devils he employed were left to their own devices, nothing would get done.

As he drew into the yard, he noticed that Daniel Searles had parked his battered old van in front of the office, and he felt a flutter of apprehension in his stomach. He quelled it immediately, putting on a smile as he walked into his office.

'Good morning, Dan,' he said. 'What can I do for you?' The smile vanished as Daniel turned to look at him and he saw the fury in his eyes. Sam glanced at his secretary. 'Fetch me some cigarettes from the pub, Milly,' he said, and he gave her a pound note from his pocket. He eyed Daniel nervously as the girl took the money and went out. 'Don't look at me like that, Dan. I had no idea what Marsham was up to at that place. I was recommended to him and I acted purely out of concern for Frances. How is she, by the way? Feeling better I hope?'

'Damn you, Sam!' Daniel said, fists balling at his side. 'You're lying through your teeth. You sent Frances there hoping that Marsham would destroy her memory with his experiments – and don't try to tell me you were afraid she might kill herself, because that would suit you down to the ground. It was because you couldn't be sure that she wouldn't talk, wasn't it – because she knew too many of your nasty little secrets? Well, I know them now too – so are you going to have me dealt with by one of your bully-boys? Maybe I should teach you some manners and see how you like being on the receiving end for a change.'

'Don't be stupid,' Sam said and backed away from him. 'Keep away from me, Dan. I'm older than you are and I don't want to fight you. If you attack me I shall go to the police.'

'You can do what you damned well like,' Dan said. 'You are like a lot of bullies – you can hand it out but you can't take it. Are you coming out into the yard to stand up like a man – or do you want me to make a mess of your office?'

'You wouldn't dare.' Sam backed away from him as Dan raised his fists. 'All right, let's do it outside.' His brain was working furiously. There were men working in the yard; he only had to call for them to drag this maniac off him. 'If you insist on settling this with brute force.'

He went out into the yard, ignoring the startled look his secretary threw him as she brought his cigarettes and was sent off with a jerk of the head. She took refuge in the office. Sam took his jacket off and laid it over a stack of crates. Daniel had already stripped his off and thrown it down. Sam put up his fists defensively. As a young man, he'd had his share of fist fights, but he knew that he wasn't up to it these days; years of good living and little exercise had taken its toll, but he couldn't lose face now, because he knew they were being watched.

'Come on then,' he said with an air of bravado. 'Let's get this over with.'

He put his fists up and stood waiting, moving from one foot to the other, weaving and ducking as Daniel came at him. He hardly saw the first punch coming, his head jerking back as Daniel's fist hit him on the chin. His head was reeling as he attempted to land one on his opponent, but Daniel was too quick for him. He was like lightning, jabbing and retreating, his next blow catching Sam in the stomach, making him wince and double up. Before he could recover, another four or five blows reined in, making him jerk and stagger back. He cursed himself for not finding a way out of this before it began, knowing that he was merely a punchbag for his opponent. He swore and flung himself at Daniel, trying to hold on to him like a bear hugging its victim, but though he used all his strength in a few moments, he was flung back and another barrage of blows to his head sent him reeling.

'That's it, Dan, give the bugger one for me while you're at it.'

'Yeah, me too!'

Sam could hear the jeering as Daniel's fists exploded in his face time after time. He looked about him desperately, hoping for a sign that one of his men would be ready to pull Daniel Searles off him, but he could see hatred in the eyes of the men, who were supporting his opponent all the way. He realised that he had taken too much for granted, using his employees as if they had no feelings, expecting them to pull caps and obey his every word if they wanted to get paid. They had given him lip service because they needed their jobs, but now they were enjoying his humiliation. When this was over, he would sack the lot of them. There were plenty of men looking for work.

The next barrage of blows sent him to the ground, where he lay winded and face down in the dirt. He sensed someone standing over him and rolled over on to his side, looking up at the man who towered above him. His thick lips pulled back in a sneer.

'Put the boot in, Dan,' he muttered. 'Enjoy your triumph while you can. You'll have a long time in prison to reflect on your folly, even longer if you kill me.'

'You're not worth the effort,' Dan said. 'I just wanted to let you know how it feels to be beaten, Sam. Do your worst. Go to the police, but I am going there now and I'm going to tell them what I saw in London. I think you're going to find yourself sitting in that prison cell right along with me.'

Dan turned and walked off, getting into his van. He drove away as Sam was rising to his feet and dusting himself down. He put his jacket on, his furious gaze moving over the small group of men that had watched the fight.

'What the hell are you staring at?' he growled. 'Get on with it if you value your job.'

'I don't think I do,' one of the men said. 'I worked for you out of respect, Danby. You're a hard man but I thought you were decent – but from what I've been hearing you're rotten through to the core. So you can keep your job and I'll be looking elsewhere.'

'Don't come crying to me when you can't find anything, Riley,' Sam sneered and looked at the faces of the other men. 'Any more of you want your cards?'

They looked at one another uneasily. One or two shook their heads, but three of them followed Tom Riley from the yard. Sam scowled at the men who remained.

'Get out, all of you. The yard is closed for today. Anyone who wants work can sign on in the morning.'

He turned and walked into the office. Milly was putting on her coat. She wouldn't look at him as she walked towards the door.

'Where are you going?'

Milly stopped and looked back at him. 'I thought this was a good job when I came here, Mr Danby. My mother heard things in the shop yesterday, but I wouldn't believe them. I thought you wouldn't do anything like that – but I was wrong and now I don't want to work for you any more.'

'Get out like the rest of them,' Sam muttered and sat down at his desk. His ribs were aching and his face felt as if it were swelling up like a balloon. He reached for the telephone, intending to contact the police and then the employment agency in Ely. Milly was the one member of staff he really needed. His hand fell back and he groaned with pain, getting to his feet. It would keep for another day.

He would go home and sit down somewhere comfortable while he planned his revenge against Daniel Searles. He had already taken measures to cover his tracks in London. With any luck it would take the police months to find the extent of his illegal dealings south of the river. He doubted that anyone knew about the gambling clubs or the other rackets. He could probably pull through this, but he was feeling too awful to deal with it just now. He had to go home.

Sam went out to the yard, getting in his car. He was moaning with the pain as he drove the short distance to his home. Rosalind looked at him as he walked into the kitchen.

'My God!' she said. 'What happened to you?'

'It was Daniel Searles. He assaulted me. I'm going to sue him. He'll be ruined and serving time when I've finished with him.'

'Serves him right for doing this to you,' Rosalind said. 'Why don't you get into bed and I'll bring you a hot whisky toddy? Have a good sleep, Sam. It won't hurt to have a rest for once. You do far too much, and this must have shaken you up.'

'Yeah, it has,' Sam said and looked at her. 'I'm sorry for what I said to you earlier, Rosalind. You've always been a good wife to me – I was just upset about things. You know I wouldn't have tried to harm Frances – don't you?'

'If you say so, Sam. I shall believe you, because you are my husband and I don't want to quarrel with you. I just want a peaceful life.'

'That's a good girl,' Sam said and smiled at her. He had known she would fall into line. 'Milly left today. You can give me a hand at the office until I get someone new – and I'll buy you something nice. A fur coat, if you like?'

'That sounds lovely,' Rosalind said. 'Up you go now and I'll bring you a soothing drink.'

She smiled as he walked out of the kitchen, and then she took a pair of rubber gloves from the dresser drawer. She set a heavy glass on the table and spooned some sugar into it, poured a stiff measure of whisky and added the hot water, mixing it well. For a moment she hesitated, and then she went to the cupboard under the sink, taking out the small packet of rat poison that Sam had bought. He had refused to let her buy it, because he said the stuff he got through his agricultural merchant was stronger.

She sprinkled a little into the glass and stirred until it had dissolved, and then she added a drop more whisky for good measure. She transferred the glass to a little tray, took off her rubber gloves and picked up the tray.

Sam was in bed when she entered the room, propped up against the pillows. She offered him the glass. He took it, smiled at her and drank it down without a murmur.

'That was good, lass,' he told her.

'Go to sleep, Sam,' she said and went out of the room.

* * *

'Oh, Dan,' Alice said as she saw the gleam of satisfaction in his eyes when he walked in later that day. 'What have you done?'

'I thrashed him, Alice.' He glanced at Frances, who was sitting at the kitchen table, an untouched mug of tea in front of her. 'I made him pay for what he did to you, Frances. I'm sorry I wasn't there for you when you needed me. I didn't realise what was going on.'

Frances smiled at him. 'I wish I had seen you beat him, Dan,' she said. 'Thank you for that, because it wasn't enough that he may be in some trouble with the police. I know how clever he is over these things. He will probably wriggle out of most of it – though the whispers will ruin him locally.'

'I think they already have,' Daniel said with satisfaction. 'The rumours are spreading, and after this morning everyone will know what he has been up to.' He glanced round the room. 'Where is Emily?'

'She went back to the house to collect some things for me,' Frances said. 'I didn't feel up to it and Emily said she would be happy if Sam called and she got a chance to tell him what she thought of him. We're leaving as soon as she gets back.'

'Yes, just as well,' Daniel said. 'He won't get a chance to do anything unpleasant to you then. I doubt if he will feel much like doing anything for a couple of days.'

'I hope it won't mean trouble for you, Dan,' Frances said, looking at Alice's worried face. 'I'm glad you thrashed him – but I don't want you to go to prison for it.'

'Don't worry,' Daniel reassured her. 'When he thinks it through he will see that it would just cause more trouble for him. If I get my day in court I'll see that he gets dragged through as much mud as I can find. That apartment building in South London isn't the only dirty thing Sam has his fingers into, don't you worry. It just needs a bit of investigating and a whole lot more will surface. Sam won't want to risk that, believe me. He will probably offer me money to sort this thing out. I shan't take it but it's what I expect of him.'

'I hope you're right,' Alice said. She turned her head as the sound of a car engine was heard outside. 'It sounds as if Emily is back, Frances.' She went to embrace her sister-in-law. 'Take care of yourself, love. We shall always be here for you if you need us.'

'Yes, I know.' Frances kissed her cheek. She gave her sister-in-law a wry smile. 'I thought I was all alone after Charlie died – but Emily moved mountains to get me out of that horrible place – and Dan has risked his future for my sake. I didn't realise that I was loved so much.'

'Of course we love you. We always have.'

'Are you ready?' Emily said as she came in at the kitchen door. 'I'll ring you, Alice. Dan – are you all right?' Her eyes went over him. 'Muriel told me there's a tale going round the village that you thrashed Sam Danby for what he did to Frances?'

'Yeah, too right I did – and I'm fine,' he said, grinning at her. 'You did things your way – I've done them mine.'

'Well, it seems to have gone down well with the locals. Muriel says that someone needed to stand up to him before this and she thinks you're a bit of a hero.'

'Nah,' Daniel said, but his eyes were bright with triumph. 'You had better get off. You've a long way to go.' He went to the door to watch them get into the car, waving until the car pulled out of the yard.

Going back into the kitchen, Dan looked at Alice. He saw the anxiety in her eyes and sighed because he didn't want her upset.

'Yes, I know it was a daft thing to do, love – and I know I could go to prison for it – but I had to do it. I couldn't let him get away with what he did to Frances.'

'I know,' Alice said. 'I understand that you had to do it and I'm glad you thrashed him. I just hope it doesn't rebound on you.'

'Connor will take care of you if I go inside for a few months,' Daniel said, but he was feeling uneasy beneath his cheerful manner. He hadn't wanted to admit it in front of Frances, but Sam was a vindictive so and so and he might well want to see Daniel behind bars.

* * *

It was Alice who heard the news first. She was shopping in the village and planning to visit with her mother for the rest of the day. Daniel had promised to fetch her at about four o'clock. As soon as she walked into the shop, she was aware that the place was buzzing, but everyone stopped talking and looked at her.

'What's wrong?' she asked, because she knew they must have been saying something that concerned her or her family. 'Has something happened?' Her heart raced because she had been anxious ever since Dan had come back home and told them that he'd thrashed Sam Danby.

'It's Mr Danby,' one of the women told her. 'His wife found him dead in bed late yesterday afternoon. She said he must have come home while she was in the garden, made himself a drink and gone upstairs. She didn't even realise he was there until she went up later to get something from the wardrobe.'

Alice drew in a harsh breath, because she knew what they must be thinking. Daniel had given Sam a thrashing and now he was dead.

'That must have been a terrible shock for her,' Alice said, her throat tight. 'Did he have a bad heart or something?'

'Mrs Danby doesn't know what he died of yet,' someone else said. 'The police came and took him away. It seems as if there was something suspicious about the way he died.'

'Oh...' Alice swallowed hard. 'I see.'

'You don't want to worry about your Dan,' another woman said, giving her a sympathetic look. 'Bill was there and he said it was a fair fight. Your husband fought with his fists. No weapons were used and Sam took his coat off and told your Dan to come on.'

'Thank you,' Alice said. She advanced to the counter and put her list down. 'Could I collect this later? I want to make a telephone call.'

She walked out of the shop as quickly as she could and ran to the red kiosk on the corner of the street, fishing in her purse for some coins. She hoped that Dan might be in the house and would pick up the phone, but though she let it ring for several minutes there was no answer.

She left the phone box and stood on the street for a moment, trying to decide what to do for the best. She was still wondering when a small van drew up near her and she saw her brother's cheery face looking through the open window.

'Want a lift, Alice?' he asked.

'Oh, Peter,' she said. 'I need to talk to Dan. Would you drive me home and then bring me back?'

'Yeah, all right,' he said. 'I wanted to have a word with Dan anyway. I bought this van yesterday and it doesn't sound quite right. He might have a look at it for me.'

'I'm sure he will be pleased to,' Alice said. She felt relieved as she climbed into the passenger seat. It was dreadful news about Sam Danby, because none of them had wanted to see him dead, even though he deserved to be punished for his crimes. What worried her most was the fact that he had been fighting with Daniel earlier in the day. If the fight had caused Sam's death, the police might come to arrest her husband. 'That's if he can...'

Peter looked at her, his brows raised. 'Something wrong, Alice?'

'Yes, there might be,' Alice said. 'Daniel was in a fight with Sam Danby yesterday and now he is dead. Apparently his wife found him when she went upstairs for something.'

Peter whistled. 'Yes, that is a bit of a worry. You're scared the police are going to come after Dan – but it was a fist fight, Alice. Dan didn't go for him with an iron bar or a knife.'

'I know, but it may still mean trouble for Dan,' Alice said. 'I have to go home and warn him – but I still haven't got my shopping. And I left Danny with Mum.'

'Well, don't worry about it,' Peter said. 'Give me the ticket and

I'll fetch it back for you. I'll bring Danny and the shopping if you like?'

'Oh, thank you,' Alice said. 'That would make it so much easier for me – and then you can tell Mum why I had to go home, can't you?'

'Yeah, of course,' her brother said and smiled at her. 'I heard what Daniel did to Sam Danby and I reckon he did the right thing, Alice. We're all on his side. Don't you worry. It will all turn out fine.'

Alice nodded, but she didn't smile, because she couldn't. Daniel had been so pleased with what he'd done – but he wasn't going to feel so happy about it when he knew that Sam Danby was dead!

11

'Stop worrying, Alice,' Daniel told her after her brother had driven off in his van. 'You should have gone back with Peter. You were supposed to have a lovely day with your mother. If I know her she has cooked a special meal and she will be disappointed. Why don't I run you back there now?'

'I couldn't rest, Dan,' Alice said. 'Don't you realise what this could mean for us?' She choked back a sob. 'I couldn't bear it if they put you on trial for murder. It was bad enough when you were in that prisoner of war camp – but...' She looked at him with tears in her eyes, because she was afraid to put the worst of her fears into words.

'Hush, love,' Daniel said, putting his arms about her and kissing the top of her head. His expression was grim, because he knew it was possible that he might be charged with assault, or even manslaughter. 'It won't come to anything like that, I promise you. It was a fist fight. He was alive when I left him and he went home. He probably died of a heart attack or something.'

'But they might say it was the fight that brought it on.' Alice looked up at him. 'I'm so frightened, Dan. Supposing they say it was murder?'

Daniel laughed at her worried face. 'They won't hang me for it, Alice. I might get a couple of months for causing an affray or something of the sort.'

'It isn't anything to laugh at,' Alice said, tears in her eyes. She heard the telephone ring. 'I don't feel like answering that.'

'Let me go,' Daniel said. Her tears made him feel guilty, because he loved her. 'Put the kettle on, love. I could do with a cup of tea and then I'll take you back to your mother's.' He went out into the hall and picked up the receiver. 'Daniel Searles speaking. How may I help you?'

'Mr Searles?' a woman's voice said. 'It is Rosalind Danby. I wanted to speak to you for a few minutes, if I may?'

'Yes, of course, Mrs Danby,' Daniel said. 'I heard the news. I am sorry for your loss.'

'No, you shouldn't be,' Rosalind said. 'My husband deserved what you did to him yesterday. It has been coming for a long time, I think.'

'I didn't intend him to die. Was it his heart?'

'No, I don't believe so,' she said. 'I wasn't in the house when Sam came home yesterday afternoon. I found him when I went upstairs later, as I told the police. I thought something was wrong with him and I called them and the doctor, because I could see that he was dead – but he looked odd.'

'I'm not sure what you mean?'

She seemed to hesitate, then: 'I've just had a telephone call from the police, Mr Searles. They asked me if I could think of any reason why my husband might want to take his own life. Well, of course I said yes. Sam was dealing in some rather dreadful stuff, Mr Searles. Some of it may have been criminal. I believe he knew it was all about to come out – and I think that is why he took poison.'

'Sam took his own life?' Daniel was astounded. 'I can hardly believe it. He didn't seem the type to do something like that, Mrs Danby.'

'No, you wouldn't have thought so,' Rosalind said in a calm, flat tone. 'But it is what the police seem to believe. Sam bought some strong rat poison some months ago. The rats had been getting in with the rabbits, you see – Sam thought we should get rid of them, because we don't need them now the war is over, do we? I asked him not to because Charlie thought of them as pets. I never did tell him that we had used them as food when meat was short. It would have broken his heart, you see.'

'Yes, I see,' Daniel said. She sounded unnaturally calm, which surprised him. He would have thought her the kind of woman who might have hysterics over a thing like this. It just showed you never knew how people would react. 'So do you think that will be the verdict then – suicide?'

'I imagine it might,' Rosalind said. 'We wouldn't want it to be anything else, would we? I would rather you weren't charged with assault, Mr Searles. My husband was not a nice man. What he did to your sister was unforgivable. I always liked Frances, you know. She thought I was an old fusspot, and perhaps I am – but I liked her. And I know that it wasn't her fault that Charlie died. We both thought he was settling down after his bilious attack and would be better in a little while.'

'No, it wasn't her fault,' Daniel said, and then added thoughtfully, 'It was very good of you to ring me, Mrs Danby.'

'I thought you should know that the police are satisfied he took his own life because of circumstances beyond his control. The detective constable was such a nice young man, and he knew all about the investigation into Sam's affairs. He was very kind to me, asked if there was anything he could do to help.'

'I'm glad,' Daniel said, feeling slightly at a loss because it all seemed a little unreal somehow. 'Alice was worried.'

'I knew she must be,' Rosalind said. 'I shan't invite you to the funeral, Mr Searles. I don't think you would wish to be there – and I intend to have Sam cremated once the police allow it. I don't want his body to come back here. It will be a very private ceremony.'

'Yes, I see,' Daniel said. 'What will you do now?'

'I have no idea,' she replied. 'I shall have to think about it. Goodbye, Mr Searles. Give my regards to your wife – and thank you.'

'For what?' Daniel asked, but she had replaced the receiver. He was frowning as he went back into the kitchen.

'Who was that?' Alice asked, looking at him fearfully. 'Was it the police?'

'You can stop worrying about that,' Daniel told her and smiled. 'Mrs Danby rang me to tell me that Sam took his own life. Apparently, he believed that everything was about to come down about his head like a ton of bricks. He couldn't face the disgrace and so he killed himself – with rat poison, apparently.'

'He killed himself?' Alice echoed. A look of relief came into her eyes. 'Oh, thank goodness! I was so afraid you would be arrested for assault, Dan.' Realising what she had said, she went bright pink. 'Oh, that was awful of me. Poor Rosalind. She must be dreadfully upset.'

'She seemed to be coping. You can forget about the police; at least, I think you can,' he said. 'If they are satisfied that he took his own life I doubt if they will come after me for giving him a smacking.'

'Is there something you aren't telling me?' Alice asked. 'You're holding something back, Dan. Tell me, please, or I shall worry.'

'It's nothing to upset you,' Daniel said. 'It was just something odd about Mrs Danby. She said thank you before she put the phone down – and she didn't seem to care that he was dead.'

'I wouldn't expect her to,' Alice said, pulling a face. 'Mary told me that he treated her like dirt. He did exactly what he wanted and she just had to go along with it. I should imagine his death was almost a relief to her – though it must have been horrid to find him like that.' A little shudder went through her.

'That will be it then,' Daniel said and smiled for her. 'And now you can tell me what you've been keeping from me, Alice. I know there's something else on your mind, apart from this business with Sam Danby.'

Alice blushed and looked at him uncertainly. 'I didn't want to tell you, because you've had so much on your mind recently, Dan – but I think I'm going to have a baby. I'm fairly certain, though I haven't been to the doctor yet.'

'Oh, Alice, love,' Daniel said ruefully. 'I've given you so much worry these past few days, and you're carrying my child. I'm so sorry. Forgive me?'

'There's nothing to forgive,' Alice said, and her eyes were shining now. Rosalind's call had relieved her mind. 'I was going to pop in to the doctor's surgery this afternoon and see what he has to say.'

'Well, that is just what you are going to do,' Daniel told her. He looked out of the window and saw that his brother-in-law had arrived with the shopping and Danny. 'I'm going to take the day off to celebrate. We'll go to Ely, have fish and chips in the café, and buy you something nice – and then we'll come back in time for the surgery. After that, you can have supper with your family and tell them the good news.'

'Oh, Dan, that's a lovely idea,' Alice said and went into his arms. 'We're so lucky! Everything is coming right after all.'

'We certainly are,' he said, but there was a strange expression in his eyes as he looked over the top of her head. If the police were satisfied with Mrs Danby's story, it wasn't up to him to challenge it. But he couldn't help feeling that it was all very convenient.

* * *

Emily answered the telephone late that evening. She smiled as she heard her brother's voice, because she had been thinking that she might ring him in the morning.

'How are you, Dan?' she asked. 'Is Alice all right?'

'Alice may be having a baby,' Daniel told her. 'She suspected it and the doctor is pretty certain she is right – so that is good news.'

'That is wonderful,' Emily said. 'I am so pleased for you both. You haven't had a visit from the police?'

'Apparently, I'm in the clear,' Daniel said, glancing over his shoulder to make sure the kitchen door was shut. 'It seems that Sam took his own life.'

'Sam is dead?' Emily was shocked. 'When did you hear this?'

'Just this morning. Alice thought the police might blame it on the fight, because it happened later that day – but apparently they think he killed himself while under strain.'

'Because it was all going to come out?'

'That is what they seem to believe.' His voice was measured, controlled.

'But you don't,' Emily said. 'Why?'

'His wife rang me. She was odd, Emily. I can't tell you why – but I think…' Daniel hesitated. 'Perhaps I shouldn't say it.'

'You think she might have done it? How – why?'

'Mary told Alice that he treated her shamefully. He is supposed to have made himself a drink and put rat poison in it. He bought the poison through his agricultural contacts and he took the drink upstairs himself – at least, that is the tale going round. Alice heard it at the village shop first, but when we spoke to him, her father had heard it from someone else and it seems to be the accepted explanation.'

'Then I should keep your theory to yourself,' Emily told him. 'It is much better for everyone that way, Dan. I've been afraid he might try to harm Frances again. If his wife did somehow get him to drink rat poison... well, as awful as it sounds, she did us all a favour. I hope she gets away with it.'

'Yes, on reflection, I think that's how I feel,' Daniel said, 'but it has been on my mind. I had to tell someone – and I couldn't lay that on Alice.'

'She doesn't need to know and nor does Frances,' Emily said. 'Whatever the truth, I'm glad he is dead.'

'Yeah, that's what his wife seemed to feel,' Daniel said. 'She thanked me – and I think she meant for thrashing him.'

Emily gave a harsh laugh. 'She had probably wanted it to happen for years. I'm not sure what the truth is about the rat poison, Dan – but if she did it, I take my hat off to her. That takes guts – regardless of the moral issues. I suppose murder can never be justified, but in this case it is a close run thing.'

'I suppose a good many might feel that way,' Daniel agreed, though he was frowning, because in an odd sort of way he had liked Sam – at least until he'd discovered what he'd done to Frances. 'Anyway, how is Frances? Is she settling in with you?'

'Yes, I think so,' Emily said. 'She is very quiet, and I think she cries when she is in bed, but that is to be expected.' She turned her head as her name was called. 'Oh, Vane wants me – I'll ring you tomorrow.'

'Fine,' Daniel said. He replaced the receiver and Emily headed for the sitting room. She had applauded the sentiments behind what Daniel had suggested, but it made her feel a bit shivery. Had Rosalind Danby really murdered her husband in cold blood? It was something that they might never know for certain.

* * *

Rosalind sat looking at the copy of her husband's will that she had found in his bureau drawer. He had left the property in London and his haulage business to Marcus or his wife and heirs. Everything else came to Rosalind. Obviously, he hadn't got around to changing it after Marcus died. She smiled her satisfaction. Most of the money was in land, this house and various other properties that Sam had bought in the area. She would be a wealthy woman and she didn't begrudge Frances what was coming to her. She deserved it for what Sam had done to her life.

Rosalind had no illusions about her late husband. She had suffered from his insults and his cruelty for years, and she knew that he had never been faithful to her. He had treated her as if she were one of his possessions with no thought or will of her own, but he had underestimated her.

She got up and looked at his picture in the silver frame that had always stood on the sideboard. It had been taken at his son's wedding, and she had seen the lust in his eyes when he'd looked at Frances then. It had made her keep her distance from her new daughter-in-law, but she had soon discovered that Frances couldn't stand him, and that had drawn her towards her son's wife – the feeling that they had something in common. Sam had disgusted her in so many ways, but for a long time she had felt trapped, unable to think of a way to free herself from his tyranny.

Normally, Sam was so strong minded, so careless of her feelings, that he ignored anything she tried to do for him. To see him vulnerable after Daniel Searles had thrashed him had given her the idea. She had offered the hot toddy out of a desire to help, but then almost immediately she had realised the opportunity it gave her. She had known that she might never get another chance.

After she'd taken the drink up to Sam she had been sick with fear. She had not dared to go near the bedroom for hours in case he was still alive and accused her of trying to poison him, but he must have died quite quickly. She had no idea of what was in the rat poison that Sam had bought, but the police officer who had rung to tell her the results of the autopsy had told her that it contained cyanide. It was of a type that had been banned for general use, because it was too dangerous. Sam had got hold of it illegally and the police had taken that as a sign of his intent to commit suicide.

She had never expected it to be so easy. If she had known, she might have done it years ago – but perhaps it was a combination of things that had led the police to their conclusion. It had all come together nicely: the police investigation into Sam's shady affairs, the fight and the rat poison being there, almost as if she had been meant to do it. She wasn't sure that Daniel Searles had believed her, but he would keep his suspicions to himself because it suited him. All in all, things couldn't have been better.

'You deserved it, you know,' Rosalind said to the photograph. 'I really loved you once, Sam, but you killed any tender feelings I had for you. I've hated you for a long time.' She shuddered as she opened the sideboard drawer and slid his picture inside. She didn't like to feel his eyes watching her, because it reminded her of the awful look of agony on his face when she'd found him. 'You did deserve it,' she said again. 'It was your own fault.'

'Did you call me?' Mary Searles said, coming in at that moment. 'I just came to tell you that I'm leaving now. I shall come in tomorrow to get things nice for the funeral.'

'Oh, you needn't bother,' Rosalind said. 'It is going to be a very private ceremony and I'm not going to invite anyone here.'

'Surely...' Mary stopped. 'Well, that is your choice, Mrs Danby.'

'I've decided to sell this house,' Rosalind said. 'I'm going to travel, I think, perhaps live abroad somewhere. I always wanted to travel when I was younger but Sam never would – so now I am going to do what I want with the rest of my life.' She smiled at Mary. 'While I'm away, would you come in now and then to look over the house – just until it is sold?'

'Yes, of course, I would be pleased to do that for you, Mrs Danby.'

'Thank you. Don't go for a moment, Mary.' She got up and went across to Sam's bureau, opening the top drawer where he kept his cash box. She took out two hundred pounds in crisp white five-pound notes and went back to where Mary was standing. 'This is for you, to say thank you for all you've done for me these past few months – and for looking after the house when I'm away.'

Mary looked at the money. 'I can't take all this, Mrs Danby. I've had my wages, and I've not done much.'

'You have been a friend, especially when Marcus and then dear little Charlie died,' Rosalind said. 'Please take it. I would like you to have it. I've never been able to do anything like this before and it feels good. Besides, Sam was bragging about all the stuff he got for nothing from your husband's farm sale. I think we owe it to you.'

Mary hesitated, but it was a lot of money to her and she wouldn't find another job as good as this easily. 'Thank you very much. When were you intending to leave, Mrs Danby?'

'Oh, the day after tomorrow, I think,' Rosalind said. 'I shall go up to London and do some shopping – and after that I'll book a nice cruise to get me started.'

'Well, I hope you enjoy your trip,' Mary said and smiled at her. 'You deserve a little happiness, Mrs Danby.'

'Oh, do call me Rosalind. I don't like the name Danby. I think I shall revert to my maiden name. Yes, I'll call myself by my father's name – Rathbone. Sam always laughed at my father for being a gentleman, but I remember him as kind and gentle. I don't think that is a bad thing to be, do you?'

'Oh no,' Mary said. 'Not at all.' She smiled and nodded. 'I'll get off then if there's nothing you want?'

'No, nothing more, thank you.'

Rosalind looked at herself in the mirror above the fireplace after Mary had gone. Did she look like a murderess? Her hand crept to her throat as she wondered what it felt like to hang, but then she checked herself. She had got away with it. The police officer had told her the inquest would be an open-and-shut case; it would be recorded as suicide, because only Sam's fingerprints were on the glass and it was clearly his intent to end his life. He had even bought the rat poison himself, because he hadn't trusted her to do it.

She had got away with it, but she couldn't bear being in this house where everything reminded her of Sam. She had to get away, to leave the past behind her and hope that in time she would be able to forget.

'Nothing lasts forever,' she told herself as she went through to the kitchen. Happiness was fleeting, and pain faded eventually, and so would her feeling of guilt. She had money and the freedom to do whatever she wished with her life.

* * *

'Sam killed himself?' Frances looked at Emily in disbelief as they were walking together in the gardens at Vanbrough the next morning. 'How – why? It doesn't seem like something he would do, Emily.'

'Rosalind told Daniel that the police were satisfied he had committed suicide because he was afraid of the consequences when the extent of his criminal activities were brought to light. It would have ruined him, Frances. Once people started talking, he would have been off the council for a start and... well, you know what folk are like in a village.'

'Yes, I do know,' Frances said and pulled a wry face. 'Some of them thought that I had neglected Charlie.'

'No one who really knows you would think that, Frances.'

'Perhaps not.' Frances caught back a sob. 'I've told myself I'm not going to think about that any more. I loved Charlie and I think he was happy most of the time. I'm going to think about the good things.'

'Yes, I'm sure he was a happy little boy.' Emily put a comforting arm about her waist. 'Don't doubt yourself, Frances. You were a good mother.'

'I didn't want him to have that wretched dog,' Frances said, a little choke in her voice. 'Sam insisted on giving it to him and now I'm glad he did. Charlie loved Toffee and that was a good thing. I think Sam really cared about Charlie, so he couldn't have been all bad, I suppose.'

'Everyone has their good points,' Emily said. 'But I shouldn't start to feel sorry for Sam, if I were you. Just remember what he tried to do to you, Frances.'

'Oh, I don't feel sorry for him,' Frances said and shivered as she recalled his threats. 'I couldn't – he was selfish and over-bearing and I disliked him even before he had me committed to that dreadful place.'

'Don't think about it, love. It's over now. You're here with me and quite safe. Vane says you're welcome to make your home here if you want?'

'I'm not sure yet,' Frances said. 'Don't think me ungrateful, Emily. I am glad to be here – but I don't think I could live in a house like this for the rest of my life. It's too big, too old and over-powering. I like Vane very much, and Amelia seems better with you than she was the last time I was here – but it wouldn't suit me.'

'No, I daresay it might not,' Emily admitted and laughed. 'When I first came here I thought the same. I had expected a home of my own and when Simon told me he thought he would live here, I was devastated – but then I started running the conva-lescent home and I was too busy to think about it. Somehow this house became my home without my realising it – and now I love it almost as much as Vane does.'

'You're very fond of Vane, aren't you?' Frances looked at her oddly. 'I think he is a little in love with you – perhaps more than a little.'

'Vane loves Amelia.' Emily frowned, because Frances was voicing thoughts that must never be admitted. 'You mustn't start imagining things, Frances. Amelia is his wife.'

'Yes, I know that, but I still think he feels something for you.' Frances sighed. 'Life is so complicated, isn't it? You married Simon before you knew him and were unhappy. I married the man I had loved for most of my life and everything went wrong.'

'I always thought you were the lucky one,' Emily said with a rueful smile. 'Out of all of us you seemed to get everything you wanted.'

'Yes, I did,' Frances said, 'but I lost it all. Marcus was never the same after the war.' She sighed. 'I had a letter from the lawyer this morning. It seems that Sam left quite a lot of property, including the haulage business, to Marcus or his wife and heirs – that means it comes to me. It sounds as if I'll have a fair amount of money when it is all sold. I shall tell them to sell for whatever they can get. I don't want any of the property in London, and I couldn't run the haulage business. Besides, I don't want to go back there.'

'Dan could run the lorries for you,' Emily suggested. 'You could make him a partner. Change the name to Searles Yard and let Dan have a chance to get on. He lost everything when the land was sold, you know. He doesn't say anything but I think he finds it a struggle to manage on what he earns.'

'Yes, I might do that,' Frances said and looked thoughtful. 'I hadn't thought about it – but it might be good for Dan to have something like that. As you said, we could change the name and I wouldn't have to go near the place.'

Emily smiled and nodded. 'That's only if you want to do it, Frances. And if Dan agrees.'

'Yes,' France agreed. 'I am thinking of buying a guest house somewhere. I was wondering if you might come in with me – if you were thinking of leaving here?'

'I don't think I could at the moment,' Emily said. 'It is something for the future though, Fran. In a year or two I might want a business to keep me busy – when the last of our guests goes. I have thought for a while that I might like to run a small hotel.'

'Yes, well, I haven't made up my mind yet,' Frances said and sighed. 'I don't feel like doing anything much yet – and I shan't know how much money I have until the lawyers have sorted it all out. Because of the investigation into Sam's affairs, it may be a while before the property can be sold.'

'There's no hurry, love,' Emily said. She linked arms with Frances. 'I was thinking we might go into Winchester one day. We could go shopping and have lunch somewhere nice.'

'Yes, that would be lovely,' Frances said. 'We never did things like that when we were girls, did we? I wonder why.'

'Oh, I suppose I was a bit younger – and then when we grew up the war came and we had separate lives,' Emily said. She smiled at Frances. 'I'm glad you're here, love. It's good that we can have some time together. I want us to really get to know each other while you're staying with us.'

'Yes, I would like that too,' Frances said. 'I feel as if I have been stuck in a long dark tunnel, Emily. It seemed as if I would never reach the end, but now perhaps I can begin to see the light.'

'That's good,' Emily said and squeezed her arm. 'Nothing is forever, Frances. It will come right again, I promise you.' She saw a car draw up outside the house. 'I wonder who that is...'

'I think... Yes, it is Dr Renton,' Frances said, her fine brows rising as she looked at Emily. 'Now, I wonder what has brought him all the way down here?'

Emily laughed. 'Perhaps he has come to see how you are, Frances.'

'Somehow, I don't think it is me he has come to visit,' Frances said. 'But he has seen us. We had better go and say hello.'

They walked towards Paul Renton, who had got out of the car and was waiting for them to join him. Emily went forward to greet him with a smile on her face. She offered her hand, but he leaned forward to kiss her cheek.

'What a lovely surprise, Paul. What brings you this way?'

'I told you I might call on you one day,' Paul Renton said with a grin that was rather engaging. 'I'm taking a few days off from work and I thought, why not.' He glanced at the house. 'I wasn't expecting this though. It's a wonderful house. Does it belong to Lord Vane?'

'Yes, it has been in his family for centuries. It does rather take your breath away when you first see it, doesn't it? I felt completely lost the first time I came here on a visit, but I'm used to it now.'

'It is a beautiful place to live,' he said. 'I'm talking more the grounds than the house here. I should imagine that is a bit of devil to run these days – must cost a fortune to heat it.'

'Yes, I expect so,' Emily agreed. 'I leave all that to Vane, of course.' She turned to Frances. 'You must say hello to Paul, love. If it were not for him I wouldn't have got you home as quickly or as easily.'

Frances came forward, offering her hand. 'I don't think I thanked you properly that night,' she said. 'It all seems a blur – but I did remember you so I must have taken some of it in. I know you looked after me when we got to Daniel's house.'

'It was the least I could do,' Paul told her and shook hands. 'I am glad to see you looking so much better. I was a little anxious about your condition, but I can see that you are fine.'

'I feel better,' Frances said. 'No one could help it in a place like this. Besides, Emily has been looking after me. I am very lucky to have her.'

'Yes, you are,' Paul said and glanced at Emily. 'I was wondering if we might go out to dinner this evening – if you are free?'

'I'm not sure...' Emily glanced at Frances. 'Would you mind being here without me?'

'I think I can manage for once,' Frances told her. 'Go out and enjoy yourself, Emily. You spend too much time working or worrying about me.'

'My work is a pleasure to me,' Emily said. 'But yes, I will go out with you this evening, Paul – but now you must come in and meet Vane. I am sure he will wish to have a few words, and you are welcome to stay for lunch, if you like?'

'Thank you, I should like that,' he said. 'Afterwards, you might take me to see the convalescent home you told me about.'

'Yes, of course,' Emily agreed. 'We only have a few guests left now, because the government is closing down a lot of the temporary homes they set up during the war. Vane didn't want our boys to lose the home they had become accustomed to so we are keeping it going in a private capacity for a while.'

They walked up to the house together, Frances following a step behind. She listened to them talking about a subject that interested them both, half envious of her sister, because she seemed so sure and confident of her place here. Frances had felt like that once, but it had all crumbled into ashes after Marcus began to drink heavily. That period of her life was over now, and it looked as if she would have enough money to do whatever she pleased with her future. She wasn't sure what she wanted yet, and sometimes the pain of Charlie's death made her want to weep bitter tears, but she was getting over it slowly. It helped being with Emily, though sometimes seeing her sister with her son could be very painful.

Emily had given her something to think about. She couldn't do anything yet, but it might be a good idea to offer Daniel the yard. She knew that he was good with engines. He had always wanted a garage. It might be that he could combine the two businesses, but she would have to see how things worked out once probate was granted.

One thing she knew for certain was that she couldn't go back to the way she had been. She had to change, to become more like Emily. Her sister was so confident, so sure of her place in the world.

* * *

'You must have been busy when this place was full to capacity,' Paul Renton said as Emily took him into her office. She had given him a tour of the building and introduced him to the few remaining guests. 'What will you do when the home eventually closes?'

'I don't honestly know,' Emily told him. 'It won't be for a while yet – and I suppose I shall find something. Probably charity work. I know Vane sits on several committees. He could find me something if I asked.' Emily laughed. 'It sounds so odd to hear myself say that, because I once thought that I would hate anything of that nature – but now it seems natural. I suppose it is living with Vane and Amelia. They are both very social minded. I must be becoming more like them.'

'I liked him,' Paul said, looking thoughtful. 'I didn't expect to, because I thought he might be a bit of a snob, but he isn't at all. His wife is pleasant, but...' He pulled a wry face. 'I thought she was not quite as friendly as her husband.'

'Amelia can be like that,' Emily said. 'She is probably wondering why you've come here. I don't usually have visitors unless they are family.'

'It won't cause a problem for you?'

'No, of course not,' Emily said. 'I am pleased you came. It is ages since I've been out to dinner with a man other than with Vane and Amelia, not since the war.'

'I suppose it takes time to get over what happened?' He looked at her awkwardly.

'Yes, it does,' Emily agreed. 'But I am over it... at least, I shall never forget him, the man I loved, but it doesn't hurt every minute of the day as it once did.'

'I'm glad,' he said and gave her an odd look. 'I've been offered a new job. I'm not sure whether I want to take it or not.'

'Is it a promotion?' Emily asked. 'You haven't been at Adden-brooks long, have you?'

'I did my training there and in a way I don't like to leave them after just a few months of service – but the job is something I am interested in doing. It is in Africa – a missionary hospital working with poor tribes in the interior. Apparently no one can stick it for long out there and they are always looking for young doctors to take over a vacant post.'

'That sounds interesting,' Emily said. 'It would be something you would never forget – a once in a lifetime chance.'

'Yes. It would be for three years, and then I would come back to England. I suppose it is something I should do. I was keen on the idea when I applied, but since then...' His voice tailed off. 'Well, I have a couple of weeks to make up my mind so I thought I would take a few days off and visit you.' He seemed to hesitate but then smiled oddly. 'I suppose I have made up my mind really.'

'And I am very glad you did come to visit us,' Emily said. 'You must promise to write to me while you are away – and come and see us when you get back.'

'Yes, I will,' he said, not looking at her. 'I am glad your sister is recovering from her ordeal. She hasn't had any side effects – no bad headaches or anything?'

'No, Frances is feeling quite well again,' Emily said. She sensed that he had turned the subject and she wondered what he had wanted to say before he changed his mind. 'She is still griev-ing, of course, but she doesn't seem so desperate now.'

'She will find her own way,' he said. 'I suppose we all do that when things don't turn out as we would like them to.'

'Yes, perhaps,' Emily agreed. 'I think we should go back now. Amelia will be waiting for us before she orders tea.'

* * *

Later that evening, as she sat brushing her hair in front of her dressing mirror, Emily looked at herself and wondered why she hadn't made it easier for Paul to say what he wanted. She couldn't be certain, because of course they hadn't known each other long, but there had been something in his eyes, and she had sensed that he wanted to ask her something. She believed he had told her about the job to gauge her reaction. Perhaps if she had told him that she didn't want him to go he would have come out and said it, but she had deliberately kept a distance between them.

She had enjoyed having dinner with Paul, and she liked him very much – but she knew that she wasn't ready to fall in love again. For the moment she was committed to Vane and looking after the convalescent home, though she knew that it could have been handed over to someone else if she had wanted to leave Vanbrough. And yet there was something about Paul that made her want to know him better. If he hadn't been going away, she might have arranged to meet sometimes. She had married in haste once and she didn't want to make that mistake again. Besides, it just wasn't possible for her to leave at the moment.

If she asked Paul to stay, told him that she liked him and wanted to get to know him better, he might think she was inviting him to begin a relationship that would eventually lead to marriage. Emily couldn't be sure that was what she wanted. Perhaps one day she would meet someone she could love – and it might have been Paul if they'd had more time.

He was coming to say goodbye to her in the morning, and then he was going off for a little holiday before he returned to Cambridge. If she tried, Emily knew she could persuade him to change his mind about taking that job. She had seen it in his eyes when they parted earlier that evening. He had kissed her cheek, but if she had turned her head...

Emily sighed. She wasn't sure how she felt and she didn't want to make another mistake. She had married Simon before she really knew him, and then she had fallen in love with Terry. It would be foolish to do something similar again, and yet she had a little hollow feeling inside when she thought that Paul was going away and she might never see him again.

She was about to get into bed when someone knocked at the door. Thinking that it might be Frances, she called out that she might enter but Amelia came in instead. She was wearing a comfortable velvet dressing gown and slippers, and looked different somehow, more vulnerable than usual.

'Were you in bed?'

'No, not yet,' Emily said. 'Did you want something, Amelia?'

'Just to ask if you'd had a nice evening. It was a long way for your friend to come just for one day.'

'Paul is going to tour for a few days before he returns to Cambridge,' Frances said. 'I think he wanted to see how Frances was getting on.'

'He came to see you,' Amelia said. 'I think he is in love with you.'

'Don't be silly, he barely knows me.'

'Well, you never know if you allowed him to get to know you better.'

'Paul has been offered a job working at a missionary hospital in Africa. He came to tell me he was going away.'

'Do you want to go with him?'

'No, I couldn't leave Vanbrough. You know that, Amelia.'

'Why don't you ask him to find a job down here?'

'I am not sure that I want to start a relationship,' Emily said. 'I married in haste once. I shan't make the same mistake again.'

'If you let him go you may never see him again,' Amelia said. 'You don't always get two chances, Emily. You like him. I know you do.'

'Yes, I like him – but I liked Simon. I was in love with Terry.'

Amelia shrugged. 'He is in love with you,' she said, 'but of course it is up to you.'

'Thank you for your advice,' Emily said. 'I haven't made up my mind yet – but if I do I'll let you know.'

She frowned as the door closed behind Amelia. Now what was that all about? It was almost as if Amelia was trying to push her into marrying Paul Renton.

12

Emily had been working in her office for an hour when Paul walked in the next morning. She looked up and smiled, laying down her pen. 'I was just about to make some coffee,' she said. 'Would you like some?'

'Not at the moment,' Paul said, looking so stern that her heart caught. 'I have to say this, Emily, or it will be too late. I tried yesterday but couldn't find the courage—'

'Paul...' Emily stood up and came round her desk. Her heart was jerking oddly, because she sensed what he was going to say. 'You know I like you very much.'

'Liking isn't enough for what I want,' Paul said, and his face was tortured with passion. 'I think I fell in love with you the first time we met, Emily. I want to marry you, but I can't offer you anything like you have here.'

'You wouldn't have to,' Emily said. She moved towards him, putting a finger to his lips as he would have spoken again. 'I do feel something for you, Paul, and I should very much like to get to know you better – but I am not ready for marriage yet. One day I may want to leave this house, but not now, not while I am needed.'

'I knew that as soon as I saw the way Vane looks at you,' Paul told her. 'He worships the ground you walk on, Emily, and you are very fond of him. I almost went this morning without speaking, because I know I can't expect you to leave all this for me.'

'Not yet,' she repeated with a smile, because his heated words were making her feel warm and happy in a way she hadn't been for a long time. 'Perhaps one day, Paul. I can't say that I will marry you, because I don't know you well enough. I married in haste once and regretted it. I won't make that mistake again – but I would like us to know each other better. If you hadn't been offered that job I might—'

'The job means nothing if there is a chance we could be together,' Paul said. 'But if you're not sure...'

'I know I want to—' Emily frowned as the telephone on her desk rang. For a moment she was tempted to ignore it but something made her pick it up, despite sensing that Paul wanted her to leave it. 'Yes, Emily Vane speaking.'

'Emily.' Frances sounded urgent. 'You've got to come back to the house at once. Lord Vane has had a heart attack and he is asking for you. Amelia is with him and in a terrible state. She asked me to get you here as quickly as possible. I think it is serious.'

'Yes, of course. I'll come now,' Emily said. She replaced the receiver with a little bang, her heart racing as she looked at Paul. 'I am sorry, I have to go. Vane is ill. He needs me.'

'Yes, of course,' Paul said. 'I'll get out of your way.'

'No...' Emily hesitated. A part of her wanted to beg him to stay, but she knew this wasn't the time. 'Yes, perhaps it would be best. I'm not sure when I'll be able to talk again. I couldn't leave Vane like this, not when he needs me.'

'No, of course not,' Paul said. 'But he will always need you, won't he, Emily?'

'Yes, perhaps,' she said. 'I am sorry, Paul. I have to go.'

She walked past him, leaving him standing there. She liked Paul, felt that there was something between them, but it was new and fragile and it didn't stand a chance when Vane needed her. The bonds between them were an invisible thread, but so strong that she felt them pulling her even when they were apart.

* * *

Emily paused to recover her breath before walking into Vane's bedchamber. She had rushed back in a panic, because the urgent summons had shocked her. It had upset her the first time Vane had been struck down like this, but it was different now. The feeling between them was so much stronger, and losing him would be a cruel blow. Her throat was tight, and she could feel a sharp pain deep inside her.

He was lying propped up against a pile of pillows, the curtains half-pulled to shade the room from too much light. Amelia was sitting on the edge of the bed holding his hand. She looked over her shoulder as Emily came in, an odd expression in her eyes.

'Thank goodness you are here. I thought you might have gone off somewhere. Vane wants to speak to you.' She got up, clearly preparing to leave the room.

'You don't have to leave,' Emily said, though she wanted her to, because she wanted a few minutes with Vane. 'Unless you want...'

Amelia gave her a mocking stare and walked out. Emily approached the bed. Vane looked old and frail against the white pillows, a dark-blue silken counterpane covering his body. He pushed the top cover back a little and smiled wearily at her.

'Thank you for coming, my dear.' He held his hand out to her. 'Amelia makes such a fuss but I think she may be right this time. We'll know more when the doctor has been, but' – he shook his head impatiently – 'I haven't time for all this. I must ask, Emily. Are you planning to marry your doctor? I know he means to ask you – will you say yes?'

'Not for the moment,' Emily said, her fingers entwining with his. His clasp was still firm despite his air of fragility, and she was a little reassured. 'Perhaps one day, if I get to know him and decide that I would like to be married. I don't really know him yet.'

'He is very much in love with you,' Vane told her. 'Believe me, Emily. I recognise the signs. It wouldn't be the way it was with Simon.'

'No, perhaps not,' Emily said. 'But I made a promise, Vane. I said that I would stay here while I was needed, and the home still has a few guests.'

'You know that we could find someone to manage it, don't you?' Vane's eyes were on her. 'I think you want to stay here, Emily. I believe you have become as much a prisoner of Vanbrough as I have been all my life.'

'What do you mean – a prisoner?'

'A house and estate like this have to be nurtured and loved,' Vane said. 'It needs new life, new blood, Emily. You brought that to us when you came, and it will live on through you and Robert – and the children you may have in the future. That is why I have arranged things the way I think best. I shan't say more now, but I wanted to make sure you understood. Robert may not carry my blood, but you carry my spirit and my hopes. I want to think of you here, carrying on the traditions.'

'Vane, please don't talk this way,' Emily begged. 'I don't want you to die.' A sob broke in her voice, her hand holding his a little too tightly. 'I don't know what I should do without you now.'

'You will go on as you did before,' he said with a gentle smile. 'I like to think that you will remember me with affection, but I know that you have the strength for what is needed, my dear. And you will carry on, won't you, Emily – for my sake?'

'You know I love you,' Emily said, realising the depth of her feelings for the first time. A wave of despair swept over her, because she was losing the one person she could rely on to love and care for her. 'Oh, Vane, I am not sure I am strong enough to do what you want.'

'You will, because you are my Emily,' he said. His eyes were softly mocking, but the mockery was directed at himself, not her. 'I have thought of you that way for a long time now. You must have known that I loved you, my dear?' He held her hand as he felt her initial reaction to withdraw. 'I care for Amelia, of course I do. She is my wife – but it was never a love match. I wanted more children, particularly another son. I think I knew from the time when Simon was quite small that he would never be my heir – and Vanessa is tied up with her husband's life in London. She doesn't even like Vanbrough. Whereas you do – don't you?'

'You know I do,' Emily said, her voice thick with emotion. 'But I want things to go on the way they are, with you and Amelia.'

Vane gave a snort of laughter. 'You want it to go on forever – but you should know that nothing lasts forever, Emily. You of all people must understand that even the best of times must fade at the last.'

'Yes, I know – but the time went too fast,' Emily said. 'All during the war with the patients and the mad rushing around, you were there and I relied on you, loved you, and hardly knew that I was happy. Now that we have come through it...' Regret caught at her throat and she shook her head. 'I shouldn't be saying these things. I am supposed to be comforting you, telling you that you will soon be better.'

'And should I pretend to believe you?' This time his mockery was for her. 'No, Emily, I don't want that from you. Amelia would have me believe that the doctor will wave his magic wand, but I know what is happening.' He put a hand to his chest, smothering a moan as the pain intensified. 'I've had a decent life. I can't expect to go on much longer.'

'Are you in much pain?' Vane shook his head but Emily knew he was lying. 'Shall I go and leave you to rest, dearest?'

'No, not yet. I just want to look at you. I don't think you know how beautiful you have become, Emily. You were always lovely, but you have such a serene beauty these days, like the Madonna but with an earthly quality that makes men want you. I wasn't surprised that your doctor fell in love with you at first sight. It came more slowly for me, but I was older and more cautious.'

'You see me with the eyes of love.' She bent forward and kissed him on the lips very softly. 'My dearest Vane. You put me on a pedestal I don't deserve.'

'Perhaps,' Vane agreed. 'Don't spend the rest of your life alone, Emily. If it isn't to be the young doctor, find someone else – but make sure that whoever it is loves this place too, because otherwise he will want you to leave it, and I don't think you will be able to. I couldn't, even though I knew it would be sensible to sell the place or tear it down and build a modern economic house.'

'I shall marry if I can find someone I love.'

'I want you to be happy,' Vane said, and his hand trembled in hers. 'Sometimes I think I wronged you, my Emily. If I had let you go instead of selfishly keeping you with me... but I wanted to see you every day of my life, so I made sure that you stayed, and now you can't leave any more than I ever could.'

'You didn't force me to stay,' Emily said, though she knew that she had stayed for his sake. 'If I had truly wanted to leave I would have gone.' She might have gone if Terry had lived, but after his death she had needed her work, and she had needed Vane. His strength and his love had sustained her, though she hadn't truly understood that until this moment.

He had closed his eyes and now his hand was slipping from hers. She felt the life draining out of him and she stood up, intending to call his wife, but the door opened as if Amelia had been expecting it to happen. She came to the side of the bed and they stood there together, watching the colour leave his face.

'I'll telephone for the doctor,' she said, feeling that Amelia would need a few moments alone with her husband. 'I am truly sorry.'

'Are you?' Amelia looked at her, cold and remote. 'I don't see why. You always get whatever you want, don't you?'

'Oh, Amelia, not now,' Emily said. 'Excuse me, I must leave you for a while. We shall talk later.'

She left the room and went downstairs to ring the local surgery again. It was too late for Vane, but it wouldn't have mattered if the doctor had come sooner. It had been Vane's time and he'd known it.

Emily felt the tears well up inside her, but she fought them down. There were things she needed to do; the tears could come later.

* * *

'I am so sorry,' Frances said when she joined Emily in the garden later that day. It was quite mild even though it was early

February. From the branches of ancient trees, a thrush was trilling its wonderful song. 'I know he meant a great deal to you.'

'Yes, he did.' Emily smiled because the first surge of grief had abated. She could still feel Vane with her, as if he were standing at her shoulder, watching over her. 'We've known for the past few years that he was living on borrowed time. His heart hasn't been all it should be, but he made nothing of it, carried on as if he were twenty years younger. He was thirty years older than Amelia, of course. Simon and Vanessa were his children by his first wife.'

Frances nodded. 'Amelia told me that he married her for a spare but she wasn't able to give him a child. I think that's awful, don't you? To marry someone just for the sake of an extra son.'

'It isn't strictly true,' Emily said. 'Amelia is feeling upset – and bitter, I suppose, because Vane asked for me at the last. She tried to take Robert over because she wanted him to be hers.' Emily sighed. 'Vane was always able to smooth her feathers. I am not sure how we shall get on now that he is dead.'

'You are going to miss him, aren't you? Not just because of Amelia – but because you loved him.'

'Yes, I did love him,' Emily said. 'I don't think I ever knew how much until today. It was a special kind of love, Frances. He wasn't exactly a father figure to me – and yet I never thought of him as a lover. I suppose I might have done if it hadn't been for Amelia.'

'He was so much older than you, Emily!'

'Yes, I know – but Vane was the kind of man who never really ages. His body got older, but his mind and spirit remained eternally young. I suppose that is why I thought he would go on for years. Even though I knew his heart was weak, I thought he couldn't die.' Emily felt the tears begin to slide down her cheeks and wiped them away with the sleeve of her light jacket. 'Damn it! I don't want to cry. Vane wouldn't want that and it's so stupid.'

Frances put an arm about her waist. 'Cry if you want to, love. It doesn't help much but it does relieve the tension. I should know. I've done enough of it lately.'

'Yes.' Emily fished in her pocket for a handkerchief and blew her nose. 'You seem a little better – are you?'

'Yes, I am,' Frances told her. 'I don't know why, because nothing has changed really – but I am thinking about the future. I had a letter from Rosalind Danby to wish me well. And Dan telephoned this morning while you were at the office. He said some of the men from the haulage yard had come to him to ask what they ought to do – apparently some orders need shifting. He told them to carry on as normal for the moment. He wanted to know if he had done right. I've asked him to take over running it. I think I shall do what you suggested, Emily. I don't want anything to do with it, but Dan seems interested so I'll give him a share of the profits and see how it works out.'

'I'm glad you've made the decision,' Emily said. 'I offered Dan money to set up his own garage, but he wouldn't take it from me. He is only accepting your offer because he thinks he is helping you – making up for his neglect when you needed him.'

'Well, he doesn't have to do it forever unless he wants,' Frances said. 'But he was concerned about men losing their jobs so I think he feels obliged to step in.'

'Yes, knowing Dan I should say that is about the size of it,' Emily said. 'I think I had better go back to the house. Amelia and I have to talk.'

'I'll walk down to the home and see if I can do anything to help out,' Frances said and smiled at her sister. 'I could never understand why you were so devoted to your work, but I think I can now I've met your guests. However much your own problems hurt, they fade into insignificance when you see what they have to endure.'

'Yes, that is exactly it,' Emily agreed. 'It stops you feeling sorry for yourself – and it gives a sense of purpose.' She kissed Frances on the cheek and they parted, Emily going up to the house alone. She was glad that Frances was feeling better, but now she had problems of her own to face.

* * *

'You can't mean it?' Emily said as she looked at Amelia. They were in the small sitting room they both favoured at the rear of the house. 'But I thought this place meant everything to you?'

'Vane meant everything,' Amelia said, and her tone was decidedly bitter. 'I immersed myself in the tradition that he cherished because he loved it all so much. I knew that he married me because he wanted a son – but I married because I wanted to be a wife and I didn't get any other offers. I'm not beautiful and clever like you.' Her face was tight with misery. 'But you see, I made the mistake of falling in love with my husband. He was kind and generous, and always considerate. Even when I failed to give him the son he wanted, he took the blame on himself – accepted that he was too old to father a child. We both knew in our hearts that it was my fault.'

'Oh, Amelia, I am so sorry. I didn't know any of this. You've always said it was just a marriage of convenience and that it was Vane who couldn't have a child.'

'I let you believe a lie,' Amelia told her. 'I believed it myself for a long time, but I always knew the truth in my heart. It was all right until Simon brought you here and then everything changed, very slowly, but quite definitely.'

'How? I don't understand what you mean.'

'Don't you?' Amelia's eyes were so accusing that Emily had to look away. 'Of course you do. Vane was in love with you. Oh, he was always courteous to me, never let me see that he preferred you – but I knew it. His face lit up whenever you came into the room. He opened the convalescent home because he had to keep you from leaving. He would have done anything for you – and he has. You and Robert get everything that matters.' Now the bitterness flared out of her, marring her face with its ugliness.

'What do you mean? Surely you and Vanessa have been left a share of Vane's fortune?'

'I've seen a draft of the will,' Amelia said. 'The estate and half the money is left to Robert. You have your own trust and the management of the estate until your son is twenty-one. Vanessa gets a few thousand pounds and a house in Dorset that belonged to her mother. I get a house in London, ten thousand pounds and an allowance from a further trust, which comes to you when I die.'

'But of course you will continue to live here,' Emily said, a little shocked by her revelations. 'You run the house so beautifully, Amelia. I am sure I couldn't do it half as well.'

'You will find it isn't as easy as it seems,' Amelia said. 'It isn't just the house. There are traditions that people expect, but I daresay you will manage. Vane thought that you would be the best person to look after things. He told me he knew that I didn't really care for the estate but that you loved it the way he did.'

'Yes, I love it here, but I'm not sure I know how to manage it,' Emily said. 'It was Vane who kept everything together. He was the heart of this place.' She looked at Amelia unhappily. 'Is there nothing that would persuade you to stay?'

'You are the mistress here now,' Amelia said. 'If Simon had lived you would be Lady Vane. Tradition says that I should move out and leave it to you.'

'I don't want your title or your place here,' Emily said. 'I just wanted everything to be as it was – you, Vane, Robert and me.'

'Well, Vane is dead,' Amelia said. 'Even you can't bring him back. I shall stay for a week or so after the funeral because it would look odd if I went at once. I'll leave you all my journals to help you – but I want a life of my own, Emily. I lived for Vane, doing the things he wanted, being the kind of wife he needed – but now I am going to live for myself for a change.'

'Then I suppose I can't hold you,' Emily said. 'I am sorry you have decided to go, Amelia – but if it is what you want you must do it.'

'Yes, I shall,' Amelia said, and there was an odd look of satisfaction in her eyes. 'I'll give you five years, Emily. If you're not up to your ears in debt by then I'll take my hat off to you.'

* * *

'I am so glad you were here for the funeral,' Emily said to Frances when most of the guests had at last taken their leave. 'I could just about manage the service, but the rest of it was almost unbearable. I had never met some of the people Amelia invited, and I felt as if I were an outsider. I am sure she was playing the long-suffering widow just to spite me.'

'You told me yourself that she loved him?'

'Yes, I didn't mean it that way – but somehow she managed to make me feel as if I didn't belong here. It was the first time I had met Vane's cousin. Actually, he is a second cousin, I think, but I'm not quite sure of the relationship. There was something about the way Amelia introduced him.' Emily shook her head. She had sensed an underlying threat but didn't understand what was going on in Amelia's mind.

'You mean Alan Leicester?'

'Yes,' Emily said, looking thoughtful. 'I've never heard Vane mention him. I didn't know he had a cousin.'

'Perhaps they had fallen out over something?' Frances frowned. 'I thought he was rather nice, Emily. Tall and good looking with that dark blond hair and blue eyes – he reminded me a little of Simon.'

'Yes, there was a family resemblance,' Emily agreed. 'But I thought he looked more like Vane must have when he was the same age – he is about thirtyish, I imagine.'

'Yes, about that,' Frances agreed. 'I wonder why Lord Vane never invited him to the house?'

'I have no idea,' Emily replied. Meeting him so suddenly had made her feel slightly uneasy. She supposed that if it hadn't been for Robert he might have expected to inherit the estate – or at least the title, because Vanessa had only a female child. 'I suppose it must have been a family quarrel. He didn't stay long after the funeral, but asked if he could call and see me in a few days.'

'I expect he just wants to talk about family stuff,' Frances said. 'You're not worried about him, are you?'

'No, of course not,' Emily said. She gave herself a mental shake. Vane had excluded his cousin from his will for reasons of his own. 'I wonder...' She broke off as Vane's daughter came up to them. She already had her coat and hat on, a fur tippet around her neck. 'Vanessa – do you really have to leave?'

'I am afraid so,' Vanessa said. 'I promised I would catch the train back this afternoon. I am flying to Paris with friends in two days so I really can't stay. Besides, I am sure you don't need me. I should only be in the way. And Amelia and I don't really get on, we never have.' She nodded to Frances. 'It was nice to meet you.'

'You won't stay for the reading of the will?'

Vanessa pulled a wry face. 'Vane wrote to me when he made it, asking if I had any objections, which I didn't, of course. I think I have done rather well actually. He was always going to leave the estate to Simon's son. Don't worry, I shan't be contesting it, though Amelia is acting oddly. I can't imagine why she thinks this house should have been hers. Father would never have left it away from Robert.' She glanced at her elegant watch. 'I must fly. Do come up to London and visit us sometime, Emily. Goodbye.'

'Yes, of course. Thank you for coming.'

'What does she mean by Amelia acting oddly over the house?' Frances said. 'She must have known Vane would leave it to his grandson?'

'Robert isn't Simon's son,' Emily told her. 'Vane knew it but he still chose to leave the estate to Robert. He told me that as far as he was concerned Robert was his heir.'

'You've never said anything about this to me before.' Frances stared at her. 'Does Amelia know?'

'She guessed it at the time, but she couldn't prove it if I chose to lie in court,' Emily said. 'Oh, Mr James is looking this way, Frances. I think he wants to read the will. I had better go.'

'I shall be in the small sitting room,' Frances told her. 'I have some magazines I want to read.'

'I'll find you there later,' Emily said and walked to where the solicitor and Amelia were standing.

'Shall we go into the study?' the lawyer asked. 'I imagine you are both aware of the main terms of Lord Vane's will – but I am required to read it to you. I shall send a copy of it to Mrs Hendry, but she told me her father had already communicated his wishes to her.'

'Yes, of course.' Emily glanced at Amelia. There was a smirk on her face, which made Emily feel uneasy.

They went into Vane's study. It was furnished with deep leather armchairs, and mahogany bookcases lined the walls. It reminded Emily so vividly of him that it brought a lump to her throat.

'It is really quite simple,' the lawyer said, smiling at Emily. 'Your own trust fund of ten thousand pounds now becomes yours entirely. You may leave it invested or take the capital as you please. The estate and half of the money – which is about eighty thousand pounds in total – invested at the moment in shares is left in three portions. One half goes to your son, Mrs Vane, the other half to be divided between Mrs Hendry and Lady Vane. Robert also gets this house, its contents and the estate. Mrs Hendry receives a house in Dorset and Lady Vane has a house in Mayfair and an income for life. There are a few small bequests to servants but they are minor and provided for from a separate fund.'

'Will you read the exact wording concerning the estate being left to Robert?' Amelia said. 'What does it actually say?'

The lawyer looked a little puzzled but obligingly picked up the will and read it aloud. '"I, Henry Vane, being of sound mind..." Ah yes, here it is. It is worded a little strangely. It says, "I leave one half of the capital invested in shares and the estate to Robert, the son of Emily Vane, my dearest friend and my son's widow. Emily is to have sole charge of the estate and money until Robert is of age." Yes, how odd. I recall remarking on it at the time but Lord Vane was most insistent that the wording be exact.'

'Let me look!' Amelia snatched the will from him, reading it herself. 'Damn him!' She threw a look of loathing across at Emily. 'I suppose you think you are in the clear now, but I haven't finished yet.' She got up and rushed from the room.

'Oh dear.' The lawyer coughed and looked shocked.

Emily sent him an apologetic look. 'I am so sorry,' she said. 'Lady Vane is under some stress. Would you excuse me? I must speak to her. Please stay tonight if you wish – or at least for dinner. I must go to Amelia.'

Emily followed Amelia out into the hall. She was halfway up

the stairs, but Emily ran after her, catching at her arm. Amelia tried to pull away from her, but Emily held on.

'What is the matter?' Emily asked. 'You knew what was in the will – why are you so angry?' Amelia glared at her, something odd in her eyes, and suddenly Emily realised what she had been hoping. 'You wanted Vane's cousin to contest it, didn't you? If Robert wasn't around he might have been entitled to something.'

'The title is Alan's by right,' Amelia said. 'The estate wasn't entailed so he couldn't have claimed that – but I might. I am more entitled to it than a bastard.'

Emily's hand snaked out, catching her across the face. 'Don't you ever dare to call my son a bastard! Vane loved him and he wanted him to be his grandson. I told him the truth but he already knew it and it made no difference.'

Amelia was holding her hand to her face. 'You witch,' she muttered. 'You think you've won – but I shall tell Alan the truth. He will claim the title and everyone will know what a cheat you are. I may not be able to contest the will – but I'll ruin your reputation. You'll find it impossible to carry on as the lady of the manor then.'

'I'm sorry I hit you. I shouldn't have done that,' Emily said, but the expression in her eyes was angry. 'If you dare tell Vane's cousin that Robert is a bastard I shall sue you for everything Vane left you. You have no proof of anything, Amelia. As far as the world knows, I was entirely faithful to my husband.'

'I hate you,' Amelia said. 'I wish you had never come here.'

'It doesn't have to be like this,' Emily said. 'We could still be friends, Amelia. You could live here exactly as before.'

'I don't want to be your friend,' Amelia said bitterly. 'You took everything I ever wanted. I couldn't give Vane a son, but he wouldn't let me adopt, even though he knew how much I wanted a child – and yet he loved your bastard. I'm leaving and I never want to see you again. And I shall tell Alan the truth.'

'Do that and I will ruin you,' Emily said. 'I'll stand up in court and lie so convincingly that you won't have a penny left.'

'Damn you to hell!'

Amelia turned and ran up the stairs, leaving Emily staring after her. She stood where she was for a moment, feeling sick and ill. Amelia must be half out of her mind with grief and hate to say such things to her. It wasn't as if Emily had turned her out. She was only too willing to carry on the way they had been, letting Amelia play the lady of the manor while she looked after the convalescent home. But that wouldn't do for Amelia. It was because Vane had loved Emily that Amelia had turned against her. Nothing she could have said or done would have made any difference. It wasn't really this house or the estate, though that had been the bitter coating on the pill.

Emily went up to the nursery. Nanny was giving Robert his tea. Emily sat and watched them for a few minutes, soothed by the normality of the scene. She had lost so much, but she still had her beloved son.

'Lady Vane is very upset,' she told Nanny. 'I want you to stay with Robert this evening please. Do not leave him at all – and he is not to go anywhere with Lady Vane.'

'Yes, madam,' Nanny said. 'I understand perfectly.'

'Thank you. I was sure you would,' Emily said. 'Excuse me. I have things to do.'

'You may rest your mind concerning Lord Vane,' Nanny said. 'I shall watch over him every minute.'

'Lord Vane...' Emily stared at her and then shook her head. 'I think we shall just stick to Robert, Nanny. He is too young for anything like that just yet.'

'Yes, madam, just as you please.'

Emily was thoughtful as she went out. She wasn't sure what she ought to do about the situation. Clearly Vane had protected Robert by the terms of his will. The money was left to her son – not to his grandson, not even to Robert Vane. He must have thought it out very carefully and with the intent of making certain Robert could not be disinherited because he was not of Vane's blood.

Vane had made his wishes quite clear to her. He had wanted her to stay on as the chatelaine of his estate until Robert was of an age to take it over. He had done it because he loved her – because he wanted Robert to be his, whether he carried Simon's blood or not. By doing so he had obliged Emily to carry on here in the traditions he upheld. It was a binding promise, unspoken but understood.

She was thoughtful as she went downstairs to find Frances. Vane had given her everything, but he had virtually made her a prisoner here. She could never walk away from the promise she had made him.

* * *

Frances looked up as Emily came into the room, seeing the expression in her eyes and understanding that something was wrong. She got up and went to greet her sister.

'What is wrong, Emily? Vane didn't turn you out, did he?'

'No, of course not. He left the estate and half the money to Robert. I have the trust he had already set up for me – and sole control of the estate and the money until Robert is old enough to look after things himself.'

'Then why do you look as if you'd found sixpence and lost a shilling?'

Emily shook her head. 'Amelia isn't very happy. She threatened to tell Alan Leicester that Robert is a bastard – and I hit her. She says she hates me and she is leaving at once.'

'Oh, Emily.' Frances stared at her in horror. 'You shouldn't have hit her.'

'You didn't see the look in her eyes. No one calls my son by that name!' Emily's expression was hard and determined, so unlike her that Frances was shocked. 'I would have let Amelia carry on here as if nothing had happened – but that isn't enough for her.' Emily lifted her head proudly. 'I didn't ask for this. I'm not sure I even want it – but it was Vane's wish.'

Frances was silent. Robert was a bastard by her sister's own admission, but she could see that Emily was upset and kept her thoughts to herself.

'You will be better off without Amelia.'

'Shall I?' Emily sighed. 'She knows all about the way the estate runs, Frances. I would rather have tried to rub along together than lose her.'

'Well, if it gets too much for you, you can always sell the place and invest the money.'

'No, I couldn't do that,' Emily said. 'Vane left it to me to manage because he knew I wouldn't let him down. I promised that I would keep things the way they are for as long as I could.'

Frances pulled a face. 'I was going to ask if you would come and look at a guesthouse I've seen for sale in Margate. It looks quite big – rooms for nine or ten guests, which is as much as I can manage. I thought you might want to come with me?' Emily shook her head. 'No, obviously you've got too much on your plate here.'

'Why don't you speak to Mary?' Emily asked. 'She wrote to me recently, told me she didn't know what she was going to do once Rosalind Danby's house was sold – which apparently it is very nearly. She needs money, Frances, and she wouldn't turn up her nose at helping to run the kind of place you're talking about. In fact, I think she would love it – and she would be company for you.'

'Mary?' Frances was thoughtful for a moment. 'Yes, I might do that, Emily. I hadn't given Mary a thought, but we always got on well. Both her sons are due to leave school at Christmas, and it will take me that time to get sorted out and moved in.'

'Why don't you go down and see her – and Daniel? You could sort out the haulage business at the same time.'

'I thought you would need me for a while?' Frances looked at her sister. 'You'll find it a bit lonely on your own here, won't you?'

'I shall have Nanny and Robert – and the rest of the staff,' Emily said. 'And I still have the home to run. I've made a lot of friends here, Frances. I expect to be too busy to be lonely. Besides, you'll need somewhere to live until your money comes through. Go and see Daniel and Mary – and then come back.'

'Yes, I shall – if you are sure?' Frances looked at her uncertainly. 'You've done so much for me, Emily. I don't want to desert you if you need me.'

'Come back when you are ready,' Emily said. 'I shall still be here.'

There was something odd about the way that Emily said those words that made Frances wonder, but she sensed that whatever was on her sister's mind was private.

'Yes, I shall,' she said. 'I'll be gone a few days, and then I'll come and stay with you until I get myself sorted out.'

EPILOGUE

Emily stood staring out at the park. Three days had passed since Vane's funeral, and Frances was on a train heading for London, where she planned to meet Rosalind Danby before going on to Daniel's home. Emily was alone in her favourite room – a room she no longer needed to share with Amelia. She had often wanted to change the furnishings in here, and now she could. She could do anything she wanted, except leave.

'Oh, Vane,' she said on a sigh. 'You never meant to let me go, did you?'

'You made me a promise, Emily,' she seemed to hear his voice saying. 'I have given you everything, but I expect something in return.'

'I owe you so much,' Emily said. 'Everything I am, I am because of you. You made me whole again when I felt there was nothing to live for – and I did lie to you.'

'But I knew you lied. If you want to go, I can't stop you.'

'Stop this!' Emily knew that what she was hearing was in her own mind. She was conjuring up Vane's voice because she wanted to hear it. 'I'm going to ring Paul.'

She went out into the hall and dialled the number Paul had given her when they first met. A woman's voice answered.

'May I speak to Paul Renton please?' Emily asked.

'May I ask who is calling?'

'Mrs Emily Vane. I am a friend of Paul's.'

'Ah, yes. Mr Renton no longer lives here, Mrs Vane. He left for Southampton yesterday, but he said that if you rang I was to give you the address at which he will be staying until the end of the week. It is a hotel, I believe – and I have the telephone number here.'

'Thank you. I have a pencil.' Emily took down the phone number and then rang off. She looked at the number she had jotted down and then picked up the receiver once more. It took a few minutes and a brief conversation with the receptionist before she finally heard Paul's voice.

'It's Emily. I thought I might have missed you. The receptionist said you might have checked out already.'

'I was leaving this morning but I decided to stay until tomorrow. My ship leaves the day after and I want to be nearer the embarkation point.'

'You are leaving so soon?' Emily felt a sinking sensation. She wasn't sure why she was ringing him, but something had driven her to it. Somehow she hadn't expected him to be leaving almost immediately.

'I saw no reason to wait and they are pretty desperate to get me there. Their last doctor died of yellow fever.'

'I see. Well, good luck. I hope you have a good trip and that everything goes as you want.'

'Emily, come with me,' he said, suddenly urgent. 'I have a double cabin. I'm sure I could swing it, especially if we got married. Or we could find another ship.'

'Come with you?' For a moment, Emily's pulses raced. She was tempted to say yes, but it was all too swift, too rushed. 'I can't, Paul. I'm sorry. There are things I have to do. I was hoping you might not have taken the job. You might have found something here.'

'I thought you weren't interested so I told them I would take it,' Paul said. 'I can't let them down. It's important, Emily.'

'And I can't leave here just like that.' She sighed. 'I shouldn't have rung you. It is the wrong time and the wrong place.'

'You could come if you wanted,' Paul said. 'If you loved me you would be willing to leave that house.'

'It isn't just the house,' Emily said. 'It's Robert and... lots of things.'

'Then there is nothing else to say, is there?'

Emily stared at the receiver as it went dead. How could he just put the phone down on her like that? He said that she should abandon her life if she cared for him, but he could have waited – he could have given her time. They hardly knew one another. She was turning away when the telephone shrilled. She snatched it up breathlessly.

'Yes. It's Emily.'

'Mrs Vane?' A voice she vaguely recognised came over the line. 'It is the Reverend Bright here. I was just ringing to ask about the Christmas bazaar. Lady Vane always let us hold it at Vanbrough. I was wondering if you would continue the tradition – and there is the orphan's party. Lord Vane always sponsored the Christmas treat we hold at the church hall for the children's home. Perhaps it isn't a good time but we usually start planning these things early and I wasn't sure...' He hesitated. 'I am sorry if I picked a bad moment?'

'No, of course not.' Emily had recovered her breath and her composure. 'I am sure Vane would wish to continue all the traditional events. You must let me know, Mr Bright, if I forget something.'

'Ah, I thought you wouldn't let us down, Mrs Vane. I'll go ahead and plan the schedule as usual – and I'll send you a copy, shall I?'

'Yes, please do,' Emily said. 'It might be as well if you and your committee came to lunch soon so that we can talk about the future. I will check my diary and let you know.'

'That is very generous of you, Mrs Vane,' he said. 'If there is anything I can do for you, please do not hesitate to ask.'

'I shall be in touch soon,' Emily said.

She replaced the receiver and went into Vane's study. He had worked at his desk whenever he had anything important to do and Emily supposed that she would find the things she needed to know in the drawers. Amelia had promised to leave her journals behind, but she had neglected to do so and it was going to take a bit of sorting out if Emily wanted to avoid disappointing people who had relied on Vane for various sponsorships.

She sat down in his chair, feeling a little tingle at her nape as she opened the top right-hand drawer. Lying on the top was a large brown envelope addressed to her. She took it out, a rueful smile on her lips. She might have known that Vane would leave nothing to chance.

Opening the seal, she took out the bundle of papers. One of them was a single sheet of Vane's special notepaper. She saw that it was a letter to her.

My dearest Emily. So you stayed and you are going to keep your promise, but of course I knew you would. I hope you know by now how much I valued and loved you, and I hope you will be happy here. This place needs you, Emily. I believe that you can bring it back to life again, make it live, as it once

*did when I was young. I know I cannot force you to stay if you
wish to leave, but I hope that you will enjoy living at Vanbrough
and relish its history. All my notebooks are at your disposal,
but you do not have to read them. I have left you some notes
to help you begin your new life – but the best part of tradition
is that it evolves. Life doesn't stand still, Emily, my love. I don't
want you to live in an isolated state and waste all that beauty
and youth. Bring your family here if you wish. Marry and have
lots of children, be happy. All I ask is that you continue to love
and care for Vanbrough for as long as you are able. I loved you
as I should not have loved you, and I made you stay with me
by whatever means I could. If I have wronged you, forgive me
and think of me with kindness. Vane.*

Emily's eyes pricked with tears as she laid the letter down.
She got up and walked over to where a small portrait of Vane was
hanging above the mantelpiece. It had been painted when he
was in his thirties, young and handsome – very like Simon but
with a stronger jawline and a more masculine appeal.

She heard the telephone ringing in the hall but didn't go to
answer it, staring up at the portrait as if trying to read Vane's
mind. He had been smiling and confident when it was painted, a
young man in love with life.

'A Dr Renton is on the telephone, madam,' her housekeeper
said from the doorway. 'I said I would inquire if you were in, Mrs
Vane?'

Emily looked at her for a moment, then shook her head. 'I
have gone out, Mrs Jones. Please thank him for calling – but I am
not at home.'

'Yes, Mrs Vane. Are you at home to anyone?'

'Not for a while – unless it is family, thank you.'

Emily went back to her contemplation of Vane's portrait as

the door closed behind the housekeeper. It seemed to her that his smile had deepened, and his eyes seemed to be slightly mocking.

'So you've won then, Vane,' she said.

'I always do, my dear,' his voice said in her head. 'But you know it is what you truly want.'

'I wish I knew what I want,' Emily said. 'You've set a trap for me, Vane. I shall be too busy to feel lonely – but whether it is what I truly want I don't know.'

She laughed and went back to his desk, sitting in his chair, feeling his presence. Whether she liked it or not, this was where she belonged. She was needed and wanted – and perhaps she was loved by some of those she helped. If this house was her prison, it was a beautiful one and she loved it. And perhaps one day she would find someone to share it with her. Until then, she had her work, just as before.

It had been the patients at the convalescent home who had taken all her time during the war and the empty years after Terry's death, easing the grief and the sense of loneliness. Now it would be the house and the community, all of them making demands that would drain her of energy and take all she had to give. She was starting at the bottom and it would be a long time before she could believe that she was filling Vane's shoes, but she had to try.

'You are not alone, my beautiful Emily.' Vane's voice seemed to be very close, his presence wrapping around her like comforting arms. 'I am always here.'

'Oh, I wish you were,' she said, and for a moment tears stung her eyes, but then she smiled, fighting them back, because she had no time for tears. Vane had chosen her because she was strong – strong enough to find her way, strong enough to keep the promise she had made. 'Damn you, go away, Vane. Get out of my head. I have work to do!' She sat down at his desk and opened his appointments diary. She had a new life ahead of her, and it had to start somewhere.

MORE FROM ROSIE CLARKE

Another book from Rosie Clarke, *A Family Fortune*, is available to order now here:

https://mybook.to/AFamilyFortuneBackAd

FROM THE AUTHOR

Dear readers. I hope you will enjoy these books as much as I enjoyed writing them. Best wishes, Rosie Clarke.

ABOUT THE AUTHOR

Rosie Clarke is a #1 bestselling saga writer whose books include Welcome to Harpers Emporium and The Mulberry Lane series. She has written over 100 novels under different pseudonyms and is a RNA Award winner. She lives in Cambridgeshire.

Sign up to Rosie Clarke's mailing list for news, competitions and updates on future books.

Visit Rosie's website: www.lindasole.co.uk

Follow Rosie on social media here:

facebook.com/Rosie-clarke-119457351778432

x.com/AnneHerries

bookbub.com/authors/rosie-clarke

ALSO BY ROSIE CLARKE

Welcome to Harpers Emporium Series

The Shop Girls of Harpers

Love and Marriage at Harpers

Rainy Days for the Harpers Girls

Harpers Heroes

Wartime Blues for the Harpers Girls

Victory Bells For The Harpers Girls

Changing Times at Harpers

Heartbreak at Harpers

Troubled Times at Harpers

The Mulberry Lane Series

A Reunion at Mulberry Lane

Stormy Days On Mulberry Lane

A New Dawn Over Mulberry Lane

Life and Love at Mulberry Lane

Last Orders at Mulberry Lane

Blackberry Farm Series

War Clouds Over Blackberry Farm

Heartache at Blackberry Farm

Love and Duty at Blackberry Farm

Family Matters at Blackberry Farm

The Trenwith Trilogy

Sarah's Choice

Louise's War

Rose's Fight

Dressmakers' Alley

Dangerous Times on Dressmakers' Alley

Dark Secrets on Dressmakers' Alley

The Family Feud Series

A Family at War

A Family Secret

A Family Fortune

Standalone Novels

Nellie's Heartbreak

A Mother's Shame

A Sister's Destiny

Sixpence Stories

Introducing Sixpence Stories!

Discover page-turning
historical novels from your
favourite authors, meet new
friends and be transported
back in time.

Join our book club
Facebook group

https://bit.ly/SixpenceGroup

Sign up to our
newsletter

https://bit.ly/SixpenceNews

Boldwood

Boldwood Books is an award-winning fiction publishing company seeking out the best stories from around the world.

Find out more at www.boldwoodbooks.com

Join our reader community for brilliant books, competitions and offers!

Follow us
@BoldwoodBooks
@TheBoldBookClub

Sign up to our weekly
deals newsletter

https://bit.ly/BoldwoodBNewsletter